Gator Bait

by Jana DeLeon

Chapter One

I was in the middle of a fabulous dream. I'd just made a HALO jump from 25,000 feet and landed undetected in Ahmad's compound. I'd weaved in and out of the collection of outbuildings, scaled a wall, traversed a roof, shinnied down a drainpipe and through an open window, and now had Ahmad in view. I sighted him in, placing his forehead directly in the center of my scope, and tightened my finger on the trigger.

"What the hell are you doing here?"

The voice startled me and I jumped straight up out of bed, reaching for my weapon as my feet hit the floor. I blinked once to clear my vision and saw a bemused Ally standing in front of me.

Ally raised her hands in the air. "Don't shoot."

Because her voice lacked the fear that a normal person would have if a gun were leveled at them, I looked down and saw that instead of my weapon, I'd grabbed my cell phone. I dropped my hand and glared at Ally.

"I ought to use it to call the cops and have you arrested."

"For what?"

"Disturbing my dream. That's probably illegal in Sinful."

"Only during full moons. That must have been some dream. You were grinning like an idiot. Was it about Carter?"

Instantly, I forced Ahmad to the back of my mind and scrambled to return my thoughts to my fake identity. "I don't know. I can't remember." I hated lying to my friend, but the less Ally knew about the real Fortune, the safer we both were.

"Bummer."

I glanced at my alarm clock and frowned. "Why are you in here yelling at a completely indecent hour?"

"The hour is indecent because I have to do the baking this morning at the café. And I was not yelling, but I was sternly asking why you were here because I rather hoped you'd finish up your date with Carter in someone's bed besides your own."

"Jeez, it was our first official date. Just because I'm a Yankee doesn't mean I'm a floozy. Or is that some kind of law, also?"

Ally sighed. "No, it's not a law, but it ought to be. Especially if your friend hasn't gotten lucky in two years and was looking to have a vicarious thrill."

"I haven't exactly been burning up the dating circuit, either." Actually, I couldn't remember the last time I'd had a roll with a hot prospect, but I had an idea my drought had been even longer than Ally's. That's what happened when you had standards such as "If I can kick his ass, I won't date him."

Ally shook her head. "We're a sad, sad lot. Two young, attractive, intelligent women and we're living together with a surly cat. If we don't jump back into things, people are going to start talking."

I shrugged. "All people in Sinful *have* to do is talk. Let them do their best. Before you know it, they'll be saying we're engaged and opening a cat farm."

"The really sad thing is, that's the best offer I've had in a while. At least tell me there was kissing, maybe boob touching?"

"Kissing, yes. No progression to boob touching."

Ally brightened. "How was the kissing?"

I suddenly felt more uncomfortable than I ever had before,

and for someone who made her living as an assassin, that was saying a great deal. It took a lot to rattle me, usually far more than one man, and definitely more than emotional turmoil. I struggled to latch onto a response that was good enough to make Ally drop the subject and not close enough to the truth—that I was becoming more of a girl every day.

"The kissing was awesome," I finally said, trying to recall a description I'd heard in one of those teen romance movies that Gertie made me watch to "broaden my horizons."

"Awesome is a great start." She looked pleased with my answer, but didn't show any indication of leaving my room.

"He has a lot of stamina. The future looks bright."

Ally grinned. "I could have told you that, and I've never kissed him." She glanced at my alarm clock. "Oh, shoot! I best get going or Francine will have my hide." She bounced out of the room and down the stairs.

Saved by the clock.

I gave the bed a wistful glance, but I knew it was hopeless. Once I was awakened to a certain level, there was no falling asleep again until I'd had coffee and breakfast, and taken care of at least one chore, such as feeding the cat. Then and only then could I contemplate napping in my hammock. I didn't want to feel lazy or something.

Then it hit me—today was Sunday.

I let out a sigh. That meant putting on a dress and makeup, fixing my hair, going to church with Ida Belle and Gertie, and then playing track and field as soon as the preacher said "amen." Lucky for me, my competition for the banana pudding sprint was a beyond-middle-aged, overweight woman with weak ankles. Lack of sleep and way too much wine wouldn't get in the way of a stellar dessert.

I had time for breakfast before I had to girl-up, so I pulled on a pair of athletic shorts and headed downstairs, following the smell of coffee. A full pot had just finished brewing and a plate with a homemade croissant sat on the kitchen table. Maybe I *should* ask Ally to marry me.

I poured my coffee and slid my laptop over as I took a seat. I wanted to check email and see if Harrison, my partner back in DC, had any updates on the Ahmad situation. So far, the summer had been eerily quiet, and that made me nervous. I was sure CIA Director Morrow wasn't any happier with the lack of movement. In his last email, Harrison implied that they'd lost sight of Ahmad, which was worrisome. I couldn't think of a single time in the last two years when we didn't know exactly where the arms dealer was located. The fact that he'd managed to give top-notch surveillance the slip was a scary proposition. I was fairly certain my cover in Sinful was still airtight, but with the CIA leak, I couldn't be sure.

I logged on to my secret email and saw a message from Harrison. I felt my pulse tick up a notch as I opened it.

To: farmgirl433@gmail.com
From: hotdudeinNE@gmail.com
I wish I were there enjoying those nice summer breezes. I was hoping to visit soon, but my dad had a car accident—hit-and-run driver—and I need to stick close for a while as he doesn't have anyone else to look after him. He broke his foot and has a mild concussion, but the doctor expects he'll be fine.

I'm still watching the weather, looking for that cool weather, but so far, no break for us.

Stay cool. I'll be in touch soon.

I logged off email and closed my laptop, my mind racing. I had worked with Harrison for a long time and knew how his mind worked. The "no cool weather break" comment meant that Ahmad was still missing and they didn't have a line on him. Even more alarming, I was certain "dad" referred to Director Morrow and "hit-and-run" meant Harrison suspected the car wreck was deliberate. But was he keeping watch on Director Morrow because he thought the attacker would try again, or keeping watch at the CIA since Morrow was out of commission? Either was plausible. Neither good.

And both were things I had zero control over.

I grabbed the croissant and bit off a hunk of it, directing my frustration at the pastry. I hated being out of the action, especially when all of the action centered on me. Why had Ahmad gone underground? Did he have a line on me, or was he simply off on other nefarious business? If the hit-and-run on Director Morrow was deliberate, who arranged it and why? So many unanswered questions.

Banging on my front door broke me out of my thoughts and I went to open it. It was too early for Ida Belle and Gertie to pick me up for church, and I hoped after last night, I was past getting early-morning angry visits from Carter, at least in an official capacity. I didn't even check the peephole, choosing instead to throw caution to the wind and fling the door open. Kinda like one of those old game shows—what's behind Door Number 1?

I paused for a moment when I saw Ida Belle and Gertie standing there, already dressed for church. Were all the clocks in my house wrong? No, that couldn't be. Ally had the morning shift at the café and she'd only left twenty minutes ago. Surely they weren't here to quiz me about my date. Then I saw the worried expressions they both wore and knew something else had brought them to my doorstep this early.

"I have a feeling I'm not going to like whatever you're here to say," I said as I waved them inside.

They trailed silently to the kitchen and poured themselves cups of coffee, and we all sat in our usual thinking and plotting spots at my kitchen table.

"Lay it on me," I said. "I've had a full cup of coffee and half a croissant. I'm as ready as I'm getting for this early in the morning."

"We've got trouble with the election," Ida Belle said.

I frowned. The previous mayor of Sinful had retired to a coffin, taking the easy way out when the skeletons came running out of his closet. At first, Ida Belle had put herself in the hot seat to be his replacement, but then her competitor was murdered, and it made her stop and rethink everything. Ultimately, she decided she could get far more things done without the rules of the job hindering her. She'd talked their friend Marie, a financial whiz, into running instead, and all signs had pointed to a positive reaction from the Sinful residents, especially given that the other candidate was a regular at the Swamp Bar, a place where the less reputable in town spent their time and money.

"What kind of trouble?" I asked.

"A new candidate threw their name in the ring last week," Ida Belle said.

"Who?" I asked, certain I wasn't going to like the answer.

"Celia Arceneaux."

"What?" I sat upright in my chair. Ida Belle and Celia were the heads of the two women's groups in Sinful. Ida Belle's Sinful Ladies Society, or SLS, required all members to be unmarried or longtime widows, and ran most of Sinful with underground influence. Celia countered the SLS with the GWs, or God's Wives, attempting to thwart the Sinful Ladies at festivals, town events, and the hallowed Sunday Banana Pudding Wars. She was one person who hadn't even entered my mind as a candidate for mayor.

Gertie nodded. "It will be the doom of the Sinful Ladies Society and ultimately of Sinful."

It was the kind of dramatic statement that would normally have had Ida Belle rolling her eyes. The fact that her worried expression didn't even shift one bit made me start to worry as well. "Surely people will vote for Marie over Celia, right? I mean, she doesn't exactly reserve her nasty nature for only a handful of people."

"True," Ida Belle said, "but she's always running all over town with her charity crap, being the hypocrite she is. And she's gonna garner the sympathy vote, given that her daughter was recently murdered."

"By the former mayor," I pointed out, "who was also her brother-in-law."

"Which she can also play to her favor," Ida Belle said. "Reclaiming family respect and all that."

"But Marie has actual business experience and knows accounting," I argued. "Surely that means something to people."

Gertie shook her head. "Marie was also accused of murdering her husband."

"And the real murderer was revealed."

"And is dead," Gertie said. "Which means there's an opening for some to believe he was the patsy used to cover for Marie."

I threw my hands in the air. "Who in the world would believe that crap?" Then I thought about the various intelligence levels I'd encountered since I'd been in Sinful. "Never mind."

"Anyway," Ida Belle said, "I have it on good authority from Beatrice that Celia is announcing her candidacy today at church."

My last remaining hope faded away. I had momentarily clung to optimism that Ida Belle and Gertie were mistaken—that they'd gotten misinformation or garbled something and none of it was true. But information from Beatrice Paulson was as good as hearing it yourself. Beatrice had been a member of Celia's group for decades, but when she was widowed some years prior, Ida Belle "turned her" and made her a secret member of the SLS. She remained in Celia's group as a spy. And boy, had she missed her calling. Beatrice had a mind like a vise. She remembered everything she heard, word for word, and even the tone of voice. It was like having a walking tape recorder at your disposal.

"That only gives her a day to get anything done. Surely that's not enough?"

"Most of the responsible people in Sinful will be in church," Ida Belle said, "and those who aren't will hear from those who were. In a place this small, it doesn't take long to mount an offense."

"Wow." I slumped back in my chair. "Okay, so I can see where Celia is less than desirable as mayor, but do you really think she'll come after the Sinful Ladies? I thought we all had sort of a truce."

Ida Belle shook her head. "Moments of quiet never last long with Celia."

"But I outed her daughter's killer," I said, "and saved her life. Has she forgotten all that?"

"No," Ida Belle said, "but she's conveniently pushed it to the 'does not matter' pile in her disturbed mind."

Gertie nodded. "She's just like that evil coach on *Glee*. No matter how much those kids do for her, she still reverts right back to the enemy. There's absolutely no doubt in my mind that if elected, she'll spend one hundred percent of her time in office figuring out how to stick it to the Sinful Ladies, especially me and Ida Belle."

"Jane Lynch is hilarious on that show, though," Ida Belle

said.

"I'll give you that," Gertie allowed.

"Unfortunately, Gertie's right about Celia, and she will definitely not be hilarious like Jane Lynch," Ida Belle said. "But what concerns us even more is that she could set her sights on you."

"What?" At first I didn't get it, but then I wasn't thinking like Celia. She'd always been at odds with Ida Belle and Gertie, and ever since I'd been in town, things had ramped up even more with the major crime wave. Even though Celia had no basis for her prejudice, I had no doubt she'd figure out some way to blame me for everything.

"And she'll have charge of the sheriff's department," Ida Belle continued.

I felt a quiver of fear in my belly. "You don't think she'd have them investigate me, do you?"

"If she thought she could find something about you that would make you leave town, yeah, it's possible."

"Crap." My cover would withstand basic police inquiry, even a fingerprint check, but it also required Morrow's tweaking things on his end to make sure nothing slipped through. With the director unable to keep his normal pace, I wasn't sure Harrison had access to everything he needed to keep me hidden from the mole.

"Exactly what I thought," Gertie said.

I looked at Ida Belle. "Then you have to ask Marie to step down and get back in the running again. You're a stronger candidate than Marie, right?"

"I can't," Ida Belle said. "The election is tomorrow. Celia played her cards well this time. She got herself on the ballot before the cutoff, then waited to announce it until no one else could challenge her."

"So we're screwed."

"I'm afraid we might be," Ida Belle said.

I sighed. "So I guess that means I can forget the tennis shoes and banana pudding today. Why antagonize the beast?"

"Hell, no!" Gertie said. "Celia was born antagonized. I don't see any reason to give up a perfectly good dessert when it's not going to change anything."

"I agree," Ida Belle said. "If she's elected, we'll be punished enough going forward. No use sacrificing the best part of our lunch until we're required to by law. And I imagine it will be one of the first things she rigs."

I rose from the table. "Then I best go put on a sundress and pack my running shoes in a handbag."

Ida Belle was right. I'd known plenty of people like Celia. If she intended to set her sights on me, she'd do it no matter what. If the end of my time in Sinful was drawing nigh, there was no sense in abandoning great dessert.

After a month in Sinful, I hadn't thought it possible, but church was even more boring today than it ever had been. Pastor Don had clearly been watching too much television and went on a rant about drug use, white-collar crime, and motorcycle gangs. He threw in some Bible verses that didn't exactly apply and indulged in lots of fist-banging on the pulpit. The latter, at least, served to keep me, and most everyone else, from nodding off.

The sermon went into even more of a lull, and my eyes were almost closed when I felt my phone vibrating in the pocket of my sundress. I pulled it out and smiled when I saw it was a text from Carter. After our great date last night, I was wondering when I'd hear from him.

I unlocked the phone and read the message.

Had a great time last night. Have to work today. Try not to get arrested after church.

I grinned. Some women liked sweet nothings whispered in their ears. I liked a man who encouraged me to avoid arrest.

I was just about to slip the phone back in my pocket when another text came through.

No sexting in church.

I looked over at Gertie, who was laid over in the pew, one hand over her mouth and her sides shaking. I didn't even know what sexting was, but not only did it sound like something that should never happen in church, it didn't sound like something I'd ever be involved in.

I looked up at the choir loft and saw Ida Belle shaking her head. It took Gertie a minute or so, but she finally sat back up, red-faced and digging in her purse for a cough drop. As if anyone was going to believe she was having a coughing attack.

The woman in the pew in front of us turned around and gave both of us a dirty look. Gertie stuffed a tissue over her nose and blew it, glaring right back at her. The woman huffed and turned around. I tried not to laugh. Between Gertie's childlike behavior and my propensity for the perverse, we probably needed to sit in different rows.

Finally, Pastor Don wrapped up his monotone monologue and the deacons began to make their way around with the offering plate. I couldn't help but think it might be better if they passed the plates before the pastor bored everyone half to death, but then I guess religious donation wasn't the same as tipping for good service.

I dug some cash out of my purse and dropped it into the plate, then passed it to Gertie. But instead of taking the plate, she began to dig around among the bills.

"What are you doing?" I asked.

"Making change."

"Are you supposed to do that?"

"You are if the teller at the bank gives you hundred-dollar bills instead of twenties."

The deacon waiting for the plate at the end of the pew leaned forward. "Get a move on. Drag racing starts at noon."

I grabbed the plate from Gertie and tossed it with a Frisbee move to the guy sitting down from her. Unfortunately, I realized after the toss that he hadn't gotten word that we'd moved on to the physical portion of church and was still snoring softly. The plate landed right in his lap and he jumped up as if he'd been shot, flinging bills and coins all over.

Gertie, who'd been looking glum—probably over the loss of the hundred—fell over in the pew, mumbling something about rain. My mind flashed back to a particularly unpleasant scene at my house when Gertie was throwing bills at half-naked men on television.

"You can't make it rain in church," I said and jabbed her in her right buttock.

The deacon scrambled for the plate and the money, managing to shoot us both dirty looks as he waved his arms at the floating bills. The previously sleeping man grabbed his hat and pushed past the deacon, apparently deciding he was done with church for the day. The song director, who was probably one of the original two disciples, squinted from the pulpit at the deacon. Apparently, he took the deacon's arm-waving as his signal to start the last hymn, and directed the congregation to rise.

The choir jumped to join the congregation and everyone sang a couple of verses of "Amazing Grace." The deacon managed to gather up all the money, then hurried back up front with his plate, barely depositing it on the table before Pastor Don launched into prayer.

As everyone bowed their heads and closed their eyes, I exchanged my sandals for tennis shoes and slid to the edge of the pew. As soon as Pastor Don uttered the "a" in "amen," I bolted for the door, Gertie barreling behind me. As we burst out of the church, I spotted Celia, already halfway down the sidewalk to Francine's, even though the church bell just started to ring.

"She cheated!" Gertie yelled.

Celia looked back and grinned and Gertie yelled a couple more things that probably weren't appropriate on the doorstep of the church. I doubled my effort and sped across the street at an angle, trying to head her off at the pass. Celia had definitely broken the rule about leaving church before the allotted time, and I had a feeling if she was elected, the allotted time might become earlier for Catholics and not for Baptists. The Sinful Ladies would never see a serving of Francine's banana pudding on their table again.

As I raced toward the sidewalk, two bloodhounds bounded down the street and locked in on me. They set off at a dead run, tails wagging and barking. I wasn't afraid for my safety because it was clear they thought I was playing a game and wanted to join in, but their size and speed could cause problems. I didn't have time to dodge playful hounds.

The hot dog vendor was setting up in front of the sidewalk for Monday's election, and I snagged two wieners from his tray as I dashed by. I chucked the first one ahead of me and onto the sidewalk, hoping to cut the dogs off before they reached me. My plan worked. The hounds caught a whiff of the wiener and immediately changed course, darting off toward the sidewalk.

Gertie, who had stepped onto the sidewalk somewhere behind me, was still pounding away and yelling "Cheater!" with every other step. Given her physical conditioning, I questioned her choice of running and yelling as it used up her limited oxygen supply more quickly, but I didn't have time to stop and throw out advice. Worst case, the sheriff's department had an oxygen tank and was across the way from Francine's.

I lifted my hand to throw the next wiener and stepped into a pothole. As I scrambled to stay upright, I involuntarily flung the wiener a little farther than I'd intended and it landed smack in Celia's huge handbag.

Chapter Two

The dogs, who'd already swallowed the first wiener, spun around and set off after Celia at a dead run. The largest hound leaped up and grabbed the purse, pulling Celia down with him. Celia screamed as she sprawled onto the sidewalk, clutching her handbag as the dogs ripped it to shreds for the elusive wiener.

I looked back to assess the damage and saw Gertie, who had surprised me by keeping her pace that long, try to put on the brakes, but it was too late to stop her momentum. She hit the first dog and went flying over him, landing on top of the flailing Celia.

I hesitated for a second, figuring I should probably stop and help, but then I heard Gertie yelling behind me, "Keep going."

I picked up pace and kept running for Francine's, completely ignoring the ruckus behind me. I flung open the door to Francine's and barely slowed as I dashed for the prime table at the front of the restaurant. Francine, who was standing in the kitchen doorway, raised one eyebrow but didn't say a word. Ally hurried over with a pot of coffee.

"What's all the commotion outside?" Ally asked as she poured me a cup.

"You don't want to know."

"Which means it probably involves Aunt Celia. Which means I definitely want to know."

The door flew open and Celia stumbled in, clutching the

remains of her handbag. Her hair stood out on end as if she'd stuck her hand in a light socket. The hem in her dress was completely torn out, leaving the bottom looking as if it had been chewed on, which made sense given that it sorta had. Unfortunately, it also exposed far too much of Celia's thighs, and I mentally apologized to Gertie for accusing her of being out of shape. Celia's thighs were pasty white jiggly masses of goo.

Gertie hobbled in the door after Celia, clutching her elbow and looking as though she'd been caught out in a windstorm. The rest of the two crews of women pushed their way inside. Dorothy, Celia's cousin, shoved Gertie to the side and stomped across the café to glare at me.

"I ought to have you arrested for assault," she said.

"Technically," I said, "I never touched her."

"You threw that wiener in her purse on purpose, knowing those dogs would attack her."

"That's a whole lot of assumptions you've made, especially the part about where I know for sure how random dogs will behave. Can you prove that?"

"Don't waste your breath," Celia said. "Even if you had the entire thing on video, nothing would happen to her. I guess when you're sleeping with the deputy, you can get away with murder in this town."

The entire diner went quiet and everyone stared at me.

"I'm not sleeping with Carter," I said.

"That's disappointing," Francine said, then glanced around. "Did I say that out loud?"

"No one believes that," Celia said. "You've been running around loose in this town since the day you arrived. It's not respectable. I didn't think it possible but you've brought Ida Belle and Gertie's stock even lower."

"That's enough," Ally said. "I won't listen to you run down

Fortune. She's helped me more than anyone else ever has, and she saved your life. How ungrateful can you be?"

Celia swung her head around and glared at Ally. "Your mother did not raise you to be disrespectful."

"No, she raised me to be her slave and a doormat. I'm neither any longer. Get used to the idea."

"It's a shame she didn't do a better job making you a lady."

"You mean like you did with your daughter?"

The café went silent. I was fairly certain everyone was holding their breath. It took me several seconds to realize that I was as well. Celia's daughter had been a sorry excuse for a human being and the kind of woman that every woman on earth loathed, but I never thought sweet Ally would slap Celia directly across the face with the one thing she had no defense for. It was both startling and beautiful. I wasn't sure whether to clap or light a candle.

One look at Celia's face, and I decided "pull a weapon" may be the best option. If looks could kill, Ally would have sunk straight through the café floor and on down to hell.

Finally, Celia took a breath. "You have the nerve to speak ill of the dead?"

"I'm not speaking ill. I'm speaking the truth. Death doesn't change who people were. Unless you want me to lie—Mother taught me that was wrong, too."

"That's enough!" Ida Belle yelled. "The bottom line is that Fortune won the race. No one but Celia's lot will believe she made that toss intentionally. Besides, one could argue that if Celia hadn't cheated by leaving church early, then none of this would have happened."

"Sounds good to me," Francine said. "If everyone will take their seats, we can get food out to you and everyone else that's held up over this spectacle."

I stared at Francine as she whirled around and headed back into the kitchen, my lips quivering with the smile I was trying to hold in. It was the most talking at one time I'd heard from the café owner. Today was two for two on the quiet ones getting their say. Maybe it was a full moon.

When the door swung shut behind Francine, it was apparently Celia's cue to give everyone one final glare and stomp out of the café, her menagerie of whipped women trailing behind her. Briefly, I wondered what they'd eat today since the café was the only place open on Sunday, but as the entire lot of them could stand to lose a pound or two, I didn't dwell on it very long.

"Are you all right?" I heard Gertie ask as the rest of the Sinful Ladies took their seats.

I turned and saw her patting Ally on the back.

"I'm fine," Ally said. "In fact, I'm better than fine. I've taken crap off that woman my entire life. It was never going to stop unless I refused to allow it. Aunt Celia will either learn to be respectful, or she won't see me."

"I hope she doesn't make trouble for you," I said.

Ally shrugged. "She'd have to work awfully hard to top last week."

She had a point. The prior week, Ally had been the victim of arson and of a particularly creepy stalker. Both seemed to have toughened her up. Now Celia might need a blowtorch to cut through Ally's leathery skin.

Gertie nodded. "Well, I guess there's nothing we can do about any of this now. We might as well talk it over with a chicken-fried steak."

"The magic words," I said, and took my seat.

Francine popped up a couple seconds later, carrying a pitcher of sweet tea. Ally began flipping tea glasses over as Francine poured.

JANA DELEON

Ida Belle looked up at her as she filled a glass. "What in the world got into you, Francine?" she asked. "If Celia is elected mayor, she'll target you straight off."

Ally sucked in a breath. "Aunt Celia is running for mayor? Oh, God. It's the end of the world as we know it."

Francine's eyes widened. "Well, Celia as mayor is certainly not optimum."

Gertie sighed. "The first thing she'll do is change the dismissal time for the Catholic church. The Sinful Ladies will never get a serving of banana pudding again."

Francine plopped the pitcher onto the table and put her hands on her hips. "If she does anything of the sort, I'll stop serving banana pudding altogether."

There was a collective intake of breath, as if someone had pulled a drawstring on all their panty hose. They all stared at Francine with so much dismay that you would have thought they'd been told Christ had already returned and they'd missed him.

Francine snatched up the pitcher and shoved it at Ally. "And if she pushes me more, then I'll sell my recipe to the Sinful Ladies." With that, she whirled around and headed off for the kitchen.

I couldn't help grinning. "The more I get to know her, the more I like her."

"Francine's always been a pistol," Gertie said.

"Why isn't she a member of the SLS?" I asked.

Ida Belle sighed. "She's still holding out hope that she'll find 'the one.'"

I frowned. "Who's the one?"

Ally laughed. "The one for her. Her soul mate. Her Carter."

"Ah," I said. "Speaking of which, I need a double order of banana pudding, and make one to go."

Gertie gave me a sly look. "Behind closed doors, there's lots of creative uses for pudding…"

Ida Belle rolled her eyes. "You haven't had a date in a coon's age. What the heck do you know about creative pudding escapades?"

"I know things," Gertie said.

"Let me be surprised," I said. The last thing I wanted to hear was Gertie's ideas for sexy pudding romps when I was about to eat lunch.

Ally looked relieved and pulled out her pad. "Let me get those orders started."

"What you do is," Gertie continued as if we hadn't spoken at all, "get a roll of Visqueen or an extra-large tarp—"

"I'll have the chicken-fried steak," I interrupted. I'd already heard enough to know that I did not want the details of the rest of it.

Ida Belle frowned at Gertie. "Sunday is probably not the appropriate day for such a discussion."

Gertie's face fell a bit. "You're right. If anyone overheard, they could have me arrested. I'll save it for tomorrow."

If I'd been anywhere but Sinful, I might have been more concerned about what words could get Gertie arrested, even on a Sunday. But Sinful had all kinds of oddball laws that appeared only to restrict the most bizarre and the most common of behaviors. I had a good idea that the founding fathers had been drunk when they wrote the town rules.

"Speaking of inappropriate Sunday behavior," Ida Belle continued, "what the heck was going on with you two in church today?"

"Fortune was sexting," Gertie said.

"I was not! Gertie was making change in the offering plate."

Ida Belle shook her head. "It's a wonder the entire building doesn't go up in flames." She tapped her fork against her tea glass and all conversation ceased as the ladies all focused on their leader.

"Ladies," Ida Belle said, "you're all aware of the situation with the mayoral race. I wish I could say otherwise, but it looks grim. I need all of you to contact everyone you can think of who is on the fence or doesn't usually vote and convince them to cast a vote for Marie tomorrow. If anyone has other ideas about how to help Marie's election chances, I'm all ears."

"We should start a smear campaign against Celia," one of the ladies suggested. "That's exactly how they do it in DC. We have to make sure everyone knows she's not a desirable person."

"Oh, oh!" One of the ladies' hands shot up in the air. "We should toilet paper her house. That's a sure sign of being unpopular."

Gertie brightened. "I haven't toilet-papered a house since I was young and frisky."

Ida Belle rolled her eyes. "You haven't done anything since you were young and we're not discussing frisky ever. Besides, that's a ridiculous idea."

"You didn't think it was a ridiculous idea when we were teenagers," Gertie argued.

"That's because back then my parents were paying for the toilet paper. Now when the kids paper a house, all I see is dollar bills hanging off the limbs."

"That wouldn't be a problem if you used something cheaper than Charmin."

"My butt and I prefer Charmin, and none of that is the point. The bottom line is that papering someone's house didn't make people turn against them when we were teens, and it's not going to now."

Gertie sighed. "Fine, but I still think it's a good idea, if only to sit across the street at Marie's and watch her clean it all up tomorrow."

I sorta agreed with Gertie on that one, but the aggravated look on Ida Belle's face kept me from tossing in my two cents.

"Given the proclivity for drama among Sinful residents," I said, "I don't think a smear campaign is the best tactic. I mean, who doesn't have some gossip floating around about them? There's not anything new you can dig up, and everyone is going to believe what they want to anyway."

Gertie shook her head. "There's always something new to dig up."

"Not by tomorrow," I said. Given all the odd criminal secrets that had started rising to the surface the day I arrived in Sinful, I couldn't argue with her in theory, but our timeline didn't allow for intensive digging.

One of the ladies raised her hand. "Maybe we could launch an appeal to the...er, less desirable citizens. Celia's never made it a secret that she'd like to see the Swamp Bar closed down. The regulars may not be model citizens, but they still have the right to vote."

Ida Belle nodded. "That's an idea we can run with to a certain extent, but we'll only be able to hit the regulars during the day to give them time to vote. If we'd known about this yesterday, we could have launched a campaign last night." Ida Belle sighed. "I hate to admit it, but Celia worked this out perfectly."

I was mulling over our seemingly nonexistent options when Deputy Breaux burst into the café and ran straight for me. "I need you to come over to the sheriff's department with me. It's an emergency."

I jumped up from my seat. "What's wrong?"

Deputy Breaux glanced around, the panic on his face

unmistakable. "I can't talk here. Please hurry."

He dashed toward the front door and glanced back to see if I was following. Ida Belle and Gertie jumped up from their seats. "We'll come with you," Ida Belle said.

I hurried after Deputy Breaux, who was moving at a rate far faster than what I'd ever seen him accomplish before. He slowed only long enough to push open the door of the sheriff's department, and we rushed in behind him.

"What the hell is going on?" Ida Belle said.

Gertie collapsed in a chair in the lobby, huffing far too much considering we'd only sprinted across the street.

Deputy Breaux locked his gaze on me. "Were you on a date with Carter last night?"

"Was it on the news or something?" I asked. "Did I need a permit?"

Deputy Breaux looked even more flustered. "No, I just wanted to know where he took you."

I frowned. "We went to some island. It had a rocky point with an open area where you could see the sunset."

Deputy Breaux shook his head. "I don't know it. Could you take me there?"

"No, and even if I could, I wouldn't until you told me why."

Deputy Breaux ran one hand across his head. "Carter came in this morning and said as how he was going to check on something he saw yesterday evening that didn't look right, then he got in the boat and left. He was at home all day until he went out with you, so whatever he saw, it musta been when you two were on the bayou."

"And when he set up the dinner," I pointed out. "It was set up when we got there."

"I didn't think about that part." Deputy Breaux ran his hand across the top of his head. "But he still would have seen it along the way to where you had dinner, even if it was before he picked you up."

For the life of me, I couldn't clue in on what was so distressing about my dinner. "Okay, so why don't you call him on the radio and ask where he is?"

He took a deep breath and blurted, "Because five minutes ago, I got an SOS call from Carter...and I think I heard gunshots."

My breath caught in my throat. Gertie jumped up from her chair and clutched my arm.

"I think I know where Carter took her," Ida Belle said and moved over to a map of the local bayous that hung on the wall behind the dispatcher's desk. "The back side of Oyster Island has a rocky edge. It's the only one I know of."

I hurried beside her and traced the channels from my house to the place Ida Belle pointed to, an island sitting in a lake. "That looks right," I said.

"Then what are we waiting for?" Gertie said. "Let's go find Carter."

Deputy Breaux held up his hands. "Ladies, I can't let you head out into a potentially dangerous situation. I've called for backup and will check it out myself."

Ida Belle put her hands on her hips. "By the time backup gets here, Carter could be dead and buried, and his mother cashing the insurance policy. Either grow a pair and get your ass out in the bayou or move out of the way and let us do your job."

Ida Belle stormed past Deputy Breaux, who stood slack-jawed and helpless as we fled the sheriff's department.

"There's a small problem," I said as I hurried after Ida Belle. "We don't have a boat."

Both Ida Belle's and Gertie's boats had met with disaster during some of our previous "work," and neither had made it out of the repair shop yet.

"We'll borrow Walter's," Ida Belle said as she turned past the General Store and headed for the pier.

"Shouldn't we ask him first?" I asked. Walter, the owner of the General Store and Carter's uncle, had been in love with Ida Belle since the crib, and would probably give her the boat if she wanted it, but it seemed only polite to ask before you stole a man's pride and joy. Walter was deeply attached to his bass boat.

Ida Belle shook her head. "If we ask to borrow it, he'll want to know why. Then he'll want to come. If something bad goes down, that won't work well for any of us, especially you. If he sees you in action, it won't take him long to figure out you're no librarian."

"Oh, right." It was a valid point, and cinched the boat stealing...uh, "borrowing" idea.

"Do you have your nine-millimeter with you?" Ida Belle asked me.

"In my purse...crap! I left it at the café."

"I snagged it when we left the café," Gertie said, huffing as she tried to keep up. "And I've got my forty-five, Mace, a dagger, and some Chinese throwing stars."

I reached back to take my purse from her as we stepped onto the dock, not sure whether to be impressed or frightened. "Is all that hardware necessary for church?"

Ida Belle waved us into the boat. "Gertie's afraid a zombie apocalypse or the rise of the Antichrist will happen Sunday morning."

I hopped into the boat, Gertie stepping in behind me. "Well, it's the best time for an attack," Gertie said. "After all, a third of the town is in church."

"And you think the Antichrist would begin his rise to power in Sinful?" Ida Belle asked as she untied the boat.

Gertie put her hands on her hips. "For all you know, she's already here and running for mayor."

"Hold it right there!" Walter's voice sounded behind us and I whipped around to see him hurrying toward the dock.

Ida Belle shoved the boat away from the dock and leaped inside. "Put it on my tab," she called out.

Walter yelled again but his voice was drowned out by the revving of the boat motor. Ida Belle glanced back. "Can't hear you!" she shouted, then gunned the boat.

I should have had a better grip on the bench, but I was too busy trying to read Walter's lips to concentrate on my balance. As the boat leaped forward, I fell backward off the bench and right on Gertie's purse. Thank goodness I put my hands down to break my fall because one of those throwing stars caught me right in the center of my butt cheek. I flew back up onto the bench as if on springs.

"If that scars," I yelled at Gertie, "you're buying me a new butt."

"Stop sitting on weapons and your butt will be fine," Gertie shot back.

There was simply no winning with Gertie, so I studied the landscape as we flew by. I remembered the little yellow house on the corner of the bayou from yesterday evening, and the shrimping barge anchored at the edge of a pond. Ida Belle whipped the boat to the right and I clenched the seat, my mind finally locked in on the task at hand.

What had happened to Carter? Was someone shooting at him? Poachers? Maybe he'd tried to arrest them? Surely not. The penalty for poaching was hardly worth killing a law enforcement officer over. Maybe it wasn't as dire as Deputy Breaux thought.

I got an SOS call...

The deputy's words repeated in my mind and I felt my

lower back stiffen. No way would Carter call for help like that, much less disappear afterward, unless things were seriously wrong. I took a deep breath and rolled my head around to loosen my neck.

Focus on the mission.

When I was on a mission, I was an efficient, nerveless, deadly machine. It was everything I'd been trained to be, and I'd been trained by the best. Missions were never personal. When things became personal, people made mistakes. But no matter how hard I tried to convince myself that this was just another day on the job, that knot of fear deep down in my stomach wouldn't go away.

It seemed like forever before I saw the jut of the island where I'd had dinner with Carter. I grabbed Gertie's arm and pointed. "That's it!"

Ida Belle glanced at the island, then cut the speed on the boat to a slow coast. "I figure what Carter saw must have been out in the lake. I didn't see anything questionable in the bayous."

"Me either," Gertie said. "The lake is huge. Where do we start?"

"Closest to the island," Ida Belle said, "with the hope that Carter came straight here and didn't meander around before setting up for dinner." She reached in a compartment below the steering column and pulled out a pair of binoculars.

"I wish we would have had time to get supplies," I said as I stood. "A scope would come in handy about now."

Gertie picked up her enormous purse and dug out a package of Kleenex, two airline samples of vodka, a remote control for her television, and finally a rifle scope. I took the scope from her and peered into the purse. "I don't suppose you have a cheeseburger in there?"

"If you'd have asked me yesterday, you would have been in

luck, but I got hungry late last night. I have a dill pickle?"

Yuck. "Pass," I said as I lifted the scope up and scanned the lake, looking for any sign of well, anything. For several minutes I moved from one position to another, hoping to lock in on something besides the miles of muddy water.

"There," Ida Belle said, and pointed to our right. "I caught a glint of something—sunlight reflecting, maybe, but it's too far away for me to see."

I moved the scope to the right where Ida Belle indicated. A minute later, I found the source of the shine. "It's the sheriff's boat, and it's sinking fast."

Chapter Three

Ida Belle shoved the binoculars into Gertie's lap and grabbed a handful of throttle. I dropped onto the bench and braced myself for the takeoff, praying that Carter was off the boat and swimming for shore. I had no idea how deep the lake was, but if he were unconscious, it wouldn't matter if it was six feet deep or sixty. By the time we reached the boat, he could run out of air.

The tension on Ida Belle's and Gertie's faces was matched by my own. Despite all the dangerous situations and close calls I'd been in since I'd joined the CIA, I couldn't remember being this worried about anything...except when my mom had gotten sick. Now my stomach was churning like that sad little girl who'd held her mother's hand as she slipped away.

Damn it! Coming to Sinful had complicated everything. For the first time in my life, I'd formed relationships with people I cared about, and it had been a lump of heartache every time one of them had been in danger. But this...this was the worst by far. I'd spent a lot of time trying to convince myself that my relationship with Carter was casual and could never amount to anything, but sometime while I was busy thinking up reasons why I couldn't fall for him, I did it anyway.

Gertie covered my hand with hers and leaned close. "He's fine. I'm sure of it."

I nodded, touched that she tried to comfort me, but I

already knew he was in trouble. I knew it just as I knew the sun was shining and that I was no librarian.

It seemed to take forever, but finally, we made it to the spot where Carter's boat had been. My heart dropped as we scanned the surface but saw no sign of him. The spotlight on the top was just dipping below the surface of the water. Without a moment's hesitation, I yanked off my tennis shoes and sundress and dived over the side of the boat.

The water was so murky, it was impossible to see more than a foot in front of me, so I swam with both arms outstretched to avoid running headfirst into the hunk of sinking metal. I latched onto the rail on the top of the boat and used it to guide myself lower until I reached the bottom of the boat. I strained to see something...anything...but the most I could manage were shadows cast by large objects in the boat.

Focus!

I cleared my mind and scanned the shadows, looking for one that wasn't made of straight edges. As I moved toward the rear of the boat, a hazy lump came into view. Using the bottom of the boat to propel myself forward, I ran straight into the lump. Immediately, I knew it was Carter.

The boat was still sinking, so I had no idea how far from the surface it had gone. Did I have enough air left to make it?

It wasn't a question I had the luxury of dwelling on. I rolled Carter on his side and grabbed him underneath his arms, pulling him to a standing position along with me. Then I bent down, and pushed straight up as hard as I could, launching us both off the bottom of the boat and toward the surface.

I kicked so hard that my thighs and hips burned from the effort, and my free arm ached from my wrist to my neck as I pushed it up and down to increase our speed. The seconds ticked by, each seeming longer than the next, but the dark water still surrounded us. The increasing pressure on my chest made my ribs ache. I let out a bit of air to ease the pressure, but the urge to let it all out and drag in a huge gulp of fresh air was so overwhelming.

A wave of dizziness washed over me, and I felt my legs and arms weaken. Carter slipped in my grasp and the remainder of my air fled my body in a whoosh. Panic set in as I tightened my grip on him and pushed my spent body even harder than before. I kicked and pushed and strained, knowing that if I didn't hit the surface soon, I'd lose consciousness and Carter and I would be together forever, but not in the way anyone wanted.

I struggled to maintain focus, but my body wouldn't comply. I felt drowsy, almost as if I'd been drugged. Above me, a sliver of light blinked through the murky water, but I knew it wasn't the surface. It was the end. Just as all those people had reported. This was it.

The light at the end of the Tunnel of Death.

I gave one last kick—one last burst of effort—before my body collapsed completely, and I slipped into darkness.

"Pull harder!" The voice drifted by as if echoing from far away.

"Stop yelling. She's heavier than she looks."

What the hell? They're insulting my weight in heaven?

I felt my body being jostled, but it was almost as if I wasn't completely inside me anymore. Then I felt a jab of something hard into my rib cage and I sucked in so much air I thought my chest would burst. A second later, I fell onto a flat, hard surface.

As I struggled to gain perspective, I heard the voices again.

"She's breathing! Get Carter."

A jolt went through me. Gertie! It was Gertie's voice.

"One, two, three, breathe."

I sucked in another breath and blinked, trying to clear my

blurry vision. I pushed with one arm, but I didn't have the strength to lift my spent body even an inch. Finally, I managed to roll on my side and blinked again.

The scene in front of me slowly came into focus.

I was on the bottom of Walter's boat. Ida Belle and Gertie were hunched over Carter, giving him CPR. My heart leaped in my throat as I saw his lifeless body. I clenched my eyes shut and prayed harder than I ever had before, then I heard a single cough. I opened my eyes and Gertie turned Carter's head to the side as water poured out. His chest moved up and down. His breathing was so shallow that he wasn't out of danger, but he was breathing.

"Get to the hospital!" Gertie yelled. "I'll watch him."

Ida Belle jumped up from the bottom of the boat and shoved a life preserver under my head. "Don't need you banged around any more than you already are," she said and gave me a pat on the shoulder. "Don't you worry. He's going to be just fine."

A second later, she hopped behind the steering column and gunned the engine. The boat practically jumped out of the water as it launched forward. Every time the boat came down on a wave, another jolt of pain rushed through my body, but none of that mattered. I was alive. Bruises and broken bones healed. The only thing that mattered was getting Carter to a hospital.

I heard Ida Belle call the sheriff's department on the CB radio. A bit of hope trickled into my stream of consciousness when I heard her demand a helicopter. Then the boat slammed against another wave, and everything went black again.

Strong arms encircled me and I felt myself being lifted, then placed onto a soft surface. I opened my eyes and saw a paramedic leaning over me, smiling as he pulled a blanket over my scantily clad body.

"Welcome back," he said.

"Carter!" I tried to push myself off the gurney.

The paramedic placed a hand on my shoulder to prevent me from moving. "They're loading him onto the helicopter now. You need to stay still."

I turned my head to the side and saw Ida Belle and Gertie, rushing behind two paramedics pushing a gurney toward a helicopter. Deputy Breaux and Myrtle ran out of the sheriff's department, followed closely by Walter, all sprinting for the gurney. Only then did I realize that I hadn't even locked in on the sound of the whirling copter blades. All my senses were off.

"They're sending a second copter for you," the paramedic said.

"I'm fine," I said. "I just need some aspirin and a cold beer."

He laughed. "You are my kind of woman—tough and excellent taste in how to treat an injury. But you're not getting off that easy. My mother is a Sinful Lady. If I don't put you on a copter to the hospital, I'll have Sinful Lady grief the rest of my life."

I groaned. Unless I was armed, there was no defense against the threat of the Sinful Ladies. Whether I wanted to or not, I was about to get a ride in a copter, be checked into a hospital, and be poked and prodded by doctors and nurses. The only good thing was that Morrow had the forethought to get me an individual medical insurance policy in case of an emergency. He probably hadn't anticipated an emergency of this scale, but at least I wasn't adding insurance fraud to my list of crimes.

The copter took off and I watched as it disappeared on the horizon. Gertie hurried up to my gurney, her face beet red. Likely, she needed to lie down more than I did.

"Ida Belle went with Carter," she said, huffing. "I'm going with you."

"Ma'am," the paramedic said, narrowing his eyes at Gertie, "I think you should sit down for a minute."

Gertie plopped down on a wooden bench near the gurney as Walter, Deputy Breaux, and Myrtle hurried over to me.

"Are you all right?" Walter asked. "What happened?"

"Sir," Deputy Breaux said, "if you don't mind, I need to ask the questions."

A red flush crept up Walter's face. "The hell you do! That's my nephew unconscious on that helicopter, and my friend lying here on a gurney looking like she just fought ten men and came up short. Law enforcement does not outrank family. Not in the South."

Deputy Breaux was smart enough to know when he was defeated. He grumbled a "Yes, sir" and took a step back from the gurney so that Walter could take his place. He leaned over to study me for a moment.

"You sure you're all right?" he asked.

"Considering everything, I'm fine," I said.

"What the hell happened?" he asked.

"We don't know. Deputy Breaux can fill you in on the beginning, but the short version is Carter was in trouble and we went after him. His boat was almost completely below the surface when we found it. I—"

I started to explain, but choked as I tried to speak. How could I put into words my dive into the inky black, finding Carter's lifeless body, and my struggle getting us to the surface, ultimately ending with my thinking I'd died?

"She dived in after him," Gertie said. "Not a second's hesitation—just ripped off her shoes and dress and went straight down after that boat."

Myrtle's hand flew over her mouth. "Oh my God."

Gertie nodded. "It's the most helpless I've ever felt, leaning over the side of that boat, clutching Ida Belle's hand and looking for any sign of life. Ida Belle wanted to go after her, but neither of us is in any shape to make that kind of dive. The boat was dropping like a stone and the water's too deep there."

Walter shook his head, looking at me. "It's a wonder you made it out yourself."

"I didn't think I was going to," I said quietly. "I thought…"

Walter reached for my hand and squeezed it. "Thank God that didn't happen."

"When we saw bubbles," Gertie said, "I squeezed Ida Belle's hand so hard it will probably bruise, but she didn't even yell. Then Fortune popped up on the surface, Carter under her arm, but she was almost unconscious but still breathing. We hauled them both into the boat and started CPR on Carter."

Myrtle dropped on the bench next to Gertie and put her arm around her. "I can't even imagine how frightened you must have been. I would have been frozen stiff."

Gertie shook her head. "I don't think so. When your loved ones are in danger, something else takes over."

Walter put his hand on Gertie's shoulder and squeezed. "It makes heroes out of normal people. Thank you…thank you both, for saving my nephew."

"I'm sorry we stole your boat," I said.

Walter let out a single laugh. "I'll let this one slide."

The sound of an approaching copter interrupted us and we all looked up the second it landed. The paramedic looked down at me. "Here's your ride. They'll take good care of you."

"Thanks," I said as two new paramedics pushed me away. Gertie grabbed our purses and hurried behind.

"I'll meet you at the hospital," Walter called out, then

headed for his store.

"Me too," Myrtle said, "I just need to call for a fill-in at dispatch." She hurried to catch up with Walter.

Deputy Breaux looked back and forth between me and the disappearing Walter, clearly completely at a loss as to how to regain control of the situation. Unfortunately, the situation was simply too far out of Deputy Breaux's skill set. Finally, he set off at a jog toward the sheriff's department, probably to head to the hospital himself, or perhaps to write his resignation letter.

The copter lurched off the ground and I watched Sinful disappear as we sped off for the hospital. My head throbbed and the rest of my body wasn't much better off, but my mind was slowly coming back into focus.

What the hell had Carter seen?

Deputy Breaux had said he thought he heard gunshots during Carter's radio transmission. Was that what sank the boat?

I bolted upright on the gurney, causing the paramedics to jump.

"Was Carter shot?" I asked Gertie.

"I don't know," Gertie said. "He was bleeding from his leg and his side, but nothing deep. If he was shot, it was only a flesh wound."

Relieved, I dropped back down. "Maybe the shots are what sank the boat."

Gertie put her hand on my arm. "Don't worry about that right now. Let's concentrate on making sure you and Carter are all right."

"We need that boat," I said. "And you said the water was deep there."

"We'll get it," Gertie reassured me. "Try to relax, Fortune." She leaned forward and whispered, "We need you at one hundred percent."

I looked at her and gave her a single nod. As much as I hated it, she was right. All indications pointed to someone trying to kill Carter. I needed to be in top form.

Because no one got away with trying to kill my man.

I was a horrible person at the hospital. I'm not a good patient, especially when my mind is focused on much more important things. Between Gertie and me, we pestered the medical staff so much that they finally sent someone to check on Carter's status. I had declared I was holding the MRI machine hostage if I didn't get answers, and since Gertie had waved around those pointy stars, people weren't all that interested in challenging either of us.

Once we were assured that Carter was stable and experiencing moments of consciousness, I agreed to proceed with the examination. By that point, I'm pretty sure the tech was ready to add more bruises to my collection. He ran me through the machines like a car on an assembly line and practically sprinted away after turning me over to the discharge nurse.

The nurse gave me a once-over and glanced at my paperwork. "Well, Miss Morrow, despite looking like you've played a full quarter in the NFL, you have sustained no serious injuries. Aspirin should help with the discomfort. Other than that, rest is the only prescription you need." She handed me a set of scrubs. "These are on the house."

"Thanks," I said, somewhat relieved over the diagnosis. I mean, other than the banging against the bottom of the boat for what seemed like forever, I hadn't thought anything else had injured me, but you never know what's going on under the surface. Medical tests always gave me a moment or two of pause, even when I hadn't made death-defying dives into creepy bodies of water and almost died saving a man that I'd only kissed.

"You can check out at the front desk," the nurse said, then took her chart and headed out of the room.

"Well, I guess that's it for me," I said. I stepped off the table and gently pulled on the scrubs. "Barefoot will have to do. Let's get this insurance crap settled and find Carter."

Gertie held up her hand and I gave her a high five, then we both winced and grabbed our elbows.

"Maybe we'll just exchange 'Hell yeahs' for a couple days," Gertie suggested.

I nodded as we headed for the front desk.

I was a little worried about the checkout process, but the clerk barely glanced at my ID before handing me a paper to sign for them to file my insurance. So far, so good. I dashed off my signature, then asked where Carter was. The clerk said he was still in emergency care and we needed to wait in the lobby.

More than a little frustrated, I shoved the door to the lobby wide open and it crashed into a table, stopping all conversation in the room. I would have apologized for all the racket, but as the only people in the lobby were there because of Carter, I figured they would give me a pass on being a little testy.

Ida Belle rushed over and gave me an up-and-down. "Are you all right?"

I nodded. "They released me."

Ida Belle looked over at Gertie. "Is she lying?"

"No," Gertie reassured her. "They told her to take aspirin and rest."

"Really?" I said. "You thought I'd lie?"

Ida Belle snorted. "If they were trying to make you stay here, hell yeah, I think you'd lie."

"Well...whatever." I couldn't really argue when she was right. "What's the word on Carter? They wouldn't tell us much."

"Damned doctors," Walter said. "We keep asking and all we

38

get is he's stabilized but no one can see him yet. They leave me hanging much longer, and I'm going to march right down that hall, opening doors until I find him."

"You really shouldn't do that," Deputy Breaux said.

Everyone glared at him.

"Never mind," he said and slid back down onto the couch.

The door to the emergency room opened and a doctor walked out. We all stared at him, and I'm pretty sure everyone was holding their breath.

"I'm Dr. Stewart. Are you here for Carter LeBlanc?" he asked.

"Yes," I said. "Is he all right?"

"Are you family?"

Walter stepped forward. "I'm his uncle, but we're all his family."

"He's stable," Dr. Stewart said, "but he's still slipping in and out of consciousness. He has a concussion, but I don't see any other damage to his head. I got very little from the paramedics about how he sustained his injuries. I could tell he'd been underwater, but can anyone give me more to work with?"

Ida Belle stepped forward and gave Dr. Stewart a rundown of what had transpired. When she was done, he rubbed his chin and nodded.

"The lengthy submersion explains the trauma to his respiratory system. It definitely shows signs of being taxed." He looked over at Deputy Breaux. "You thought you heard gunshots?"

Deputy Breaux nodded. "The transmission wasn't real clear, but that's what it sounded like to me."

"I think you're probably right. There are two injuries on Mr. LeBlanc that I couldn't explain—both clean removal of the tissue. A bullet would account for both and is consistent with other flesh wounds I've treated."

Myrtle gasped. "So he *was* shot? Oh my God." Her knees buckled and she started to slip to the floor, but Ida Belle caught her before her knees hit the tile.

"Get a grip," Ida Belle said as she righted Myrtle. "What caused the concussion?"

Dr. Stewart shook his head. "Until Mr. LeBlanc is able to tell us, I can't say. My best guess is that he fell and struck his head on something in the boat, rendering him unconscious."

"Maybe when he was shot..." Gertie suggested.

"Perhaps," Dr. Stewart agreed, "but given the situation, I'm not ruling out the possibility that someone struck him on the back of the head."

"Good Lord," Myrtle wailed. "You think someone hit him, too?" She started to wobble again and Ida Belle poked her in the ribs.

"If you buckle again," Ida Belle said, "I'm letting you hit the tile."

Myrtle straightened up and shot a dirty look at Ida Belle.

"We're keeping a close watch on him for now," Dr. Stewart said, ignoring the exchange. "If you're sticking around for a while, I'll pop back in and update you if there are any changes."

Walter reached out to shake the doctor's hand. "We'd appreciate that. His mother is on her way. I know she'll want to talk to you, directly."

Dr. Stewart smiled. "Mothers always do." He gave us all a nod and left.

I looked over at Gertie, a sliver of fear running through me. "Carter's mother?"

I'd known he had a mother, of course, but as she'd been out of state visiting her sister, I'd never run into her. Meeting the mother of the guy you may or may not be in a sorta-relationship with was stressful enough under ordinary circumstances. But when he'd been shot and almost died, it kinda ticked things up a notch. I'd only ever made it far enough into a relationship to meet one mother, and she'd been one of the primary reasons that relationship had ended.

"Don't worry," Gertie whispered. "Emmaline is a lovely person. You'll like her, and more importantly, she'll like you."

"You can't know that."

"Yes, I can. You saved her son's life."

"There is that." Some of the tension in my neck slipped away. Surely I got permanent brownie points for rescuing Carter from a murky death. But how many brownie points? And did they expire? I walked over to a chair and sank into it with a sigh. This relationship stuff was so hard. Getting shot was easier.

Gertie sat next to me and pulled aspirin and a bottled water out of her purse. "Good. Take a couple of these and rest. And have a cough drop. It will help numb your throat a bit. It's got to be sore."

I took the aspirin and washed them down with the water. Now that she mentioned it, my throat was sore. I guess I'd been too wound up to notice. I popped the cough drop in my mouth and sat the water on a table next to my chair. "You know, if you unloaded at least fifty items from that purse, your back would probably stop hurting."

"Yes, but then you wouldn't have aspirin, water, or a cough drop." She pulled a bottle of Sinful Ladies cough syrup out and handed it to me. "Take a good swig of that. Takes the edge off."

I removed the cap and took a huge swig, then blinked a few times as my eyes watered. Sinful Ladies cough syrup was really their homemade hooch, and it was strong enough to strip paint off a bumper. I'd had it before, but usually mixed with another liquid. This huge gulp, undiluted, had practically made my eyes cross.

"You guys should really think about making a light version," I said, coughing.

Gertie brightened. "That's a great idea. All kinds of applications—teething babies, noisy children, and long airline flights."

I leaned back and closed my eyes. I was pretty sure those "applications" would get someone arrested, but I knew back in Gertie's day, it was the norm. I didn't do much travel by domestic flight. Mine wasn't the sort of travel you wanted reported on a passport, but the excruciatingly long hours I'd spent on my bus ride to Sinful, most of them with my seat being kicked by the small boy behind me, were reason enough to wish for the good ole days.

Guns. Missions. The good things in life.

Chapter Four

I must have dozed off because the next thing I knew, Gertie was shaking me. Normally, I would have bolted up, grabbing weapons and preparing to take down a small army, but I was actually too tired to move that quickly. Instead, I opted for opening one eye.

"Carter's mother is here," Gertie whispered.

That got my attention. I snapped into an upright position, jolting my injured limbs and jostling my lightly throbbing head into a harder throb. I looked across the lobby and saw a woman hugging Walter. Emmaline LeBlanc. I had absolutely no doubt. She was wearing Carter's face. Or he was wearing hers—whatever. It was obvious where Carter had gotten his looks.

According to Gertie, Emmaline was in her fifties, but she could have easily passed for early forties. She was trim but not too skinny, like a lot of older women seem to aim for. Her long dark hair was pulled back in a ponytail, its glossy waves trailing midway down her back. Her facial features had the same fine bone structure as Carter—high cheekbones, wide-set eyes.

When she released Walter, he inclined his head toward me and she locked her gaze on mine, her green eyes sparkling. I rose from my chair and she rushed over and gave me a quick hug.

"Please, sit back down," she said. "You've done enough physical activity today."

I didn't even attempt to argue with her. The truth was, my

body had taken a beating, and I felt every inch of it. I slid back down to my chair, my muscles practically sighing with relief as they relaxed.

Emmaline sat next to me and squeezed my hand. "I'd hoped to meet under better circumstances, but I have to say, I don't think I've ever been happier to know someone as I am right now. Thank you for saving my son." She sniffed and wiped tears from her eyes with her free hand. "'Thank you' sounds so underwhelming. I wish there were better words for something like this."

"It's okay," I said. "I understand. I'm just glad I got to him in time."

"It was a huge risk," she said, her brow creased with worry. "You could have both been killed."

"But we weren't, and the doctor said Carter will be fine."

She managed a small smile. "Thanks to you. As far as I'm concerned, it's a Sunday miracle. You've done so much. You should go home for a hot meal and a comfortable bed."

"What about Carter? I wanted to talk to him."

"I know, honey. I do, too. But he's still not completely awake and it's past visiting time. Dr. Stewart said we wouldn't be able to see him tonight."

I glanced at the clock on the wall, surprised to see it was a little past 9:00 p.m. I'd been asleep in that chair for hours. I rose from the chair, Emmaline still clutching my arm.

"Gertie sent Ally home an hour ago," Emmaline said. "She's preparing you soup and pot roast as we speak. You need a good meal, a hot bath, and a lot of sleep."

"Oh, wow," I said. "I must have really been out. I didn't hear a thing." As I couldn't see a single flaw in her argument, and my mouth had started watering at the words *pot roast*, I started my barefoot shuffle out of the lobby.

The ride back to Sinful was awkwardly quiet, but then given that we were riding with Walter, I figured Ida Belle and Gertie were hesitant to say too much lest Walter get the idea that we planned on investigating again. Even though I hadn't discussed it with Ida Belle and Gertie, I had no doubt that my partners in crime weren't going to let this one quietly slip away. Mentally, they were mounting the cavalry, except we rode in on bass boats, or motorcycles, or stolen cars...anyway, I was sure the silent process was in motion.

"What do you think happened?" Walter asked, breaking the uncomfortable silence.

"I don't know," Ida Belle said.

Walter glanced over at her and frowned. "Don't give me that crap. You three have been up to your eyeballs in every criminal act that's happened in the last month. You must have some idea what's going on. This is Carter, damn it."

His voice broke on the last words and my heart clenched. I knew Carter's dad had died when he was young, but I didn't know the details. I had always gotten the impression that Walter viewed him more as a son than a nephew. I couldn't begin to imagine how worried he was.

"We really don't know anything," I said. "I swear."

"She's telling the truth," Gertie said. "If we had any idea who did this to Carter, we would have skipped out of the hospital, stolen a car, and popped a cap in them."

Walter looked at her in the rearview mirror and gave her a small smile. "I believe you would. What does it say about me that I wish you could have?"

"It means you love Carter," Ida Belle said. "We all do. If there's anything we can do to fix this, we will. You have my word."

Walter looked over at Ida Belle and nodded. "If it were

anyone else, I would ask you not to, but this time...this time, I'll only ask that you be very, very careful."

I watched his expression shift as he looked at Ida Belle, then away, and realized that in that brief look, he had conveyed so much—his desire for justice for Carter, his concern for the three of us, and the enormous conflict going on inside him as he felt he was risking one for the other.

Oh my God. I was actually getting good at this. The whole girl/emotion thing.

I frowned. Was that good or bad? Logically, having an emotional side would be a hindrance at my job, but then, I didn't have deep feelings for anyone I worked with. I liked Deputy Morrow and Hadley and I probably even liked Harrison more than I was willing to admit, but none of them tugged at me.

I let out a breath of relief. Thank God. At least I didn't have to find a new job when this whole fiasco with Ahmad was over.

"Are you all right?" Gertie asked.

"Yeah. Just tired."

She patted my hand and leaned over toward me. "I'm so proud of you," she whispered. "What you did was extraordinary, and I don't believe anyone else could have done it."

"Why do you say that?" I knew I had skills far beyond those of the typical woman, but I wasn't the only person equipped to handle such a recovery.

"Not for the reason you're thinking. It's because of your connection with Carter. I don't think anyone else could have found him, assuming they had even been willing to try. That far under the surface, visibility must have been zero. I believe it was your emotional tie to Carter that led you to him. That led you to save him."

She sniffed and reached for her purse, pulling out a tissue.

I watched as she dabbed the tears from her eyes, but didn't

say a word. I could have told her that I could make out shapes. That my training included deep sea diving and recovery, and I'd been taught to look for shapes rather than individual objects. Instead, I gave her hand a squeeze. If Gertie wanted to believe in some sort of karmic magic that saved people you cared about, who was I to spoil it for her?

"Don't go sniffling now," Ida Belle said. "Carter's going to be fine and we've got a busy day tomorrow."

I nodded. "I hope he remembers everything."

"Oh!" Gertie's eyes widened. "I didn't even think about that, but with a concussion, he may have lost some of his memory."

"It's usually temporary," I said, "but the sooner he can provide details, the better." I left the rest unsaid. We all knew that timing was a key component in catching criminals. The sooner you could set out on their trail, the more likely you were to find them.

It was long past dark when Walter pulled into my driveway, and my house was lit up inside and out.

Gertie shook her head. "That girl needs to talk to someone about that stalking mess. The repairs to her house will be finished soon, and it's far more isolated than yours."

I frowned. It had never crossed my mind that all the lights were on because Ally was afraid. I'd figured she was distracted by what happened to Carter and with cooking and simply forgot, but now that Gertie mentioned it, I realized lights were on in all the upstairs rooms, even the ones no one used.

"I'll talk to her," I said as I climbed out of the car. "Are you guys coming in?"

"Not tonight," Ida Belle said. "We all need to get some rest. We'll regroup at your house first thing in the morning."

I nodded and closed the door. In the morning, Ally would

be at work and Walter wouldn't be sitting next to Ida Belle. We'd be able to speak freely and make plans that it was probably far better others didn't know.

Before I could even slip my key into the lock, Ally flung open the door and threw her arms around me. "Gertie told me what you did. You could have been killed."

"But I wasn't," I said, hoping the hugging part was over soon. My bruises did not appreciate all the attention.

Ally let go of me and sniffed. "And you saved Carter." She waved me inside and immediately locked the door and drew the dead bolt. She paused to peek out the living room blinds before heading to the kitchen, and that was when I noticed she had a butcher knife in her hand. I trudged behind her, worried that Ally's fear was worse than even Gertie had imagined.

"Sit," Ally ordered. "You look like you're ready to drop, but you haven't eaten since breakfast. So food first, then shower and bed. I was just about to check the pot roast." She waved the knife and I felt a bit of relief pass over me. Maybe she wasn't completely gone.

She opened the oven and gave the pot roast a peek then filled a huge bowl with soup. When she placed it in front of me, my mouth watered as the smell of potatoes and herbs wafted up to my nose.

"Baked potato. My favorite." I took my first bite and almost sobbed. The creamy, cheesy sauce might have been the best thing I'd ever eaten in my life. "You should be awarded a medal or something."

Ally smiled. "It's good, but you're also starving." She prepared herself a bowl and sat across from me. "You were out cold when I was at the hospital. Are you feeling all right...I mean, considering?"

"Yeah. My body feels like I was jumped by a street gang,

and I have a nagging headache that seems to almost go away then pop back up, but given everything that could have gone wrong, I'm lucky this is the worst of it."

"Do you have any idea what happened?"

I shook my head. "I don't think we're going to know for sure until Carter wakes up."

Ally dropped her spoon in her bowl and it clanged on the side of the dish. "What is going on in this town? It used to be so mundane and uninteresting and…safe. I don't understand."

I lowered my spoon. "Are you worried about moving back into your house alone?"

Her eyes widened a bit and she opened her mouth, then closed it. After a couple of seconds of silence, she finally sighed. "I guess I am. I'm fine when I'm there looking at the repair progress. It's really all going to be quite lovely and my new kitchen is going to be fabulous—practically gourmet. But then I start thinking about being there after dark, and this knot forms in my stomach."

"I wish I had answers for you," I said. "I don't know what's happening here. It seems like an awful lot of issues for such a small place, but maybe when the first thing happened, the rest just fell in line. Like dominoes."

"More like a loose thread on a knitted blanket. Before you know it, the entire thing is unraveling."

I frowned. *Unraveling* was a particularly accurate description of what seemed to be happening in Sinful. I couldn't help but feel a twinge of guilt that my arrival seemed to have set it all in motion. If Bones hadn't dug up part of Marie's missing husband, maybe none of this would have happened.

"Don't even go there," Ally said, pointing her finger at me.
"What?"

"You were thinking it's all your fault because it started with that bone, but that's not true. You just happened to be there. You didn't cause any of it."

"Yeah, I guess not."

"The pot roast should be ready. Do you want more soup?"

"No. Now that I'm not starving, I think I'll take a quick shower before the roast."

"Good idea."

I rose from the table and headed upstairs, my aching body protesting with every step. When I entered my bedroom, I walked over to the window and opened the blinds, looking out across the neighborhood. Pretty houses with beautiful landscaping all in neat little rows. It didn't look at all like the place where someone would shoot a deputy and leave him to drown.

What the hell was going on in Sinful?

It wasn't even 7:00 a.m. when I heard banging on my front door. I kicked my legs over the side of the bed, groaning as every muscle in my body protested. The banging started up again, making my head pound, so I headed downstairs as quickly as my thighs allowed me to go. I'd barely gotten the front door unlocked before Ida Belle and Gertie pushed the door open and rushed inside.

"We got trouble," Ida Belle said.

I felt my back tighten. "Did something happen to Carter?"

"No, he's fine," Gertie said. "Physically, anyway. He's awake, but someone else got to him first."

"What do you mean?" Maybe it was the early hour, or my pounding head, but I hoped someone got to the point soon.

"Feds," Ida Belle said. "Emmaline stayed at the hospital last night. She said two men in dark suits showed up in the middle of the night, demanding to see Carter. She told them in no uncertain terms that the first person to see Carter this morning would be his doctor and the next was her."

"What agency are they with?"

Ida Belle shook her head. "They didn't offer any ID, but I know the type—black suits, tight butts, sunglasses indoors. Emmaline said they backed down after she came at them, but they returned at 5:00 a.m. She caught them trying to sneak down the hall to Carter's room and sent them packing again."

"It doesn't make sense to me," Gertie said. "Why would Feds care about a small-town deputy getting shot?"

"They wouldn't," I said, "unless they think he stepped in the middle of something big and that's what got him shot."

Ida Belle and Gertie glanced at each other, their concern apparent. "That's what I figured," Ida Belle said. "But I was hoping you had a different idea."

"I'm afraid not," I said. "If they're interested in Carter, then that means they think the shooting had something to do with their case. All Feds care about is their case. And they're highly protective of any other law enforcement creeping in. They pretty much think anyone who isn't a Fed is an idiot. Add small town to that, and it's even worse."

"Which means they'll be barking orders and keeping everything to themselves," Ida Belle said. "I don't like it. Their goals will have nothing to do with catching whoever shot Carter—at least, not for shooting Carter."

"No. They will think whatever they're working on is far more important than one small-town deputy."

"They're wrong," Gertie said. "And they suck."

Ida Belle raised an eyebrow.

"Just sayin'," Gertie grumbled.

Ida Belle put her hands on her hips. "We've worked our way around Feds before. We can do it again."

"True," I said, but we'd gotten lucky the last time. The Feds hadn't really locked onto the three of us as suspects, so they'd never had any reason to run my background. But with Carter being shot, and us being...close...or whatever, they might take a harder look. I figured my fake identity was good enough for regular law enforcement scrutiny, but I wasn't so sure it would hold up to a federal check.

"I have to be really careful with this one," I said.

Ida Belle's eyes widened. "Crap! I hadn't even thought about that. We'll play it cool—the concerned friends and new girlfriend. Play the cute ditzy blonde and they won't take a second look at you."

"Ditzy?" I shook my head. "I wouldn't even know where to begin. I barely manage capable librarian. Ditzy is so far out of my element it's not even in this universe." I sighed. "But if it means finding out who tried to kill Carter, then I guess I'll manage."

Gertie smiled. "That's the spirit. Now, get upstairs and put on something girlie—I'm thinking the yellow sundress. And put your hair in a ponytail. It makes you look younger, which means less experience and knowledge."

"And be fast about it," Ida Belle said. "We've got to get to the hospital. Emmaline can't keep the Feds away from Carter forever. We need to talk to him first."

"I'll fix us some breakfast for the road," Gertie said, and headed for the kitchen.

I dashed upstairs and made a quick change into my girl persona, even slipping bright pink lip gloss into my purse to don after breakfast. I'd thought the color horrid when Gertie selected it, but it was perfect for what I needed to do. I gave myself a final look in the full-length mirror and hurried downstairs, saying a quick prayer as I went.

We were going to need all the help we could get.

Emmaline jumped up from her chair when we entered the hospital waiting room and gave Ida Belle a hug.

"They're sitting in the corner by the plant," she whispered.

I appreciated the effort, but didn't need her to point them out. In a rural area hospital, black suits and sunglasses looked completely out of place. Clearly, they'd been watching too many movies.

Two of them. First one six feet even, 185 pounds. Second one six feet two, 200 pounds. Needed to lose a few pounds, but both in decent shape. Bummer.

Emmaline gave Gertie and me quick hugs, then motioned us to the side. "The nurse said Dr. Stewart is in with Carter now. I'm praying we get to see him."

"Is he awake?" I asked.

Emmaline nodded. "The nurse said he was awake for fairly long spurts during the night. I slipped back there once to take a peek, but he was sleeping then. I didn't want to wake him."

"Of course not," Ida Belle said. "He needs his rest, and besides, Dr. Stewart will let you see Carter before he turns a couple of Feds loose on him."

"Do you think so?" Emmaline asked.

"Definitely," Gertie said. "Otherwise, he'd be giving up his official Southerner card."

The waiting room door opened and Dr. Stewart stepped into the room. The two Feds jumped up from their chairs and flashed their badges at him. I hurried over to see the badges, but they closed their wallets quickly and shoved them back in their pockets.

"We need to speak to Mr. LeBlanc immediately," the first Fed said.

Dr. Stewart glanced over at Emmaline, then looked back at

the Feds. "He's my patient. I'll say who speaks to him and who doesn't. He's asking for his family and friends."

"I don't think you understand the gravity of the situation," the second Fed argued.

"And I don't think you understand Southern hierarchy. Mothers are always first. Anything else could get you shot." He winked at Emmaline and waved us toward the door.

"He's still weak," Dr. Stewart said as we walked down the hallway, "but doing quite well given his condition. There is still a good bit of swelling, but it's decreased significantly since yesterday. I don't anticipate any long-term effects. I'd like to keep him another day for some additional tests and observation. If he's raising too much hell and the swelling is gone, I might be convinced to release him tonight, but only if he has someone staying with him."

"I think you can pretty much count on the raising hell part," I said.

Emmaline smiled. "You know my son well." She looked at Dr. Stewart. "Once you release him, he'll insist on going to his own house, but I'll insist on staying there for as long as you think I should."

We stopped in front of a door and Dr. Stewart turned to face us. "He got banged around quite a bit, so his appearance will be somewhat distressing. But I assure you, the surface injuries are just that and will fade quickly."

Emmaline took a deep breath and pushed the door open, Ida Belle close behind as she entered the room. I hesitated and grabbed Dr. Stewart's sleeve as he started to walk away.

"I'm sorry," I said, "but those men in the lobby. Who were they?"

Dr. Stewart shrugged. "I didn't bother to look at their ID, but Feds, if I had to guess. I'm certain the government issues them all the same suits and superior attitude."

"Oh," I said, working up my best surprised look. "What in the world could they want with Carter?"

"No telling," Dr. Stewart said, "but don't worry. I'll have my nurse keep them from barging in for as long as she can." He gave Gertie and me a nod and headed down the hallway for the front desk—probably to instruct the nurse to stall the Feds. He looked almost happy at the prospect.

"I've decided I like Dr. Stewart," I said.

"Me too. And I have an idea."

Uh-oh. Gertie's ideas never worked out the way she thought they would.

She pointed to the door across from Carter's room with "Cleaning Supplies" stenciled on the front. "I'm going to grab some supplies and head to the lobby. If the nurse aggravates the Feds enough, they may let slip why they're here."

I stared at her, fairly certain that this time she really had lost her mind. "That will never work. They just saw you with the rest of us in the waiting room."

She waved a hand in dismissal. "Please. Young people never pay attention to seniors. They glance long enough to classify us as 'old' and move on."

"Normal people, maybe, but regardless of agency, they wouldn't be in the field unless they were investigators."

"*Government* investigators. They're wearing sunglasses inside. How much of me could they have possibly zeroed in on in the half second they looked my direction? Besides, I'll put on a disguise."

Before I could protest, she slipped into the supply room. I looked back at Carter's room and Ida Belle poked her head out. "What the hell's the holdup?" she asked.

"I don't think you want to know."

"Well, hurry up." She ducked back into the room, leaving the door open a crack.

I reached for the handle and as I started to pull it open, the supply room door opened and Gertie came out. I froze and did a double take.

Her rose-print dress was gone and now she was clad in green scrubs, complete with the plastic booties that medical staff wore over their feet for surgery. She had a purple bandanna wrapped around her head and her silver hair stuck out the sides, making her look like a geriatric chicken.

"What's with the booties?" I asked.

"I can't exactly wear my red pumps. Oh! I almost forgot." She reached back into the room and stuck a hand in her purse. Then she pulled out a pair of black glasses with the thickest lenses I'd ever seen in my life and slipped them on.

"You got new glasses! Why don't you wear them?"

"How many times do I have to tell you that I don't need new glasses? I only got these for undercover work."

"Yeah, right."

She glared at me and I held in a smile. It was like looking at an owl, really close up. She reached into the room once more and pulled out a rolling bucket and mop. Gertie plus a rolling bucket of water brought all kinds of possibilities to mind, and none of them good. "Do you think…"

"What?"

"Never mind. Just be careful, and don't be obvious."

I slipped into Carter's room before Ida Belle poked her head out and stopped Gertie altogether. I didn't think it was a great plan, but if there was even a 1 percent chance of finding out something that helped us catch whoever had tried to kill Carter, I was willing to roll the dice. Besides, it was Gertie. If things went south, she could always do the fuzzy-headed old lady thing she was so good at.

Chapter Five

Carter was propped up in bed and gave me a weak smile as I walked in. Emmaline stood next to his bed, clutching his hand and biting her lower lip as she studied the bruises on his face. I was glad Dr. Stewart had issued a warning. The discoloration didn't worry me, but I was used to seeing such injuries on others as well as myself. Someone who lacked exposure would automatically assume the injuries were far worse than they were.

"How are you feeling?" I asked as I stepped next to the bed.

"Like I got shot twice and almost drowned." He locked his gaze on mine. "I hear I owe you big."

I shook my head. "I did what anyone else would have done."

"Not true," he said, "and even if they'd tried, I doubt many would have been successful."

I felt a blush creep up my face. "I just got lucky. I mean, I'm a certified scuba diver, but that doesn't exactly qualify you for this sort of thing."

He reached for my hand and squeezed it. "I'm not sure anything qualifies you for this sort of thing. Thank you."

The words were simple, but the depth of emotion in his eyes had my heart beating a little harder and faster. The alternative ending flashed through my mind and I slowly drew in a breath, trying to shift my thoughts from what could have happened to what did.

"I would say 'anytime,'" I said, "but I'd really prefer if we didn't do this again."

Emmaline looked up at the ceiling. "Lord, I hope you heard that."

"Amen," Ida Belle said, then glanced at the door. "Where's Gertie?"

"She's, uh…had to make a pit stop," I said, grasping at the first excuse that might pass muster. "She'll be along in a minute."

Ida Belle frowned and I knew she didn't believe me for a minute. Then a wrinkle of worry appeared across her brow and I gave her an imperceptible nod. The wrinkle deepened and I could see her lips moving, probably in prayer.

"Mom says there's Feds in the waiting room," Carter said and looked at Ida Belle and me.

"That's the general assumption," I said. "Dr. Stewart stalled them but they're demanding to see you. What happened yesterday?"

Carter frowned. "It's all kind of fuzzy. I remember leaving the dock at the sheriff's department, and I remember calling for help when the first bullet hit me…" He shook his head. "But I don't remember anything after that."

Emmaline's brow creased with worry.

"It's the concussion," I said. "In a day or two, it will probably all come back. What were you looking for?"

"I can't remember that, either. Damn it!" He banged his hand on the railing and we all jumped. "Sorry." He gave Emmaline an apologetic look. "Do you have any idea how frustrating it is to know that somewhere in your foggy brain is the answer to why someone tried to kill you and not be able to access it?"

I glanced over at Ida Belle, who looked even more worried than Emmaline, but for entirely different reasons. I had no doubt

Carter would be okay, physically, but the longer Carter's memory took to return, the more likely the perpetrator would be long gone.

"Deputy Breaux said when you came in that you said you'd seen something the day before that you wanted to check out," I said. "That's why we looked for you near where we had dinner."

Carter frowned. "It's like it's right there, and just when I think I have hold of it, it's gone again."

Emmaline patted his arm. "It will come, dear. Don't strain yourself. Those federal agents are here for a reason. Maybe they'll tell us what's going on."

"Maybe so," Carter said, but I could tell he was humoring his mother. He knew there was no way Feds were going to give him any information on their investigation. And boy, were they going to be pissed when they found out he didn't know anything.

I was about to ask him about the depth of the lake when I heard loud voices outside the room. Ida Belle and I hurried out of the room and saw the Feds arguing with a nurse at the end of the hall. Gertie was about five feet away, mopping one side of the hallway. Ida Belle glanced at her, then the fact that it was Gertie registered with her and she jerked her head back around and uttered a strangled yelp.

"We're not waiting one minute more," the first Fed said and pushed past the nurse.

A burst of anger ran through me as I saw the nurse stumble backward, and I started down the hallway, but before I made it two steps, Gertie pulled a well, Gertie.

Fed One approached swiftly and when he got to Gertie, she whipped the mop around, striking him in the shins. It was a hell of a good blow. Fed One went sprawling onto the tile floor. Fed Two, who'd been following right on his tail, tried to put on the brakes, but his shoes slid on the wet floor and he ran straight into the now-prone Fed One. He flailed about, waving his arms as if he were going to attempt flight, but finally lost the battle and fell right on top of Fed One.

"Oh my!" Gertie dropped her mop back in the bucket, feigning innocence and concern.

She took a step toward the prone men but while she'd been busy acting, hadn't noticed that the mop handle had fallen in front of her. She tripped over the mop handle, which wouldn't have been a disaster if the end of the mop hadn't been wedged between the side of the bucket and the handle. As she fell, the entire bucket flipped over, sending a wave of dirty mop water over the three of them.

Ida Belle and I rushed down the hall and pulled Gertie off the two cursing agents. Fed Two jumped up and glared at Gertie. Fed One flailed around in the dirty water for a bit before gaining his footing and finally making it back to a standing position.

"What the hell are you trying to do?" Fed One yelled. "Kill people?"

"Don't shout at her," I shot back at him. "She's just trying to do her job in a place that you don't even have any right to be, I might add. Are you all right, ma'am?"

Gertie pulled off her glasses and blinked several times. "I think so."

Fed One glared at me and whipped around, grumbling something about the hospital hiring more competent staff as he stalked off toward Carter's room, Fed Two falling in step right behind.

The nurse, who'd been staring openmouthed at the entire scene, finally shook herself out of her stupor and focused in on Gertie. "You're not an employee," she said.

"She's my great-aunt," I said. "She used to work in a hospital." I leaned toward the nurse and whispered, "Sometimes she gets confused."

The nurse frowned. "But when you spoke to her just now, you sounded like you didn't know her."

"I wasn't about to let those two know she was with me. They didn't seem overly friendly."

The nurse's face cleared in understanding. "No, they're definitely not friendly. I won't file a report, but do you think you can get your great-aunt out of those scrubs and back into the clothes she was wearing when she came in? There's liability and all."

"Of course." I put my arm around Gertie's shoulders and headed for the storeroom to retrieve her clothes and handbag. "Get changed and meet us in the car."

Gertie started to protest, but Ida Belle pointed to the bathroom, then tugged on my sleeve. "Hurry or we'll miss the questions."

Ida Belle pushed open the door to Carter's room just as the dripping Feds stepped up to Carter's bed.

"Ma'am," Fed One said, "we're going to have to ask you to leave." He looked back at us. "All of you."

Carter gave them both an up-and-down, frowning at their disheveled appearance. When he glanced over at me, I mouthed "Gertie." His bottom lip quivered, but he managed to hold in the grin I knew was straining to break out.

"It's okay," Carter said and motioned his mother to the door.

Emmaline wagged her finger at the Feds. "If you boys compromise his condition, you'll answer to me. And trust me, you don't want to answer to me." She gave Carter a kiss on the forehead, then whirled around and followed us into the hallway.

Gertie popped out of the restroom and drew up short when she saw us all standing there. "What happened?" she asked.

"They kicked us out," I said.

"Crap," Gertie said. "They didn't talk in the waiting room, but when they were complaining to the nurse, I heard one of them say ATF."

I nudged Ida Belle in the ribs. "Maybe they got wind of Sinful Ladies cough syrup."

"I don't think we're big enough to draw the attention of the ATF," Gertie said.

"She's joking," Ida Belle said, and frowned. "They wouldn't be here unless they think whoever they're after could have attacked Carter."

I nodded. "The question is, who are they after and why did they attack?"

"Exactly," Ida Belle said. "They're not going to be happy when they find out Carter can't remember anything."

Gertie's eyes widened. "He's brain damaged?"

"No!" I said. "It's probably temporary, but those two goons aren't going to want to hear that. They'll be hounding Carter until he remembers."

"Over my dead body they will," Emmaline said.

I smiled. I really, really liked Carter's mom.

The door to Carter's room flew open and slammed right into Gertie, who grunted. Fed Two stuck his head out. "Who's behind the door?"

"No one," I said. "Just one of those laundry carts." If he looked behind the door and saw Gertie standing there, the gig was up.

"Then who made that noise?" he asked.

Gertie, who was holding in position lest the door open any wider, held up one hand behind the door, middle finger extended.

"Me," I said. "You startled me throwing the door open that

way."

"Whatever," he said. "You're the girlfriend, right? Get inside."

I raised my eyebrows. "Please?"

"Please, what?" he asked.

"Ask me politely, and include the word 'please.' I'm a lady, not your employee."

I glanced over at Ida Belle, who was giving me a thumbs-up and struggling to hold in a laugh. Playing the Southern belle might not be as horrid as I'd originally thought.

He blushed and I could tell he was hacked. Finally, he sputtered, "Can you step inside, please?"

"I *can*, and you're in luck. I will."

I gave him a smile and stepped inside the room. Then I stopped short and drew in a breath so hard, it made my chest hurt. Thank God, Fed Two was mostly blocking me from view and neither Carter nor Fed One had seen my reaction. Fed One had taken off his sunglasses.

And I knew him.

You look completely different. You don't even recognize yourself.

I drew in a breath and slowly blew it out. All of that was true, and I'd only worked with the agent briefly, but I wasn't about to leave anything to chance. Time to turn on the girl charm as I never had before. No way could he confuse a regular girl with the shaved-head, militant assassin he'd worked with before.

"Miss Morrow?" Fed One—Agent Riker as I knew him—gave me an intense once-over as I stepped up to the bed.

"Yes?" I replied, struggling not to cringe as he stared. "And you are...?"

"You can call me Agent Riker. That is Agent Mitchell."

"Oh! Secret agents?" I widened my eyes and put one hand

over my chest. "I hope I didn't do anything wrong."

Carter stared at me, his brow scrunched. Awesome. If I had Carter confused, that meant my ploy was working.

"No, ma'am," Agent Riker said. "I'd just like to get some information from you."

"Well, okay, I guess."

"I understand you pulled Mr. LeBlanc from the sinking vessel."

"Yes, that's right."

He gave me a skeptical look. "That must have been quite an effort."

"Oh, well, I'm a librarian."

He frowned. "And that qualifies you as a marine recovery specialist?"

I giggled. Carter's jaw dropped and he stared at me as if saying "Who *are* you?"

"No, of course not," I said. "It's just that the library isn't busy a lot of the time so I read. If I find something that interests me a lot, I take lessons. I read this great book about pirate's treasure and decided to take diving lessons."

"Uh-huh. You had dinner Saturday night with Mr. LeBlanc near the location his boat sank. Is that correct?"

"Yes."

"Did you see anything out of the ordinary?"

"It was a first date, Agent Riker. I don't like to see out-of-the-ordinary things until I get to know a man a little better."

Carter launched into a coughing fit, covering his mouth with one hand and reaching for a glass of water with the other, but I could tell he was covering a grin.

Agent Riker's frustration began to show. "No. That's not what I meant. I mean did you see anything out of the ordinary in your surroundings."

"Well, sure. Hardly anything in Sinful is what I would call normal. There's alligators and frogs that sound like they're using amplifiers, the most enormous mosquitoes I've ever seen, and none of the people are normal, at least not compared to home back east."

Agent Riker's face fell a bit. "I see. You're not from here."

"No. I'm just here for the summer to settle up my great-aunt's estate. I can't even remember the last time I was here—probably too young to recall." I frowned. "What's all this about, anyway? Do you know who shot Carter?"

Agent Riker's expression went from contemplative to blank. "I'm not at liberty to talk about that."

"Not at liberty, my foot," I complained. "If you know who shot Carter and don't tell, you'll have to answer to his mother."

Agent Riker looked mildly disturbed, then pulled a card from his pocket and handed it to Carter. "As soon as your memory clears, give me a call."

"Sure," Carter said and placed the card on the tray next to him.

"I can't express enough how important this is, Mr. LeBlanc," Agent Riker said. "Attempting to handle this matter yourself is not advisable."

"Got it," Carter said, not bothering to look at Riker.

Agent Riker frowned. "I wonder if you do. In case you're fuzzy on the law as well as what happened to you yesterday, if you interfere with my investigation, you'll be arrested so quickly, it will probably give you another concussion."

Carter looked up at him. "Since you haven't told me what you're investigating, you might have trouble making charges stick. I can hardly be expected to sit in my house until you decide it's all right for me to do my job."

Agent Riker smiled. "If you give me any reason to doubt

your intentions, that can be arranged." He motioned to Agent Mitchell and they left the room. The door hadn't even closed before Ida Belle and Emmaline hurried inside.

"What a douche bag," I said.

Carter laughed.

I whirled around. "Did I say that out loud?"

"Yes," Ida Belle said, "but I was thinking it."

Carter looked at me and grinned. "You were a maniac. That whole airhead routine made Agent Riker crazy."

I nodded. "It also made him leave. So what the hell is going on?"

Carter shook his head. "I couldn't get a thing out of them except that they're with the ATF. I threw out some comments and questions that I thought would elicit a response, but I didn't even get an eye twitch. Lobotomies must be required for government agents. I swear, they've all had their personalities scrubbed."

Ida Belle glanced at me, looking a little worried. I probably should have been offended, but I couldn't muster up the energy to be. His statement held entirely too much truth, even about myself. My entire career, I'd essentially been a machine. Granted, a highly reliable and extremely efficient one, but personality hadn't played into any of my accomplishments. At the CIA, personality was usually considered a detriment.

"So all we know is that the ATF thinks you might have stumbled into their investigation," I said, "but we have no idea what that investigation is about."

"Well," Ida Belle said, "we know it's alcohol, tobacco, or firearms. Tobacco seems a stretch. There's plenty of illegal stills around here, but I can't imagine the ATF cares about them."

Carter shook his head. "The sheriff doesn't even care about them."

"That's because one of them is his," Ida Belle said.

Carter stared at her in dismay.

"Oops," Ida Belle said. "Anyway, I suppose someone could be running the high-end stuff through the Gulf from Central and South America."

"Yes," I agreed, "but they could be running any of the three, or even from Cuba. The ATF is on high alert in Florida. Someone smuggling cigars may have decided on an alternate drop point."

Carter studied me for a moment.

Crap. That sounded way too much like law enforcement and not at all like a librarian.

"I saw this special on television," I lied.

Carter blew out a breath. "Most of television is crap, but I happen to know that tidbit is accurate."

"So we're back to not having a clue what we're up against."

Carter straightened up in his bed. "Wait a minute. *We* are not up against anything. This is a police matter. How many times do I have to tell you to stay out of the way of law enforcement?"

Ida Belle raised one eyebrow at him. "You mean like you intend to do?"

"That's different," Carter argued. "I *am* law enforcement so that makes it my business."

"Agent Douche Bag told you to stay out of it," I pointed out. "I don't think he believes it's your business."

Carter's face turned a bit red. "That's not the point. The bottom line is that something big is going on in my town—apparently right under my nose—and no way in hell am I letting some Fed screw up the investigation."

Emmaline gave him a stern look. "No way in hell are you running around chasing criminals until your brains are unscrambled."

"But—" Carter started to protest.

"The way things are right now," Emmaline said, "you could walk right up to the bad guy and not even know it. You have to wait until you remember."

"She's right," Ida Belle said. "Whoever took a shot at you isn't going to know that your memory is fuzzy. Any proximity to them or whatever they're hiding, even accidental, would prompt a repeat performance."

I could tell Carter wanted to argue, but he probably couldn't find a line of reasoning good enough to trump logic. He shook his head. "So you just want me to sit here while anyone in Sinful could be at risk from an unknown enemy with an unknown agenda?"

"I'm sorry," Ida Belle said, "but until your memory returns, I just don't see any other way."

"There's got to be some way to hurry this up," he said. "Call that doctor back in. Surely they can make the swelling go down faster, right?"

"The only way to make the swelling go down faster," Emmaline said, "is for you to rest."

"Great," Carter groused. "So the only contribution I can make is to do nothing. That's not what I get paid to do."

Emmaline put her hands on her hips. "I don't remember 'getting shot and almost drowned' being in your job description either, but you managed that one. I worried and prayed every day of your military service. And you know I wasn't happy when you decided on law enforcement when you left the military. When you settled in Sinful, I thought, 'How bad can it be?' Now…"

Emmaline sniffed and Ida Belle put her arm around her shoulders. "It's going to be all right," Ida Belle said. "I know things are strange here lately, but they also have a way of working themselves out."

Ida Belle glanced at me and I gave her an imperceptible nod. They had a way of working out all right.

This was another mission for Swamp Team 3.

Chapter Six

All three of us started talking at once when we got into Gertie's car.

"With Carter's memory fuzzy, we have no place to start," Gertie said.

"If only we could figure out what the Feds are after," Ida Belle said.

"Agent Riker knows me."

Gertie yanked her head around so hard that her arms followed and the ancient Cadillac lurched onto the shoulder of the road. Ida Belle clung to the headrest and stared at me, her eyes wide as Gertie forced the car back onto the pavement, apologizing the entire time.

"Holy...wow," Ida Belle said. "I never saw that one coming."

"Me either," I said. "When I walked into Carter's room and saw him without those sunglasses, I almost bolted out the window."

"That might have been a bit suspicious," Gertie said.

Ida Belle rolled her eyes. "I take it you met on a professional basis?"

"Yeah, an arms dealer established in Florida was moving product in from Cuba on cigarette boats. He had a tourist business as his cover, but drew attention with his lifestyle. Most guys running boat sightseeing tours don't live in ten-million-dollar estates in Miami."

"And this Agent Riker was on that case?" Ida Belle asked.

"The ATF was the agency of record. It was American soil, but included international waters, so we were able to insert ourselves into the investigation."

"Do you think he recognized you?" Gertie asked.

"I don't think so. I mean, I look completely different than I did then, and I played up the ditzy girlfriend as much as I knew how to." I cringed a little at the memory.

"I would have paid money to see that," Gertie said.

"Me too," Ida Belle agreed.

"Carter stared at me like I'd lost my mind," I said, smiling at the memory, "but then he figured out I was trying to get rid of them. I think he enjoyed the show."

Ida Belle snorted. "I bet he did."

"I called Riker a douche bag at the hospital, and I have a perfect memory, so I know I'm right on that one. But he's not incompetent."

"The advantage we have," Ida Belle said, "is that Riker has no expectation that he would run into you here."

"True, but the more time he spends around me, the more likely he is to lock in on facial structure or the more likely I am to slip with my voice affectation. He won't make a connection immediately, but if he latches onto the idea that he knows me from somewhere else, he'll keep working on it until he figures it out."

"Just like a dog with a bone," Gertie said.

"And that's not all," I said. "The guy we busted in Florida…he worked for the arms dealer who has the bounty out on me."

Ida Belle and Gertie exchanged worried looks.

"That ups the stakes even more," Ida Belle said. "We need

to make sure we keep you off Agent Riker's radar."

"Yeah." I flopped back against the seat. "I have a feeling that's going to be harder than we think. Riker and Mitchell are going to be all over this, and Sinful isn't exactly a metropolis. Everywhere we need to be, they're going to be."

"We've worked around Feds before," Ida Belle said, "and Riker may not be incompetent, but in Sinful, he's definitely out of his element."

Gertie nodded. "We got this!"

I felt my spirits rise. I'd worked with some of the best in the world at infiltration and combat, but I'd never been as confident as I was now. Gertie and Ida Belle were unconventional, way past their physical prime, and had little regard for rules, other than Southern etiquette, but they got results. The steps taken to resolve a case mattered to the CIA, but here in Sinful, results trumped everything.

I smiled. "Damn right, we do."

"So what's first?" Gertie asked.

I pulled out my cell phone. "First is asking Deputy Breaux to see if he can get Carter's boat up from the bottom of the lake."

"Why the boat?" Ida Belle asked.

"Because it might have taken a hit from whatever was used to shoot Carter. If I can identify the weapon it might help us profile our bad guy."

I punched in Deputy Breaux's number and told him what I wanted. It took several minutes of detailed explaining, but finally, he agreed to send some local shrimpers out to the lake to see if they could get the boat up.

I disconnected and shook my head. "That was so much more work than it should have been."

"Young Deputy Breaux has never set the world on fire,"

Ida Belle said, "and he's never going to."

"He set the chemistry lab on fire once," Gertie said.

"Anyway," Ida Belle continued, "the good thing is that Riker and company aren't going to get anything out of Deputy Breaux either. Even if he thinks he knows something, he won't tell without getting permission from Carter."

"He's sorta afraid of Carter," Gertie said. "On account of Carter threatening to shoot him."

"Why would Carter threaten to shoot him?" I asked.

"Because as long as Deputy Breaux is worried about being shot," Gertie explained, "he never questions anything Carter asks him to do. Deputy Breaux is terrified of being shot."

"Probably because someone shot him once," Ida Belle said.

"That was an accident," Gertie protested.

"Regardless," Ida Belle said, "the bottom line is that Deputy Breaux won't be a factor. If a clue flies into his face—which is the only way he's going to find one—it will go straight to Carter and nowhere else."

"Perfect," I said. "So next up is figuring out what Carter saw Saturday that made him suspicious. Without knowing what he was after, we have no idea where to start."

"That makes sense," Ida Belle said, "but how do we do it?"

I leaned forward. "Deputy Breaux said Carter came into the office yesterday morning to get the boat keys and headed straight out to the dock, right? So he already knew where he was going and why when he got up that morning."

"Yeah," Ida Belle said, "but how does that help us?"

"What that tells me is that Carter did all his thinking at his house. His mind was already made up when he arrived at the sheriff's department. When I'm contemplating a mission, I sometimes make notes, look at maps…"

Ida Belle's face brightened. "You think we might find some

clues about Carter's thought process at his house."

"There's no guarantee, but it's a better place to start than aimlessly cruising the bayous with the potential to be shot at ourselves."

"Carter's not going to let us in his house," Gertie said. "He'll know right away why we want in."

"I don't recall saying we would ask permission," I said.

"All kinds of ways into a house," Ida Belle agreed.

"We could always ask Emmaline for the key," Gertie suggested.

I considered it for a moment, then shook my head. It would definitely be easier to stroll right in the front door, especially given that Carter's Rottweiler, Tiny, guarded the backyard, but it opened the door for too many risks.

"The more people we involve," I said, "the more likely Riker or Carter will find out what we're doing."

"She's right," Ida Belle agreed. "Emmaline wouldn't think twice about keeping something from Carter if it was for his own good, and she's used to our meddling around in things, but Fortune is new in town and dating her son. If she gets even an inkling that Fortune isn't exactly who she claims to be, Emmaline has the contacts to track down the real Sandy-Sue. And then the gig is up big-time."

"Crap," I said. "I hadn't even thought about Emmaline checking up on me."

Gertie frowned. "If she thinks Carter is serious about you, sooner or later, she's going to. That's what mothers do."

I sighed. "Why couldn't I find a nice, orphaned fisherman to date?"

"You could always stop dating Carter," Gertie said.

That was true, and the easiest solution to both current and future problems. But the thought of turning Carter loose now made my heart clench with a tiny feeling of loss that I hadn't experienced since my mother passed.

"I don't like that option," I said finally.

Gertie grinned. "I wouldn't like that option either if I were you. If ever there was a man worth risking your life over, it's him."

"We're going to be careful," Ida Belle said. "No one's life needs to be at risk."

"It wouldn't take much to jimmy Carter's front door," I said. "Give me an ice pick and a credit card, and I can get the door opened in a matter of seconds. Do you think someone will notice?"

"Of course," Gertie said. "Sinful is full of the nosiest people in the world, but by now, everyone has heard about what happened to Carter. They will just think we're picking up some things for him at the hospital. Likely no one will ever mention it to Carter or Emmaline."

"And even if they do, we can deny it," Ida Belle said. "With everything else that's going on, no one's going to dwell on the questionable musings of a nosy neighbor."

"Great," Gertie said. "We can swing by my house for an ice pick and I can change clothes. I'm starting to smell."

"You're probably molding, you old coot," Ida Belle said.

Gertie shot Ida Belle a dirty look and wheeled around the corner into the neighborhood. As she was about to turn onto her street, I grabbed her shoulder. "Keep going."

Gertie yanked the steering wheel back straight and continued on down the road before pulling to the shoulder and stopping. "What's wrong?"

"Riker and Mitchell are parked in front of Carter's house." Which also meant they were parked across the street from Gertie's house.

"What for?" Gertie asked. "They know where he is."

"I bet they have a warrant to search his house," Ida Belle said. "Looking for the same thing we are."

"Well, they can't show it to him if he's not there," Gertie said.

"They don't have to," Ida Belle replied. "They can present it to the sheriff and force their way in."

"We have to get inside before the sheriff gets there," I said. "And our easy front door entry is out, which only leaves the back door. Unless Tiny is off visiting relatives for the summer or has had counseling for that killer disposition, then I'm afraid the life-threatening part of this plan is now unavoidable. And I'm going to need a change of clothes and tennis shoes, which will take up even more time we probably don't have."

"You have a spare pair of yoga pants, socks, and a T-shirt in my laundry room," Gertie said. "We wear the same size tennis shoes, so you can borrow my new Nikes."

"We can't just pull up in your driveway without Riker and Mitchell seeing us," I said, "and I'd rather they didn't."

"We can park around the block," Ida Belle said, "and get in through the back door."

"Isn't it just easier to go to my house?" I asked. "And there's still the issue of the dog to address."

"I've got the dog covered," Gertie said. "I got a whole slab of meat on Saturday. Put most of it in my freezer, but there's a plate of steaks in my refrigerator."

I wrinkled my nose. "Why would you buy an entire slab of meat for one person?"

"I didn't really plan to?"

"You can't accidentally buy half a cow," I said.

"You can if you hit it with your car."

Ida Belle shook her head. "Is that why your bumper is duct-taped on again?"

Gertie's eyes widened. "No. The bumper fell off when I hit Big Leonard Vincent. He didn't budge so much as an inch."

I pondered the details of a man who tore a bumper off a car without moving an inch versus the cow, who didn't get nearly as good a deal, but I couldn't form a decent mental picture of such a giant.

"Okay, so we use the steaks to distract Tiny, and I jimmy the back door. Ida Belle comes with me to handle Tiny, and Gertie will keep watch up front, but some distance from Riker and company in case they recognize you from the hospital."

"I'm telling you they won't," Gertie said.

"She's probably right on that one," Ida Belle said. "Aside from a quick glare, they barely looked at her."

"Let's hope that's the case," I said. "Gertie will alert us when the sheriff arrives." I looked at Gertie. "If necessary, distract him for as long as possible so Ida Belle and I can make a clean getaway."

"Perfect," Ida Belle said as Gertie wheeled the car around the corner and parked behind her house, one street over.

We hurried in between the houses and into Gertie's backyard. Gertie let us in the back door and we split off in three different directions. I ran to the laundry room and threw on my own clothes, then headed into the kitchen for the ice pick and meat. Gertie went upstairs to change clothes, and Ida Belle practically sprinted for the downstairs bathroom, grumbling something about daily water requirements and old bladders. A box of Nikes sat on the kitchen table, so I pulled them out and tried them on. A perfect fit.

Five minutes later, we reconvened. As Gertie bounced down the stairs, I drew up short and stared. Ida Belle exited the hallway, took one look up the stairwell, and uttered an "Oh my."

During some era—one before my birth—the outfit Gertie had on was probably considered sexy. But a historical artifact worn on a, well, historical artifact, didn't elicit the same response. The bright red fabric was more suited for a brothel than the sidewalks of Sinful. The fitted waist strained against fat forced into the restrictive fabric, creating creases where I was pretty sure it was supposed to lie flat and smooth. The poofed-out skirt hit just above the knees and looked oddly like a tutu. I was fairly sure the scoop neckline was supposed to provide a hint of the cleavage below, but the currently inserted cleavage and gravity had conspired to tug it down a good two inches below optimum range.

"What the hell are you wearing?" Ida Belle asked.

"Fortune said to distract the sheriff," Gertie said.

Ida Belle cringed. "She meant start a conversation or fake a heart attack or something benign. Not dress like an Old Testament street walker. And what's with the tennis shoes? Weren't you wearing red pumps earlier?"

"My feet hurt and you never know when I'll need to run. Besides, the tennis shoes have a red stripe."

"Uh-huh," Ida Belle said. "Where the hell did you get that getup, anyway?"

Gertie put her hands on her hips. "It so happens that this is the dress I bought for our high school homecoming."

"I don't ever remember seeing it," Ida Belle said. "Maybe I was drunk."

"In high school?" I asked.

Ida Belle shrugged. "Small town. Not a lot to do. You either got married, drunk, or pregnant, not necessarily in that order."

"You never saw the dress because I didn't get to wear it," Gertie explained.

We didn't have time to waste, and I knew the answer would

be something that either strained credulity or made me blanch, but I couldn't seem to stop myself. "Why not?" I asked.

Ida Belle sighed.

"Back then," Gertie said, "I wasn't exactly in hot demand."

"You're not in hot demand now," Ida Belle grumbled.

Gertie gave her the bird. "So when that idiot Fingers Marcantel asked me to the dance, I started to say no."

"His name was Fingers?" I asked.

"Yes, on account of him losing two of them in a fight with an alligator," Gertie said.

"That's not true," Ida Belle said. "Everyone started calling him 'Fingers' because he couldn't do math without using them to count—and I'm talking high school, not elementary. He made up that story about the alligator to sound like a tough guy. What really happened is he stuck his hand under the lawn mower when his dad was working on it."

Gertie waved a hand at Ida Belle. "Whatever. Anyway, I wanted to go to the dance, and Fingers was my option, so I took it. I snuck off to New Orleans with two other girls and we bought dresses our mothers would have never let us out of the house in."

"Your mothers would have been right," Ida Belle said. "I wish yours was still around to stop this tragedy."

"Anyway, I was walking home from school one day and heard someone moaning behind the big oak at the west side of the park. I thought someone was hurt, so I ran around the tree and there was Fingers and that slut Jasmine Arceneaux."

"Great-aunt of Pansy Arceneaux," Ida Belle threw in.

I nodded. Pansy Arceneaux, Celia Arceneaux's daughter, wasn't exactly a vestal virgin, and her less-than-moral ways had gotten her killed. "So it runs in the family. I take it you were so disgusted you didn't go to the dance with Fingers?"

"I would have still gone," Gertie said. "I mean, I'd already bought the dress, but Fingers's mother found out. She pumped him full of penicillin and sent him off to military school the next day."

Ida Belle threw her hands in the air. "All that to explain why you're dressed like a Halloween hooker. You know what? I don't even care anymore. Let's just get this over with." She stalked out the back door, Gertie trailing behind, her skirt swishing as she walked.

I gripped the ice pick and package of raw meat and set out after them, wondering how my life had gotten so complicated all over again.

Chapter Seven

I perched on top of one corner of Carter's back fence and studied the giant sleeping dog on his patio. I motioned to Ida Belle, who was sitting on the opposite corner, and she pulled out a piece of steak and whistled.

Tiny opened one eyeball and Ida Belle whistled again, waving the hunk of meat in the air. Realizing his perimeter had been breached, Tiny jumped up and trotted straight for Ida Belle. She scooted back on the fence and tossed one of the hunks of meat about five feet out. The smell of the meat had Tiny skidding to a stop beside it. He took a single sniff then gobbled the entire thing up in two bites.

I worried for a moment that I hadn't brought enough meat. The bait had to give me enough time to get in and out of Carter's house. In and no out was fraught with issues I didn't even want to consider.

Ida Belle waved and pulled out a second piece of meat. Tiny stretched his entire body up the fence, whining for Ida Belle to provide him with more raw treats. As soon as she dropped the next piece, I dropped into the bushes, then burst out and sprinted for the patio. Tiny's head jerked around, and for a moment, I thought it was all over but the trip to the hospital, but Ida Belle whistled again and dropped another piece of meat on the ground.

I jabbed the ice pick into the door lock and shoved the

credit card down the slot between the door and the frame. A couple seconds later, the lock clicked open and I bolted inside, closing the door on the now-charging Rottweiler. Tiny slammed into the door and dropped onto the patio. For a moment, I thought he'd broken his neck, but finally, he rose and wobbled over to his bed, where he flopped down.

I ran to the front of the house and peered out the window. Riker and Mitchell were still parked at the curb. Riker was arguing with someone on the phone. I wondered if it was the sheriff's department. I eased the blind slat back into place and headed for the kitchen. I wasn't sure if Carter maintained a separate office, but if he didn't, I figured he might work at his kitchen table like I did.

Sure enough, some maps of the bayous and a pad of paper and pen were sitting there next to his laptop. I scanned the maps and recognized some of the channels surrounding Sinful, including the one that led to the place we'd had our romantic dinner, but I didn't see any notes on the maps or the notepad.

Come on, Carter.

I opened his laptop. The password box flashed at me and I groaned. I typed in "Tiny" and hit Enter.

Failed.

I tried "Emmaline" and hit Enter again.

Failed.

Crap. One more try and I'd be locked out completely. I pulled out my phone and texted Ida Belle.

Need password to Carter's laptop. Already tried Tiny and Emmaline.

A couple seconds later, Ida Belle replied.

Try Fortune.

I frowned. Surely not.

A second text came through.

Trust me.

I took a breath and typed "Fortune," then hit Enter before I could change my mind.

The screen flashed, then the desktop appeared.

I froze for a moment, my hands poised over the keyboard. Carter had changed his password to my name. Had he done it before our date? Was he just due for a change or had he changed it because he wanted to use my name? If so, what did that mean?

I shook my head and focused on the laptop again. All of those questions were better explored later and over a beer or three. I took a look at the bottom of the screen and saw that a Word document was open. I checked the date and felt my pulse tick up a notch when I saw it was created Saturday, well after midnight. Bingo. I clicked on it and it filled the screen.

HE shouldn't have been there.

That was it. The entire document contained only those five words. And I had zero idea what they meant. I went to his Internet history and saw that he'd accessed the sheriff's department around the same time he created the document, then the local newspaper shortly after, but I couldn't tell what he'd read within the newspaper site. Clearly, he was looking for something.

Something about the man who shouldn't have been there.

I closed the laptop and started toward the hallway, but drew up short in the middle of the kitchen. At casual glance, it looked completely normal, and quite frankly, neater than I'd expected for a single man. Pretty curtains with yellow daisies above a window over the sink, matching yellow rug on the stone floor below, a set of white canisters lining one side of the countertops.

But something was off. Something I couldn't put my finger on.

And then I saw it. A single blue dish towel hanging on the refrigerator, its matching partner hanging over one of the two cabinet doors under the sink. I stepped closer to the refrigerator—a massive stainless steel block that could probably hold a month's supply of beer—and took a closer look at the surface. Sure enough, the fingerprints I expected to see appeared on a good bit of the stainless steel surface, which was exactly why I had a black refrigerator. But the handle, which should have been littered with fingerprints, was completely clear.

I pulled the rag off the refrigerator and squeezed it. It was still damp.

Someone had already searched Carter's house!

They used the rag to wipe where they touched and failed to put it back in its correct spot. If not for that one slipup, I might never have noticed. I stared at the refrigerator again and frowned. Did people really hide stuff in there? I'd never known someone who did, but I supposed if you were searching a house, you opened everything. I used the dishrag to open the refrigerator and smiled at the store of beer and hamburger patties.

My curiosity piqued, I closed the fridge and headed for the hallway to check out Carter's bedroom. I didn't anticipate finding anything more, but it would be remiss not to look, and if I was being honest, I kinda wanted to see what his bedroom looked like. I headed down the hallway, poking my head into doors as I went. Guest room. Hallway bath. Exercise room...nice equipment. I slipped inside to check the weights on the bench press bar. Three hundred. I'd figured as much. He had a three-hundred-pound-bench-press sort of chest.

Only one door remained, and it had to be the master bedroom. I pushed it open and stepped inside, scanning the room. It was a nice large room with big manly sort of furniture. A four-poster bed with giant columns like a building in the Roman Empire, and matching dresser and nightstands, all in a dark wood. The walls were painted light brown and the comforter and pillows were all navy. Navy rugs with cream stripes were on each side of the bed, covering a small piece of the natural hardwood that stretched everywhere in the house except the kitchen and bathrooms.

I crossed the room and peeked into the master bath, expecting to find it somewhat dated, as my house was, but clearly Carter was not holding fast to history. The bathroom had been completely updated. It looked like a sea of brown swirling marble with brown and navy glass tile accents. Quite frankly, it was the nicest bathroom I'd ever seen except for that one hotel in Morocco where I stayed while pretending to be the arms dealer's girlfriend. That place had gold fixtures that I was pretty sure were real.

But it was the little touches such as the navy vase with fake white flowers—the kind that looked real, not the cheap ones—the matching candles, and all the other decorations that were absolutely perfect for the space that had me suspecting a woman had been involved. No one had alluded to Carter's being seriously involved with anyone since he'd returned to Sinful, so I was going to hazard a guess that it was Emmaline's touch. She had that refined, elegant look about her. This room looked the same way. The yellow accents in the kitchen were probably her as well.

I was just about to check out the closet when I heard noise out front. I hurried back to the living room and peered in between the blinds. At the same time, my cell phone buzzed. It was a text from Gertie.

Sheriff Lee is rounding the corner.

Time to bail. I hurried to the back door and scanned the patio. Tiny was in the same spot he'd collapsed in before, eyes closed and chest moving rhythmically. I sent Ida Belle a text telling her to fire up the bait and watched as she whistled and waved a piece of meat. Tiny opened one eye, then rolled over and closed them both again. I swear he looked like he was snoring.

I saw Ida Belle whistle again, then she rapped on the fence, but the sleeping Rottweiler didn't so much as flinch. The voices out front started to get louder and I realized they were approaching the front door. There was no place to hide. Once Riker and Mitchell got inside, they'd toss the place upside-down looking for a clue. My only option was to sneak out the back door and hope I could make it over the fence before Tiny decided naptime was over.

I eased open the back door, got Ida Belle's attention, and put one finger over my lips. She stopped rapping on the fence and nodded. I took a step outside the door and paused, but Tiny never flinched. I inched forward again and made it almost to the end of the patio before Tiny stretched and rolled over. I froze, praying that the dog didn't open his eyes. I was right in his sight path. The seconds ticked by and finally, Tiny began to snore. I stepped off into the grass and picked up my pace as I crossed the lawn. Ida Belle gave me a thumbs-up right before I slipped into the bushes.

And stepped on a squeaky ball.

It might as well have been a gunshot. Tiny bolted up as if he'd received an electrical jolt, his eyes instantly locking on mine, then a second later, he launched off the patio with speed I had hoped he didn't possess. I leaped for the top of the fence but miscalculated the first jump and came up an inch short. I could hear the dog racing across the lawn, exhaling a breath every time his front feet hit the ground.

I squatted and jumped again, this time giving it 200 percent.

And overshot the top of the fence by a good foot and a

half.

I reached for the fence, but my upward momentum was so strong that I couldn't break the forward progression. The only option I had was attempting to redirect it so I clutched the top of the fence and folded myself over it, knocking my breath out as my ribs crashed onto the top rail. I heard Tiny jump behind me and felt the fence sway as his entire weight crashed into the slats. I could hear Ida Belle whistling, but Tiny wasn't having any of it. As I swung my leg up, Tiny jumped again, and this time, he caught my shoe.

The only thing that kept me from falling back into Carter's yard was the fact that I was literally bent over the fence at my waist. I grabbed the fence rail on the other side and jerked my leg as hard as I could, trying to shake the tugging dog off my shoe. I felt myself start to slip backward and tugged harder, this time putting my entire body into it.

The shoe popped off my foot, and I flew over the fence like a rubber band being shot off a finger. I didn't have the time or the body positioning to prepare for a drop-and-roll, so I crashed onto the hard ground behind the fence, jarring every bone in my body and making my teeth hurt. I heard Tiny growl and slam himself into the fence again.

Then there was a loud splintering sound.

I stared in horror at the split that appeared in three of the fence slats, then spun around and ran for the corner of the fence Ida Belle occupied. If Tiny made it through that fence, my only saving grace would be the steak. Tiny must have mounted another attack because I heard the boards crack again, but this time it was less of a splinter and more of a sonic boom.

Time was up.

I ramped up my speed, but I could hear Tiny closing in on me. Ida Belle was still perched on top of the fence and gesturing wildly at me to hurry. When I was a couple feet away from the fence, I jumped, and not a moment too soon. Tiny leaped at the same time, barely missing snagging my one remaining shoe. I scrambled on top of the fence next to Ida Belle and looked down at the angry dog.

"We can't sit here forever," Ida Belle said. "Someone will hear the racket and call the police."

"If we're lucky, that's all that will happen. I'm more worried that Riker and Mitchell will hear the racket and come to investigate."

Ida Belle's brow creased in worry. "I only have two pieces of meat left, and that's not nearly enough time to get away. That dog practically inhales them."

I scanned the fence, the woods behind Carter's house, and the roofline, looking for a potential out. I'd escaped from heavily guarded arms compounds in the Middle East in 110-degree weather and without having food or water for two days. If I couldn't work around one suburban pet, I needed to turn in my agent badge.

"We need a distraction," I said. "Something more interesting than us."

"Good luck with that."

I pulled out my cell phone and sent a message to Gertie.

Make a lot of loud noise. Tiny is loose and we need a distraction.

I hit Send and then had a second thought.

Take cover after making the noise.

I hit Send again and waited. A couple seconds later, Gertie answered.

I got this.

Holy crap. I was more than a little afraid.

"What are you doing?" Ida Belle asked.

"I think I just unleashed the kraken."

"Huh?"

"*Pirates of the Caribbean*. You know, that pirate movie Gertie made us watch last week."

"Oh." Ida Belle's eyes widened. "Oh!"

A second later, the loudest whistle in the history of man echoed through the neighborhood. Tiny froze for a moment and cocked his head to the side. Then a second whistle rang out and he took off for the front of the house.

Ida Belle jumped off the fence, gesturing wildly. "Those Feds will shoot that dog. We have to rescue him."

Crap! I hadn't even considered the douche-bags-with-weapons part of the equation. I bailed off the fence and grabbed Ida Belle's sleeve as she started to run. "Wait! I've only got on one shoe and Tiny's still got the other in his mouth. They'll know it was us."

Ida Belle stared at me for a second and I swear I could see the wheels turning in her mind. She reached down and pulled off her shoes. "Take the other one off," she yelled as she ran for the woods and chunked her shoes into the bayou.

I had zero idea where she was going with this, but since I didn't have anything better, I yanked off the remaining tennis shoe and hurled it into the swirling water.

"This way." Ida Belle took off down the fence line of the house next to Carter's. I sprinted behind her and followed her around the house to the sidewalk around the corner.

"We're taking a walk," Ida Belle said.

"Without shoes?"

"It's good for the arches."

"No, it isn't."

"They don't know that! Get a move on before this becomes an episode on *Cops*."

I stepped onto the sidewalk and rounded the corner next to

Ida Belle, trying to appear as if we were on a nonchalant stroll around the neighborhood...without shoes. But the scene in front of us precluded any requirement for being calm.

Gertie was running down the sidewalk in the opposite direction screaming bloody murder. Tiny was locked in on her from half a block away and closing the distance fast. Agents Riker and Mitchell both whirled around and stared at Gertie, probably in an attempt to figure out why she was running. Tiny shifted his gaze to Riker and altered course. For a split second, I figured he deserved being hit by the oncoming tank, but I was more worried about what might happen to Tiny if he made it undeterred to Riker.

"Dog!" I yelled as we broke out in a run. It wasn't the most descriptive warning but it was easier to belt out than "slobbering man-killer."

Riker whirled around, his eyes widening at the approaching Tiny, and yelled at Mitchell to get back into the car. Mitchell spun around and with only a glance at the dog, ran for the car and jumped in the driver's side, then scrambled to the passenger's seat before Riker leaped in and slammed the door. Tiny skidded to a stop next to the car and jumped up on the driver's door, shoving his face against the window, still clutching the shoe in his giant jaws.

I grabbed Ida Belle's arm and slowed to a stop about twenty yards from the car. "We can't just run up there."

Ida Belle glanced at the jumping, growling Tiny, then looked back at me. "Right. But we have to do something."

I looked down the street in time to see Sheriff Lee rounding the corner at the end headed straight for Gertie, who was still at a dead run. But instead of the ancient horse he usually rode, he was perched atop something smaller and with long gray hair.

"Is that a burro?" I asked.

Ida Belle's eyes widened. "What the heck?"

Gertie hit the brakes and tried to stop, but she tripped over a lip in the sidewalk and went sprawling right into the burro, then hit the pavement, her tutu skirt flipped up over her back, exposing her camouflage underwear. Tiny swung his head around to see what all the racket was and launched off the car door, setting off down the sidewalk toward the burro-Gertie wreck at high speed.

I took off running again, no idea what I was going to do, but no way could I let Tiny maul an old woman or a cute furry animal. Riker and Mitchell jumped out of their car as I sped by. Riker yelled something, but I didn't slow down enough to make it out. I shouted at Gertie, who looked up and saw the speeding Tiny.

She grabbed the burro's halter, struggling to get up, and then the burro caught sight of the rapidly approaching dog. The burro yanked his head up so hard that he dragged Gertie completely upright. Sheriff Lee clutched the saddle horn, swaying like a drunk and yelling at everyone to calm down. Clearly, he hadn't noticed the real threat.

Tiny dropped the shoe, letting out an ear-splitting bark, and Sheriff Lee's head whipped around. His eyes widened and he began to yell even louder. Gertie scrambled on top of a transformer that wasn't tall enough to save her from a Chihuahua, but at least it got her out of the line of sight. The burro locked in on the dog and reared up. I cringed, expecting Sheriff Lee, who I suspect was born somewhere around the Mesozoic Era, to launch off the back of the burro and break into a million pieces, but he flung his arms around the burro's neck and managed to maintain his seat.

Unfortunately, there was no time to admire Sheriff Lee's neck-hugging ability, because as soon as the burro's feet hit the pavement, he took off like a rocket. Tiny, who'd just reached the rearing beast, spun around and set out after him, both of them racing straight toward me. I whirled around so fast, I was pretty sure I gave myself a bit of whiplash, and sped back toward the car, wishing I'd concentrated more on interval training.

I needn't have bothered with any of it. The burro sped past me, Sheriff Lee still clinging to its neck and the dog right on its heels. Riker and Mitchell jumped back into the car as the burro barreled straight toward them. Just when I thought the burro would veer right or left to avoid the car, the situation went from bad to completely absurd.

The burro ran right up to the back of Riker's car and jumped onto the trunk. Without pause, he climbed from the trunk onto the roof and stood there, glaring down at the confused Rottweiler.

Chapter Eight

I could see Riker and Mitchell yelling as the roof of the car started to sag. Ida Belle ran up beside me, gaping at the scene in front of us.

"I called Walter," she said. "Tiny listens to him."

"I hope he gets here before the roof collapses or Riker starts firing."

I'd barely finished my sentence when Walter's truck squealed around the corner. I pulled out my cell phone and texted Gertie to get the hell out of here before Riker made her. She waited until Walter parked before climbing off the transformer and hobbling around the corner and out of sight.

Walter jumped out of his truck, looking more than a little startled at the sight of Sheriff Lee and the burro on the top of the car. After a couple seconds of jaw-dropped staring, he whistled and called Tiny. The dog, who had both feet on the trunk of Agent Riker's car, gave him a sorrowful look but finally relented and climbed into Walter's truck.

As soon as Walter slammed his truck door shut, Riker jumped out of the car and stared in dismay at the collapsed roof. "Get that beast off my car!"

Sheriff Lee looked down at him, completely unfazed. "Who the hell do you think you're yelling at? You should learn some respect for your elders and for law enforcement." He pulled his badge out and flashed it at Riker.

"You've got to be kidding me." Riker looked fit to be tied. "Is everyone in this town crazy?"

"That's a loaded question," Ida Belle said, "and probably not one we have time to delve into at the moment. Sheriff Lee, I don't think that roof is going to hold much longer. Let's get you off of there before you and the burro need knee replacements."

"Hhhmmph," Sheriff Lee grunted. "Had both knees done three times already and my darn hip twice. Ain't looking to do either again." He picked up the reins and gave the burro a kick. The animal swung his head over to peer at the barking Rottweiler in the truck, but must have decided it was safe to leave the questionable safety of the roof because he took a step down on the hood and continued onto the street.

Riker stared at his demolished car in dismay. "You're going to pay for that."

"Not me," Sheriff Lee said. "I'm here on official business. You'll have to take that up with the mayor…as soon as we have one, anyway."

"The election!" Ida Belle grabbed my arm. "I have to go vote."

"No one is going anywhere," Riker said, "until I get this sorted out. Who does that dog belong to?"

"My nephew," Walter said. "Deputy LeBlanc."

Riker's eyes widened a bit. "Is he normally running loose in the street threatening citizens and…" He looked over at the burro and frowned. "Donkeys, or whatever the hell that is?"

"No," Walter said. "He's usually penned up in the backyard, but I suppose he found a way out."

"Why would he want to do that?" Riker asked, then pinned his gaze on Ida Belle and me.

"How should we know?" Ida Belle asked.

Riker shifted his gaze to only me. "I thought you were the

girlfriend. You should have been able to control the dog. Why were you running from it?"

Riker's scrutiny had me squirming internally but I hoped I looked every bit the innocent damsel that I was pretending to be. "Hello? Is anyone listening? It was a first date. I haven't been in his house. I've never met his dog. We're not sleeping together. And everything in this town is strange."

"That's a bold statement coming from a woman with no shoes on. What are you two doing here, anyway?"

"We live here," Ida Belle said. "Couple blocks over."

"And you thought you'd walk past the deputy's house with no shoes on? At the exact moment a dog came running up with a shoe in its mouth?"

"What's your point?" I asked. "The shoe doesn't belong to one of us or we'd be wearing its partner."

"Besides," Ida Belle said, "if that dog had wrangled a shoe off of either of us, we'd probably be missing a leg up to the knee."

Riker didn't look as if he believed a word we'd said, but he had no proof that we had on shoes prior to now, and he couldn't exactly argue with Ida Belle's missing leg theory. "I'm supposed to believe that story?"

"Exercising is hard to believe?" Ida Belle asked. "You've heard of exercise, right?"

"Walking barefoot is good for the arches," I threw in.

Walter covered his mouth with his hand and coughed. I could tell he was trying not to laugh. No doubt he figured we had something to do with Tiny's being loose.

Riker stared at me in disbelief. I knew he wanted to say something about how stupid that statement was, but he must have decided it would be a waste of time. "Fine. Who was that woman the dog was chasing? The one who whistled?"

"Crazy Annie?" Ida Belle said. "She's not all there."

"I don't care about her mental state," Riker said. "I want to talk to her."

"Good luck with that," Ida Belle said. "She can't talk, hence the whistling. The last time someone tried to talk to her, she screamed until the paramedics came and sedated her. Look, all this has been far more interesting than our walk usually is, but we'd like to get going. I've got to go vote."

"And I'm hungry," I said. "All this excitement has done a number on my metabolism and my feet. I think I need to soak them."

Ida Belle nodded. "Soak them in salt water, then cover them with lotion and wrap them in hot, damp towels."

"Oh, that sounds wonderful."

"Enough with the feet," Riker said. "I don't know what you are up to, but I don't buy for a minute that you were out for some barefoot stroll. If I find out you're helping Deputy LeBlanc withhold information, I'll have you all jailed in New Orleans until you decide to talk."

"Road trip!" Ida Belle stuck her hand up and I gave her a high five.

Riker shot us a disgusted look before yanking a piece of paper out of his pocket and shoving it at Sheriff Lee. "This is a warrant to search Deputy LeBlanc's house. He'll need to replace the lock and maybe the front door once we're done."

"That won't be necessary," Walter said. "I have a key. I'm sure my nephew would appreciate arriving home from the hospital with his home still intact." Walter stressed the word *hospital* and gave Riker a dirty look before pulling the keys from his pocket and heading for the front door.

Ida Belle and I took advantage of the lull and hightailed it away from the angry Feds.

"My house," Ida Belle said. "I have to grab some shoes and go vote."

I hopped off the sidewalk and onto the grass. "This cement is getting hot."

"I know. It was all I could do to stand there pretending this barefoot thing was normal." She hopped into the grass next to me. "So did you find anything?"

"There were bayou maps on the kitchen table and a pad of paper, but he hadn't written anything on it or the maps."

"Damn. What about his computer?"

"His laptop was on the table and he had a Word doc open, but it only had one thing typed on it."

I told her the strange notation.

"He shouldn't have been there," Ida Belle repeated. "That's it?"

I nodded. "Yeah, it's not much to go on."

"No, but it tells us two things—he's male, and Carter saw someone in a place he wasn't expected to be."

"Out in the lake? But if Carter knew him, he's local. Why would a local on the lake raise so much as an eyebrow?"

"I don't know. Maybe he was supposed to be at work or out of town. Or maybe he was doing something on the lake that he wasn't supposed to."

"Like poaching or something?"

"Sure, poaching oysters or something like that."

I frowned. "Would someone really try to kill Carter over poaching? It seems kind of extreme."

"I agree. But what if Carter went out to check on the poaching, or whatever, and got in the way of whatever the ATF is here about."

"So it was a wrong-place-wrong-time sort of thing? Do you really think it could be that simple?"

"There's nothing simple about it," Ida Belle said. "Something bad is going on in Sinful. Something worth killing a law enforcement officer over. You realize what that means?"

"They wouldn't hesitate to kill anyone else."

"Yeah."

It was only one word, but it contained all of the gravity of the situation.

"There's something else," I said. "Someone beat us to the house. I'm certain it had been searched already." I told her about the dishrag and the missing fingerprints.

"What do you think he was looking for?" Ida Belle asked.

I shrugged. "Maybe the same thing we were—some indication that Carter was onto him?"

"He would have had to break in. Did you find any sign of forced entry?"

"No, but I couldn't check the front windows or door with Riker and company out front. That has to be where he entered. No one would be foolish enough to attempt the backyard with Tiny on duty."

"Except us," Ida Belle said.

"We're special," I said.

"We have to figure this out fast," Ida Belle said, "but I have no idea where to look next."

"If Deputy Breaux can get Carter's boat up, maybe it will tell us something."

Ida Belle gave me a single nod and we picked up our pace.

It sounded good, but I couldn't help feeling the boat was a real long shot. I didn't know how deep I dived to rescue Carter, but I did know it wasn't the bottom of the lake. I had my doubts they could even get the boat up from the bottom, and even if they managed to, I wasn't convinced it would give us answers that led anywhere.

But I'd get those answers. If it was the last thing I ever did.

While Ida Belle went to snag a pair of shoes, I called Gertie and asked her to pick us both up at Ida Belle's house. She pulled up at the curb a couple minutes later, just as Ida Belle emerged wearing a pair of navy flats that didn't quite match her turquoise-and-black dress.

"I know," she said as she grabbed her purse. "I threw my only pair of black shoes in the bayou. Unless you count my motorcycle boots."

"Probably not a better look than the navy."

As I reached for the door, Gertie burst inside. We both stared at her in dismay.

"Why didn't you change clothes?" Ida Belle asked.

The dress was bad enough before, but apparently Tiny had gotten a piece of the tutu skirt. A big hunk was missing out of the back, exposing Gertie's camo underwear.

"The zipper is stuck," Gertie said. "I think it got stripped when I jumped onto the transformer."

"So cut it off," Ida Belle said.

Gertie looked horrified. "I'm not going to cut up my homecoming dress."

Ida Belle threw her hands in the air. "High school was barely invented when you bought that dress. Put it out to pasture where it belongs."

Gertie put her hands on her hips. "All I want is one day in the dress. Then I'll store it so that I can remember it when I'm old."

"You're old now!" Ida Belle said.

Gertie stalked past her. "I have to pee."

She stomped down the hall, the tutu swinging back and

forth over the camo undies.

Ida Belle sighed. "She could have at least changed underwear."

"Look at the bright side," I said. "If Celia's downtown, we can get Gertie to stand in front of her."

Ida Belle's lower lip quivered and I could tell she was trying not to smile, but finally, the mental picture of Celia staring at Gertie's underwear-clad bottom shining in Celia's face won out and she broke out in a grin. "That would be stellar."

"What would be stellar?" Gertie asked as she entered the living room.

"Nothing," I said. "Just talking about the election."

"Let's go grab Fortune some shoes," Ida Belle said, "and get to the church to vote."

"You vote in the church?" I asked as I followed them outside. "Doesn't that go against the whole separation of church and state thing?"

"We used to vote at the library," Gertie said as we climbed into her car. "But they only have one bathroom—for men and women. The Catholics put in new bathrooms with five stalls each a couple years ago."

"Show-offs," Ida Belle grumbled.

I started to ask why the Baptists didn't put in more restrooms, but decided against it. Everything in Sinful had some convoluted and often completely illogical reasoning behind it. Asking questions about how the town operated was like asking why Santa Claus was late delivering gifts.

We made a quick stop at my house and I snagged some sandals, then Gertie directed her car downtown. I did a double take when we inched to a crawl blocks away from Main Street to avoid the sea of people walking in the middle of the road. And everywhere I looked, there were more. People on the sidewalks.

People on lawns.

"Where did all these people come from?" I asked.

"There's thousands of houses out in the bayous," Gertie said. "Most of them aren't much to speak of, but people live in them."

"A lot of the men work construction in New Orleans or on oil rigs in the Gulf," Ida Belle said. "When they're home, they tend to prefer their recliners, beer, and television remotes. They're not out much for us regulars to see."

"Apparently, everyone puts down the remote and the beer to vote," I said.

"Of course," Ida Belle said. "These men ask to be home specifically at election time. We take voting seriously here in Louisiana."

Gertie nodded. "If only our elected officials took it as seriously as the voters do. We tend to elect a bunch of fools."

"Everyone does," I said, "but then my opinion of politicians isn't all that high."

"You'll have to revise that if Marie is elected mayor," Gertie pointed out.

"Goes without saying," I agreed. I pointed to a large gathering at the end of Main Street opposite the church. "What's going on down there?"

Ida Belle rose on her tiptoes to look over the crowd and frowned. "Nothing good. I see Celia standing on a park bench. Her mouth is open, which means trouble."

"She's not supposed to be campaigning within six hundred feet of the election place," Gertie complained. "We should get a tape measure."

"Waste of time," Ida Belle said, "but we should probably go see what she's up to. We can vote afterward."

We headed down the street, threading through the mass of

men talking about sports and women pushing strollers and clutching screaming children. Finally, we made it to the end of the street where someone was handing Celia a microphone attached to a small amplifier on the ground next to the bench.

"Something has got to change," Celia boomed into the microphone, causing the amplifier to screech.

"Sorry," she said, lowering her voice about a hundred decibels. "This was always a safe town filled with good people, and look what has become of it. We've had more crime this year than we have my entire lifetime."

"Maybe if you were five years old," Gertie yelled.

Celia leveled her gaze at Gertie, flinching a bit when she took in Gertie's outfit. "And what is law enforcement doing to protect us? 'Nothing' is the answer."

"You're still alive and mouthing off, aren't you?" Gertie yelled.

Celia glared at Gertie, then continued her rant. "Sheriff Lee is so old he falls asleep reading people their rights."

"I'll give her that one," Gertie grumbled.

"Deputy Breaux is likable enough. So is Daffy Duck, but I don't see anyone asking him to join law enforcement."

I leaned toward Ida Belle. "I'm confused. Did she just call Deputy Breaux stupid or funny?"

"I think she was going for stupid," Ida Belle said.

"That was rude," I said. Deputy Breaux wasn't any Einstein and he wouldn't make it in law enforcement in a big city for a day, but calling him out as an imbecile in front of the entire town was a special kind of unpleasant. "I hope his mother didn't hear that."

Ida Belle pointed to a horrid-looking woman standing next to the park bench and holding a "Vote for Celia" sign. "That's his mother."

"The one nodding?"

"Yep."

"Jesus." From now on, I was going to make an effort to be nicer to Deputy Breaux.

"Right now," Celia continued, "Deputy LeBlanc is in the hospital, a victim of yet another criminal that he failed to catch."

I felt a flush run up my face. "He was shot and almost drowned, and you have the nerve to complain about him, you ungrateful bitch."

The crowd went silent.

Celia locked her gaze on mine. "Maybe if he was concentrating on his job, instead of making time with Yankees, we wouldn't have any crime in this town. We didn't before you came."

"You can't blame Fortune for anything going on in this town," Ida Belle said. "Everything that has happened since she's arrived started years before she got here."

"Maybe so," Celia said, "but the first thing I plan to do as mayor is clean house at the sheriff's department. This town needs law enforcement that will keep us safe. Men that criminals fear so much they won't even try to get away with something in this town."

"You mean criminals like your daughter? Or the former mayor?" I asked. "Or were you only referring to criminals not related to you?"

There was a collective intake of breath and the entire crowd froze, only their eyes moving back and forth between Celia and me. Celia turned white, then whiter, then the blood rushed back into her face and turned her as red as a tomato.

I waited for the twinge of guilt I should have felt, but it never came. The part about Celia's daughter was a low blow, but I was tired of hearing her vitriol. Carter wasn't responsible for criminals choosing their way of life, and no law enforcement officer, no matter how scary, was going to turn criminals straight. It was a ludicrous thought and highly insulting to every man and woman who worked to protect the general population.

Finally Celia gained her voice back and she pointed a finger at me. "When I win this election, I'll make it my first order of business to find a way to get you out of this town. You may not have committed any of the crimes here, but I know bad luck when I see it. It wasn't here before you arrived. The solution for returning this town to normal seems clear to me."

I stared at her, trying to understand how anyone could be so superstitious and stupid and downright mean, but it escaped me. Even worse, some of the residents were starting to study me as if Celia might be onto something.

Gertie drew herself up straight and glared at Celia. "Fortune saved your life. If she hadn't been here, you would have died. That seems awfully lucky on your part, although some of us might have a differing opinion."

Ida Belle shook her head at Celia and spun around, grabbing my arm as she went. "Let's get out of here. This can only get worse, and we've got bigger fish to fry."

I hesitated a moment before setting out after her. Finding the man who'd tried to kill Carter definitely took priority over Celia and her nonsense, but I was worried about this election. If Celia was elected and made good on her promise, Carter might be released from the hospital to unemployment. I shuddered to think of what Celia would deem a suitable replacement. I was certain no one else in Sinful was better qualified to manage the town than Carter. And anyone who wasn't a Sinful resident would be at a gross disadvantage.

"Where's Marie?" I asked. "Shouldn't she be down here duking it out with Celia?"

Ida Belle shook her head. "Marie would never do something like that. She'd consider it crass."

"Well, maybe she needs to consider getting a bit of crass," Gertie said. "She might need it to beat Celia."

I worried that Gertie was right, and Marie's refusal to fight dirty could result in her losing the election. With Celia in charge of Sinful, all kinds of things would change, and not for the better. Celia just thought things were bad now, but if she fired Carter, I had no doubt things would go from bad to way, way worse.

.

Chapter Nine

Gertie and Ida Belle made quick work of the voting, skirting the locals who tried to hold them up with questions about Carter and Celia and anything else they wanted gossip about. In an attempt to avoid the nosiness, we took the long route to the sheriff's department, making a beeline for the bayou behind the row of shops on Main Street and working our way back toward the other end of the street where the sheriff's department was located. We wanted to check with Deputy Breaux about the boat and to see if he'd discovered anything of use.

When we walked into the sheriff's department, Myrtle gave us a halfhearted wave before dropping her hand back onto the desk. She looked exhausted.

Ida Belle frowned. "You look like you've been up all night. Where's your backup?"

Myrtle nodded. "Sick. And I have been up all night, but I can't leave Deputy Breaux to handle everything. Between Carter, the Feds, and the election, this town's a madhouse. You guys been to see Carter?"

"We went this morning," Ida Belle said.

"How's he doing?" Myrtle asked.

"Good, considering how things could have gone," I said.

"Did he say what happened?"

Ida Belle shook her head. "The concussion is causing memory loss. It's probably not permanent, but for now, he's as much in the dark as the rest of us."

"Unless Deputy Breaux has found out anything useful?" I gave Myrtle a hopeful look.

She shook her head. "Between the election fights he keeps having to break up and those Feds who keep trying to force him to do anything but his job, he's had his hands full. Even if there was something to be found out, he wouldn't have had time to listen to it."

"Did he send someone to try to recover the department's boat?" I asked.

Myrtle frowned. "Oh yeah. That's the current round of issues. You're not going to believe—"

The door to Deputy Breaux's office flew open and a young woman carrying a baby hurried out, tears streaming down her face. "I can't hear any more of this," she said. "If you find a…you know, let me know."

Deputy Breaux stood in the doorway to his office, a stricken look on his face. "I'm so sorry, ma'am."

"It's not your fault," the woman said. "I appreciate your efforts. I just have to get home. Tommy needs his nap."

As if on cue, the little boy's face contorted, his giant blue eyes almost squeezed shut, and he let out a wail that practically shook the walls. I cringed and forced myself not to put my hands over my ears. The woman hurried past us, giving Ida Belle and Gertie a nod as she rushed out of the sheriff's department.

"What's wrong with Laurel?" Gertie asked.

Deputy Breaux sighed. "She's upset."

"Doesn't take a detective to figure that one out," Ida Belle said. "What did you say to upset her?"

"Wasn't so much what I said as what the shrimpers found when they went to pull up the sheriff's boat."

"Are you going to tell us?" Ida Belle asked, her impatience

evident, "or do I have to pull it out of you one sentence at a time?"

Deputy Breaux's brow creased and I could tell he was trying to decide if he should tell Ida Belle what she wanted to know or if he wasn't supposed to tell. Finally, he must have decided that whatever he knew wasn't confidential, or he was more scared of Ida Belle than the rules. Either way, he started talking.

"The shrimpers took a couple of roughnecks with them to help with the boat. One of them is certified to dive and had all the equipment and stuff. They lucked out because the place where the boat sank wasn't one of the deepest parts of the lake, and he found the boat right where your coordinates said it would be..."

"But?" Ida Belle prompted.

"But there was more wreckage down there."

Gertie shrugged. "There's probably a hundred or more boats at the bottom of that lake."

"It was *The Calypso*," Deputy Breaux said.

Ida Belle's eyes widened and Gertie sucked in a breath.

"I get the feeling I missed something important," I said.

Ida Belle nodded. "*The Calypso* is...was Hank Eaton's shrimp boat."

"Laurel Eaton's husband," Gertie said.

"Oh! The woman who just left?" I asked.

They nodded.

"I take it he didn't make it off the boat?"

"When he didn't come in from shrimping one evening," Ida Belle said, "we all assumed that was the case."

"But it's still a shock when you find out for sure," Gertie said. "Kinda like losing them all over again. And Laurel so young and that baby with so many problems."

"The baby has problems?" I asked.

"So sad," Gertie said. "He was born with something wrong with his heart. Hank didn't have medical insurance on them, and I heard through the grapevine that the medical costs ate up what little life insurance he had pretty quick-like."

Ida Belle sighed. "Laurel's an aide at the hospital. She had to drop out of college and couldn't finish her nursing degree. They don't pay much, but they let her off whenever she needs it to see the specialists in New Orleans."

"People seem to disappear around here," I said. "More than other places, I mean."

"It's bayou country, so not exactly surprising," Ida Belle said. "Men have dangerous jobs in unpredictable terrain."

"Besides," Gertie threw in, "Malaysia lost an entire plane, so we're not doing bad."

"Did he normally shrimp in the lake?" I asked.

"Sometimes shrimpers push through the lake," Ida Belle said. "The catch is smaller than the deeper waters, but the day Hank went missing, a big storm blew in. My guess is the storm carried his boat into the lake."

Gertie nodded. "He could have fallen off the boat before it got to the lake, or hit his head and gone down with the boat like Carter did. Lots of things can go wrong when you're caught on the water in a storm like that one."

After my trip to the bottom of the lake to rescue Carter, I couldn't think of a worse way to die than drowning. I felt sorry for Hank and his wife. The mental image of what must have happened to him would probably be rolling through her mind for a long time to come.

"You said they found the sheriff's boat, right?" I asked. "Were they able to get it up from the bottom of the lake?"

Deputy Breaux nodded. "Took some doing, but they were able to get it up and attach it to some big blocks of Styrofoam, then drain it enough to tow it in."

"Can we see it?" Fortune asked.

"No."

"Jesus," Ida Belle said, "this is no time to start playing the confidential card. We just came from voting and Celia's standing at the end of Main Street telling everyone how incompetent this department is and how she's going to replace every one of you as soon as she's elected. Trust me, you need all the help you can get right now."

Deputy Breaux's face contorted with frustration as Ida Belle relayed Celia's words. "I'm not saying no because I have some illusions about solving this myself or anything. Those damned Feds showed up when they pulled up to the dock with the boat. They said the boat was evidence in their case and they were taking it."

Gertie mumbled a couple of curse words I recognized and a couple more I didn't.

Deputy Breaux gave her an appreciative look. "I felt the same way, ma'am. I tried to tell them that Walter had a place for it in his garage where it would be safe and they could look it over, but they refused."

Ida Belle sighed. "That would have been perfect. At least we could have gotten access on the sly."

"And I'm sure that's exactly what they figured," I said. Especially now that they knew Walter was Carter's uncle. "Did you see anything useful on the boat before they hauled it away?"

"What looked like a bullet hole in the side," Deputy Breaux said, "but they wouldn't let me close enough to check it out. I asked the men who brought it in about them, but all they said was it looked like gunshots. No idea what caliber, if it was even gunshots."

"I don't suppose you know where they were taking the

boat?" I asked.

"Yeah, I overheard that one in charge on the phone. He was talking to someone at Southwest Storage."

Gertie perked up. "That's off the highway going toward New Orleans, right?"

"Yeah," Deputy Breaux said, "but what does it matter? If they won't let me inspect the department's boat at our own dock, they're not going to let me look at it somewhere else."

"Oh, I wasn't—" Gertie started and Ida Belle jabbed her in the ribs.

"The whole thing was weird, really," Deputy Breaux said. "After you called and asked about the boat, the only people I talked to were the shrimpers and the roughnecks they had helping. I asked them all to keep it quiet, and I don't have any reason to believe they didn't." He frowned. "But they'd no sooner docked when those Feds showed up. Like someone had alerted them, but I have no idea who it could have been."

"That is weird," Ida Belle agreed. "I can't imagine a Sinful resident who would willingly go into cahoots with the Feds, especially when things involved a local."

"Celia would," I said.

Everyone stared at me, their dismay apparent, then everyone spoke at once.

"Son of a bitch."

"Figures."

"That woman is a disease."

Gertie covered her mouth with her hand. "Did I say that out loud?"

"Yeah," I said, "but it wasn't as bad as what I was thinking."

Deputy Breaux's expression shifted from aggravation to worry. "Does the doctor think Carter's memory will come back soon?"

"He has no way of knowing," I said. "Hopefully, it will start coming back the more the swelling goes down, but there's always a slim chance he never remembers."

"That would be bad," Deputy Breaux said. "I know Sheriff Lee is supposed to be in charge, but everyone knows Carter is running the department. If Celia got him fired, she wouldn't have to bother doing the paperwork on me. I'd resign before I'd work for anyone she picked out."

"Of course you would," Gertie agreed.

I gave him an approving nod. Perhaps Deputy Breaux wasn't quite as foolish as he appeared to be. "Let's just hope Carter remembers soon and the whole mess is wrapped up."

"And that Celia isn't elected mayor," Gertie said.

We exchanged looks, but apparently no one wanted to verbalize their thoughts on Celia in charge of Sinful. I had a feeling that only Celia's cronies would fare well if she took over, and even then, only if she felt like it. Everyone else's life as they knew it would be changed forever, especially mine. If Celia got control, I had no doubt she'd make good on her promise to run me out of town. I couldn't risk my cover over the ravings of a crazy woman. If Celia came after me, I'd have to request extraction.

Which meant leaving Sinful—and Carter—for good.

"So what's the deal with the storage facility?" I asked after we exited the sheriff's department. "I figure you two know where it is, right?"

Gertie perked up. "It's just up the highway. Maybe a twenty-minute drive."

"Then I guess we're talking a night trip?"

"Whoo-hoo!" Gertie hooted, causing a flock of pigeons to launch off a bench. "Road trip."

Ida Belle frowned. "There may be a problem with the storage facility."

"What kind of problem?" I asked.

"It's owned by Big and Little Hebert."

"Oh," I said, mulling over this particular piece of information. We ran across Big and Little during a recent trip down investigative lane. They were part of a mob family based in New Orleans, and according to the rumor mill, worked the loan shark end of the business for the area. But we really had no way of knowing what all they had their fingers in.

Then I started to smile, and the more I thought about it, the more it tickled me.

"So," I said, "the ATF just parked evidence in a storage facility owned by mobsters."

Gertie began to giggle, and finally a grin broke through Ida Belle's stern expression.

"Okay," Ida Belle said, "I can see the hilarity on the part of the Feds, but any plans we had of visiting that facility need to be considered from all angles. We have no way of knowing what the Heberts are using the facility for, but my guess is that some of it is the kind of business they don't want anyone to know about."

"Which means really good security," Gertie said. "Like maybe dogs."

"Or that Hulk of a security detail they had at their office," I said.

"The bottom line," Ida Belle said, "is it's not the church or the sheriff's department or someone's home. If we do this, we have to be prepared, and armed."

"Okay," I agreed. "So where do we start?"

My cell phone signaled that I'd received a text and I pulled it out to check. It was from Carter.

Can you come back to the hospital as soon as possible?

I frowned and showed the text to Ida Belle and Gertie. "What do you think he wants?"

Gertie grinned. "You have to ask?"

Ida Belle waved a hand in dismissal. "Your mind is always in the gutter lately. The man is hardly in any condition for romantic liaisons, and even if he were, the hospital is hardly the location for such things."

"Especially with his mother in the room," I added.

"Ick," Gertie said. "You two really know how to spoil the mood."

"So hospital dating aside," I said, "any other thoughts?"

Ida Belle nodded. "My guess is he's trying to remember."

"And he thinks I can help? I don't see how."

"You were the only other person on the lake Saturday evening. You might have seen whatever it was that troubled Carter. You just wouldn't have known something was amiss."

I stretched my mind back to that evening, trying to focus on our boat ride to the island and the things I'd seen along the way. "I just don't see how…"

"It's a long shot," Ida Belle said, "but in that hospital bed with a memory that's not working properly, it's also the only thing Carter has."

"It must be killing him to just sit there," Gertie agreed. "Carter was never the sort to watch things happen."

"So what do I do?" I asked.

"Go," Ida Belle said. "Tell him everything you can remember about that night. I know it's grasping at straws, but there's always the slim chance it will jar something in his memory—something that we can use to get to the bottom of this."

"And if you see he's having a thought," Gertie said, "then you will have to lure it out of him."

"True," Ida Belle said. "His natural inclination will be to keep anything he recalls from you, especially given our past involvements where we weren't supposed to be involved."

"So I get to be charming, too? This is looking like more fun by the minute. Hey, I wonder if what he wrote on his laptop would jar his memory?"

"Maybe, but you can't risk telling him about it," Ida Belle said. "It would compromise everything we did today and put you right back in an uncomfortable spotlight. As soon as he's released from the hospital, Carter will check for notes. We'll know soon enough if what he wrote jars his memory."

"And the break-in before us? At some point, we have to tell him that his home was compromised."

Ida Belle shot an anxious glance at Gertie. "I have to be honest. The break-in concerns me most, but we still need to play our cards close...at least for now. Once Carter is released, Emmaline will stay with him and one of us will insist on staying as well."

"Won't they think that's strange?"

"I'll tell Emmaline it will make us feel better, given the strangeness of the situation," Ida Belle said. "And with Carter not physically up to par, she'll agree. There's nothing Emmaline cares about more than her son, and she'll do whatever necessary to protect him."

"And she won't ask questions," Gertie said. "Not of us."

"That's handy," I said. "What about tonight?"

"Don't worry about that," Ida Belle said. "Gertie and I will do the necessary reconnaissance on the storage facility. We'll have a plan by the time you get back to Sinful."

"Then I will head to the hospital to deceive, inveigle, and obfuscate."

Gertie pointed at me. "*X-Files* reference. Very nice. You're really coming along on this pop culture thing."

Ida Belle shook her head. "*The X-Files* is hardly pop culture. Some of the seasons are so old they didn't even have cell phones yet."

"But it's classic investigation," Gertie argued. "It never hurts to bone up on our skills."

"They're investigating unexplained phenomena," Ida Belle said.

"This *is* Sinful," I pointed out.

Ida Belle sighed. "Carry on."

It went against all my better judgment, but I changed into jeans and a turquoise top before heading to the hospital. Normally, I would have gone in whatever I had on, which in this case was yoga pants and a T-shirt, but when I'd reached for my car keys earlier, I had this twinge that maybe I should look more presentable.

I'd hurried upstairs to throw on another outfit, all the time wondering if I should just shoot myself. All this pretending to be a girlie girl was making me, well…girlie.

It's because of Carter.

I shut that thought down as quickly as I could. The last thing I needed to become was one of those women who thought she had to attract a man with her looks. If a man couldn't lock onto far more important things than a pretty face, then he lacked substance and was of no interest to me.

Who the hell are you fooling?

I sighed as I pulled my Jeep onto the highway.

"Nobody," I said out loud.

But I was trying to fool myself. Sometimes I tried to fool myself into believing this was just another undercover job and when the time came, I'd pack my duffel bag and skip out of Sinful as quickly as I rode in. Sometimes I tried to fool myself into thinking that if I wanted it, I could have a more normal life. *Normal* being one with friends, hobbies that didn't include death, and maybe even a relationship.

Then reality set in and I realized how big a mess I'd made of everything. I'd broken the first rule of undercover engagement and formed real attachments. Granted, the people in Sinful weren't anything similar to my CIA targets, but when my time in Sinful was done, the feelings I'd formed for all of them would make it hard to go.

And even harder to tell Carter the truth.

That was the real kicker. And it was something I knew I'd have to do one day. No way could I leave Sinful without telling Carter about the real me. That was one conversation I'd give anything to never have, but it was unavoidable. And the deadline for having it was approaching rapidly. The situation with Director Morrow already had Harrison on alert. If he suspected any danger other than the norm, he'd yank me in a second and place me somewhere else. And even if I stayed my term in Sinful, that only gave me until the end of summer. Sandy-Sue Morrow had a full-time librarian job when school started up again. She was only in Sinful for three months.

One month had already passed. It seemed like a lifetime, and also only a second.

As I turned into the hospital parking lot and rolled into a slot in the visitors' section, I forced my mind to shift gears. Right now, I had to focus on helping Carter remember, and making sure he thought I was only a visiting librarian who was concerned about his well-being. I'd played that role a million times before already, but I knew this time was going to be so much harder than the others.

Emmaline smiled at me when I walked into Carter's room. Carter's eyes were closed and his chest rose and fell in rhythm.

"He finally dozed off after he called you," Emmaline said. "I've been trying to get him to sleep, but he's so stubborn."

I walked over to the bed and nodded. "He wants answers."

"We all do," Emmaline agreed. "But exhaustion will only make his memories harder to retrieve."

I looked down at her. Even with her makeup half worn off and her hair mussed from sleeping in a hospital chair, she was still a beautiful woman. "You look like you could use a break, too," I said. "Why don't you go home, have a shower and a change of clothes? Grab a decent meal and maybe even a nap."

The spark in her eyes when I mentioned a shower let me know she really wanted to go, but she was still in protective mode. "Don't worry," I said. "I'll stay with him until you get back. Take your time. I don't have anything to do until later tonight."

"You're sure?"

"I'm positive. I imagine when he wakes up, he'll want to grill me, trying to remember what he saw Saturday. You can't help with that, and it will likely be frustrating for both of us when I can't help. No use for you to feel the frustration of the situation any more than you already do."

Emmaline smiled and rose from her chair. "You're a wonderful person, Fortune. I can see why my son set his sights on you." She leaned over to kiss my cheek. "Thank you for looking out for him. I know he thinks he doesn't need any help, but even the toughest of men benefit from a strong woman who's got their back."

"What was his father like?" I didn't mean to blurt it out, but all of a sudden, I really wanted to know. Carter never spoke of him, so I had always been afraid to ask. And I wasn't about to ask Ida Belle, Gertie, or Ally such personal things about Carter. Not when I was busy trying to convince them that I wasn't interested in a relationship.

"Carter's father...he was a complicated man. All stoic and strong and never willing to ask for help. Now you know where Carter gets it. But there was also the other side of him—the side no one saw but me and Carter—the gentle and fun-loving side." She sighed. "He was the most loyal, the most honest person I've ever met. Not a day goes by that I don't miss him. The memories are so vivid that sometimes it seems he just passed yesterday."

"What happened to him? I mean, if you want to tell me."

"Nothing scandalous or interesting. Just a simple heart attack, but he was offshore fishing with some buddies when it happened and they couldn't get him help in time. His family has a history of that sort of thing. It's probably why Carter eats healthy most of the time and is always exercising. His father was better about it when he was young, but as he got older he slacked off the exercise and indulged in too much of Francine's food." She smiled. "Not that I'm not guilty of that myself."

"Me too. That woman's cooking should be a controlled substance."

Emmaline laughed. "And now that we've talked about it, I think I'll call in an order and pick it up on my way home."

She gave me a wave and headed out of the room. I grabbed an automotive magazine from the nightstand and took a seat in the chair Emmaline had vacated. I opened up to an article on restoring old cars and nodded off to sleep before I'd finished the first paragraph.

Chapter Ten

I awakened with a start and bolted up from my chair, completely unaware of my surroundings and brandishing the magazine like a bat. Then Carter started to chuckle and I remembered I was at the hospital, currently poised to strike an unknown assailant with paper.

"Unless you're going after a dog with that," Carter said, "I don't think it's going to be a big deterrent."

I tossed the magazine on the nightstand and took a breath to steady my racing pulse. "I don't know, the articles might bore someone to death."

"I can agree with you there. Put me out like a light last night. Worked better than the painkillers."

I stretched my arms up and rolled my head around. "Apparently, it had the same effect on me. I must have dozed off."

"If that was dozing, you were doing a mighty fine job of it. And you snore."

"I do not snore."

"Like a freight train. The nurse even looked inside once to make sure it wasn't an earthquake."

"Now you're just being mean. Why didn't you wake me up?"

"It's not like you had the easiest time of it yesterday. I have a good idea of what it physically took to get me up from the boat. And I bet you didn't sleep all that well besides, with everything that happened."

"Hmmm," I said and nodded. The reality was that Sunday hadn't even been the most strenuous day I'd had since I'd been in Sinful, and certainly not the most stressful. Compared to my day job, it was a walk in the park. Truth be known, I'd slept like the dead, just not as long as I would have liked. But I couldn't exactly relay any of those truths to Carter, who thought I'd had a librarian-turned-Wonder-Woman moment.

"Do you always leap up from a dead sleep ready to attack?" he asked.

"I do when I'm in unfamiliar territory, or think there's an intruder in the room."

"Or a raccoon in your attic? I'm probably lucky you aren't armed with more than a magazine."

I shifted my weight from one leg to the other, ready to change the conversation to things I was more comfortable talking about. Like anything not related to me, especially since I was currently saying a silent prayer of thanks that I'd decided to leave my weapon at home. If I'd jumped up in a ready position with my pistol, that would have been very, very bad. Average civilians did not have weapon response time anywhere near what I did.

"How are you feeling?" I asked.

"Like I got shot and almost drowned," he said. "Other than that and the fact that I can't remember a thing since Saturday night, everything's peachy."

"At least you don't snore."

He laughed. "And I remember Saturday night. The real tragedy would have been forgetting our dinner."

I felt a blush run up my neck. "It's only a pleasant memory because I didn't do the cooking."

"The cooking was spectacular," he agreed, "but the company was better."

He cocked his head and studied me. "You're actually blushing."

"Am not."

"It's nice...and different, to be around a beautiful woman who isn't vain."

I shook my head. "I'm not beautiful."

"The fact that you don't know it only makes it more so."

I was so uncomfortable that I was about to fake a bathroom call when a nurse pushed open the door and walked inside the room.

"Time for a checkup," she said, then looked at me. "You can stay if you'd like. It's just a routine heart, bandage, and machines sort of thing. No forced nudity."

"If there's no nudity, I don't see any reason to stay," I said.

The nurse laughed and Carter grinned. "You got a live one here," the nurse said. "Now, sit still for a minute and let me check those bandages."

"Where did my mom go?" Carter asked as the nurse went about her duties.

"I sent her packing. She looked like she could use a break. I promised her I'd stay until she got back."

"Thank you for that. Hopefully she'll take advantage of your kindness and get some sleep. I know she hovered all night in the lobby. Probably drove the night shift crazy."

I shrugged. "She's your mom. That's her job." I thought it was nice the way Emmaline fussed over Carter. I liked to think that if my mother had lived, she'd be the same way with me.

The nurse made notes on Carter's clipboard and hung it back on the end of the bed. "All done, and looks good. Do you need any pain meds?" she asked.

"I'm fine right now," Carter said.

She held up a plastic tube with a remote attached to it. "Well, if the pain gets too bad, just push this little button and help will be on the way." She gave us both a nod and exited the room.

"You sure you don't need the pain meds?" I asked.

"They make me sleepy, and we need to talk."

I must not have looked convinced.

"I promise I'll take them as soon as we're done."

"Okay," I said. "Have you talked to Deputy Breaux today?"

"Yeah, a couple of times. He said you called this morning and told him to try to get my boat up from the bottom of the lake."

"Sorry. I know you told us not to interfere, but when Ida Belle, Gertie, and I got to talking about it, we thought it might be a good idea."

"It was an excellent idea, and one I didn't grasp onto until hours after you did, which just goes to show how unfocused I am."

"Give yourself a break. You almost died. You get several Delayed Mental Reaction free cards for that."

"I hope I don't use them all up today."

"Have you talked to Deputy Breaux since they got the boat up?"

"No!" He sat up straight in the bed. "He was supposed to call me as soon as he had the boat secured...assuming they could manage that in the first place. You know something about the boat?"

"Ida Belle and Gertie had to vote and we stopped by the sheriff's department afterward. Some shrimpers and a couple of roughnecks—one who dives—got your boat up and towed it in to the sheriff department's dock." I took a breath and blew it out, knowing Carter was going to be seriously pissed when I told him the next part of the story. "Then those ATF agents showed up and kinda forced Deputy Breaux to give up the boat."

"Damn it!"

I cringed a bit as Carter continued his rant. Finally, he came up for air.

"Does he know where they took it?"

"Some storage facility up the highway a bit."

"I know the place. Maybe when I get out of here, I can sweet-talk the owner into letting me give the boat a look-over."

"Anything's possible." Except convincing Big and Little Hebert to run up against the ATF as a favor to another cop. But that was another piece of unfortunate information that wouldn't do Carter any good to have at the moment.

"Why hasn't Deputy Breaux called and told me this?"

"There's probably three reasons, and all of them good."

"I'm listening."

"First off, when the diver went down to secure your boat, he found wreckage of another boat nearby. It belonged to a guy named Hank Eaton. His wife was there when we walked in, and she was pretty upset to hear the news."

"Hank Eaton's boat is in the lake? Man, we searched every bayou and channel for weeks looking for any sign of Hank and his boat, but that storm was so fierce, it was impossible to know what direction to look, especially given we didn't know his whereabouts when the storm hit."

"That whole 'looking for people lost in the swamp' is definitely one of the suckier parts of your job."

"Yeah. Poor Laurel. I mean, we all knew the score when Hank never returned, but..."

"Gertie said hearing this was probably like hearing it all over again for the first time."

Carter nodded. "I think until people have proof, they still have this tiny sliver of hope that their loved one isn't dead."

"I can see that. I mean, you hear about those strange reunions decades later on the news. I guess it's like the lottery—you figure it has to happen to someone, so it may as well be you."

"That's one good reason for Deputy Breaux's delay, but you said you had three."

"Number two is that the election has proven to be a bit of a hassle for law enforcement, and with the Feds muddying up the local waters, you out of commission, and Sheriff Lee moving at negative light speed, Deputy Breaux has been stretched a little thin."

Carter cringed. "I wasn't in Sinful for the last election, but I've heard the horror stories. With Celia running, I can imagine it's worse than anything Stephen King has ever written."

"She was making a public spectacle of herself downtown. I mean, that's nothing new, really, but with every citizen in Sinful down there crowded into one spot, there's bound to be trouble."

"And the third reason?"

"That one's easy. Deputy Breaux knew how mad you'd be when you found out the ATF agents confiscated your boat, so he left that last on his list of emergencies to handle."

"Ha. You nailed that one."

"I told you I had three good reasons. So now that you're up to date on the unfortunate Sinful situation, what can I do to help?"

"Get comfortable," he said and pointed to the chair. "This could take a while."

I poured us both a glass of water and slipped into the chair. "Then let's get started."

Carter reached for a pad of paper and pen on his table. "I

made some notes about Saturday. It's all there. At least I think it is. But for the life of me, I don't remember thinking something was off-kilter."

"And whatever you saw happened Saturday, so it makes no sense that you wouldn't remember that when you remember everything else."

"Exactly."

"Okay. So what is the last thing you remember from Saturday?"

He stared at the wall for several seconds, his brow creased. "I remember taking you home, and I definitely remember our kiss at your front door."

"That would be impossible to forget."

He smiled for a moment, then his expression turned thoughtful again. "I remember going home and taking a shower. Then I poured myself a beer and turned on the television in the living room."

"What was on?"

"Huh?"

"What was on the television?"

He frowned. "I think...no." He looked at me. "I don't know. Why don't I know?"

I was pretty sure I knew what had happened to him. In my line of work, it wasn't exactly an uncommon problem, but I needed to present my thoughts in a way that screamed *nerdy librarian who reads all the time* and not *CIA agent who deals with this on a regular basis.*

"I read a book on how the brain works once. It had this section on amnesia, specifically when associated with traumatic events. Most were victims of crimes and forgot the circumstances at the point of attack."

"But that's not what's happened to me. I can't remember

but a minute or two after Saturday night, and the attack wasn't until Sunday morning."

I nodded. "There was an investigator they did a case study on. He was closing in on a serial killer and ended up being kidnapped by him. He was rescued, but the serial killer was long gone, and the investigator couldn't recall anything after dinner the night before."

"Sounds familiar. But how does any of that help me?"

"He finally remembered, and when he did, he realized that his memory blanked at the exact moment he put together who the serial killer was. Something on television triggered a thought and all his clues came together with the identity of the killer."

Carter nodded slowly. "Then he was kidnapped and his memory flashed back to the first unrelated event."

"That's what the doctor's theory was."

"But the investigator still remembered that he was working on the case. If I saw something that I thought was suspicious before our dinner, then why didn't my memory shoot all the way back to that moment?"

I leaned forward in my chair. "Okay, this is just a theory, but what if you saw something suspicious, but it didn't register that way to you at the time. What if it was sitting in your subconscious and when you turned on the television, you saw something that brought whatever you saw into your consciousness because it put it into perspective."

Carter stared at me for several seconds, and I began to wonder if he was going to call for the nurse, but for me this time. Finally he shook his head. "It's a bizarre theory for sure, but it makes more sense than anything I can come up with."

"It's just a guess. I mean, we have no way of knowing for sure. Not until you remember, anyway."

"True, but at least this gives me something to start with."

"But what can you do with that information?"

"For starters, I can call my mother and ask her to swing by my place and tell me what channel the television is on. Then I can backtrack to what was playing Saturday night when I turned it on."

"Oh!" I sat up straight in my chair. "That's a great idea."

Carter grabbed his phone and called his mother, explaining what he wanted her to do. I could hear the anticipation in his voice as he told Emmaline why he wanted the information. I felt my excitement brew for a moment, then wane when reality hit. Whoever had searched Carter's house could have easily changed the channel during their poking around. And even if the channel was still the same, it could have been a commercial that prompted his breakthrough. If that was the case, the television idea would be a complete bust.

"What's wrong?" Carter asked.

"What...oh, nothing. I was just trying to process it all. It's sort of overwhelming."

He gave me a sympathetic look. "You've been tangled up in some pretty awful stuff since you arrived in Sinful. I imagine your life back east isn't nearly as dramatic."

"No, the drama level is pretty low there." It wasn't a lie. Drama had no place on a CIA mission. Everything was calculated and clinical. Bringing drama into that line of work was exactly what had landed me in Sinful.

"Things will settle down," he said. "I know it seems overwhelming now, but I swear this used to be a pretty quiet place. Whatever this current upheaval is, it can't last. Pretty soon, I'll be back to poaching and drunk-and-disorderlies."

"I'm sure you're right." What else could I say? It's not like I could blurt out that if Celia was elected mayor he wouldn't even have a job to return to. His health was already stretched enough.

Until that bomb dropped for sure, no way was I even going to bring up the possibility.

I slumped back into my chair, holding in a sigh. This not giving away anything was so much harder when you cared about the person you were keeping secrets from. Especially when the secrets were about them. "So what now? We have a starting point, but is there anything else you thought I could help with?"

"I'm not sure it will help, but I wanted you to tell me everything you saw on our boat ride to the island."

"Okay." At least this was something I could do comfortably and without lying. "Where do I start?"

"Start with everything you saw after we left downtown Sinful and got down the bayou past the residential area."

I closed my eyes, hoping it would help me remember, and the bayou appeared in my mind as if I were back on that boat ride. I relayed a description of every boat we passed and a description of the occupants if I didn't know their names. I recalled the fishing camps I'd seen on the way and which ones had a boat docked out front. I remembered passing a shrimp boat as we entered the lake and Carter waving at the captain as we went by.

"You've got a good memory," Carter said. "Do you recall the name of the boat?"

"*The Neptune.*"

Carter frowned. "That's Lucas Riley's boat. He usually doesn't shrimp the lake."

I nodded, now remembering where I'd seen Riley before— at the Swamp Bar. He was one of those tall, muscled guys with a shaved head, piercing blue eyes, and far too many tattoos. "He was dumping ice on a chest of fish when we passed. I don't know what kind—they were long and had dots on them."

"Speckled trout. He must have been fishing."

"Is the lake a good place to catch speckled trout?"

"Oh yeah. If you hit a school of them feeding, you'll be eating fish for a week."

I shrugged. "Then that's it. I don't remember seeing any other boats after that one. No camps, either."

"No, there aren't any more until you get across the lake. The banks on the other sides shift too much to be stable." Carter slumped back in his bed, and I could tell he was disappointed.

"I'm sorry I couldn't help."

"No. It's not your fault. It was a long shot anyway. It's far more likely that whatever I saw was when I was setting up for our dinner and not after I picked you up."

I had a feeling he was probably right. Part of my makeup was watching people very closely, looking for any shift in their expression that might indicate a branching thought that could be followed by a new and unexpected action. But I'd never seen a shift in Carter's expression that night. He was entirely focused on me and our date. I never saw a twitch of indication that he'd left "us" for even a moment and returned to police work.

"I wish I could do more," I said.

Carter narrowed his eyes at me. "Don't go getting any ideas about doing anything more than you are already. I was in the sheriff department's boat. Whoever shot at me had to know I was law enforcement. If he'll take that kind of risk, he wouldn't hesitate a moment to take out anyone else who got in his way."

"I know," I said, raising my hands in surrender. "Besides, I wouldn't have any idea where to start. And I'm not foolish enough to take that chance." Unless one considered breaking into a public storage facility owned by mobsters to access a boat confiscated by the ATF a foolish move.

He stared at me several seconds more, but I had been trained to look someone directly in the eyes and lie without flinching. Carter was a good cop, but the CIA trained assassins for an entirely different skill set.

"I want you to promise me you'll be doubly careful," he said finally. "It doesn't look like you saw whatever prompted my search, but we can't be certain. If the shooter suspects you saw whatever I saw, then you could be in danger, too."

"I promise to sleep with all the lights on and a pistol on my nightstand."

"I'm not sure whether to be happy or frightened. Just make sure you don't shoot Ally or that stray cat you took in."

"Merlin is smart enough to duck. I'll give Ally fair warning."

"Maybe if she needs you and you're sleeping, you should have her call your cell phone."

I nodded. It actually wasn't a bad idea. Ally had narrowly escaped my misdirected attacks on several occasions.

Thinking about narrow escapes flashed me back to my eventful relay with Tiny. That was a sticky one. I had no intention of telling Carter I'd been inside his house—ever, if I could avoid it. But Riker, Mitchell, Sheriff Lee, and Walter all knew Ida Belle and I had been on location for the dog-running, burro-climbing festivities. I doubted Sheriff Lee or Walter would call Carter about the incident while he was in the hospital, but I was certain he'd hear about it as soon as he was released.

"There was a sorta…um, incident at your house earlier today."

"What kind of incident?"

"I'm not really sure about all the particulars. Ida Belle and I were taking a walk, mulling everything over, and when we rounded the corner to your block Tiny was loose and running down the sidewalk."

"How did he get out?"

"I have no idea." I went on to tell him about Riker and

company being there, and on to the glorious conclusion with the burro atop Riker's car.

At first, he stared at me as if I were joking, but when I kept going, he realized it had happened exactly as I was describing. He started to grin, then chuckle, and by the time I got to the part when the burro climbed onto Riker's car, he was laughing so hard he was clutching his injured side. I glanced at the monitors, worried that any moment an alarm was going to go off and the medical staff would rush in thinking Carter was having a seizure.

Now that I thought about it, it sorta looked as if he was having a seizure.

"Are you all right?" I asked and rose from my chair.

He nodded and waved a hand at me before downing half his water. "I would have given anything to see that."

"Oh, you can see most of it. Ida Belle filmed it with her phone."

"Nothing fazes that woman, does it?"

"Not that I've seen so far. It's kinda scary."

"No shit," Carter said. "I bet Riker was fit to be tied."

"Oh yeah. He was completely apoplectic. So mad I thought he'd burst into flames."

"So how did you get the burro off the car?"

"We didn't. Far as I know, he's still up there."

Carter's mouth dropped open and he stared at me. I tried, but I couldn't keep my poker face on more than a couple of seconds and my grin broke through.

"You're joking," he said.

"Yeah, but for a couple of seconds, I had you." I went on to explain Walter's arrival and procurement of the angry Tiny and the dismounting of Riker's car.

Carter chuckled some more, then shook his head. "What was Riker doing at my house, anyway? He knows where I am."

"This is another one of those things that's going to make you mad, but he had a warrant to search your house. Sheriff Lee was there to make his access legal. Riker was going to break down the door but Walter said he'd let him in so you didn't have to return home from the hospital and worry about fixing your front door."

"You called Riker right with that douche bag label."

"I've met enough of the type. He's hardly original. Anyway, I have no idea what happened after that because Ida Belle remembered she needed to vote and we figured it was best to hightail it out of there before Riker could find something to blame us for besides witnessing his less-than-manly response to a dog and a burro."

"Smart. So I guess Riker doesn't believe my lost memory claim."

I shrugged. "Or he does believe it and hopes you made notes somewhere about what you went looking for."

Carter frowned. "I guess I could have…I wish I could remember. All of this would go away if I could just remember."

"I don't think it's going to be as simple as that. Whatever is going on, someone shot a law enforcement officer and left you to drown. And if whatever happened involves the ATF, it must be something big. Even once you remember, my guess is there's still a lot that has to happen before the ATF would move on the shooter."

"True." He smiled at me. "You're pretty sharp for a librarian. I would tell you to consider a job in law enforcement, but then you'd be allowed to tote a gun around all the time."

"What difference would it make in this town? Everyone here seems to be packing. Heck, Gertie carries more weapons around in that huge purse of hers than they probably have down at the pawnshop."

A monitor behind Carter beeped and I saw his blood pressure shoot up. Ooops.

"I really didn't need to know that," he said.

"Know what?" I put on my best innocent face.

He reached his hand out toward me and I placed my hand in his. He winced as he squeezed my hand. "Do you need one of those pain medicine shots?" I asked.

He shook his head. "But I'm pretty sure a kiss would make me feel better."

"I can call the nurse back in, but I doubt your PPO is going to cover the charges for kissing."

"I had something a little less clinical in mind."

He tugged on my hand and I stepped closer to the bed, but as I began to lean over to kiss him, the door opened and Emmaline walked in. I planted a frozen smile on my face, feeling like a kid who'd just been caught with her hand in the cookie jar. Fortunately, Emmaline didn't seem to notice she'd almost interrupted our medical attempt at reviving Carter.

"Mom," Carter said, "I thought you were going to get some rest."

She waved a hand in dismissal. "I tried, but every time I closed my eyes, all I could see was you lying here with those awful bruises. Then I'd get mad all over again. I finally gave up. When I get tired enough, nothing will keep me from it."

She placed a brown paper bag on the table. "This is from Francine."

The smell of chicken and dumplings wafted past me and my stomach grumbled. I suddenly realized I hadn't had anything to eat except for croissants that Gertie had thrown together for our ride to the hospital.

Carter laughed. "Sounds like you can use it worse than me."

"No, you go ahead," I said. "Unlike you, I can go get

refills."

Carter looked at Emmaline. "Did you check my television?"

She nodded. "The History channel."

"Was anyone at my house when you stopped by?"

"No, and it's a good thing. The place is a mess. I swear I raised you better than that."

Carter stiffened. "Assholes."

"Good Lord." Emmaline's eyes widened. "What in the world has gotten into you?"

Carter's jaw flexed and I could tell he was steaming mad. I explained to Emmaline about the ATF and the search warrant.

"You mean those rude men are the ones who made a mess in your home?" Emmaline asked. "Is that even legal?"

"Probably," I said. "I think if someone isn't a suspect then they're supposed to be more considerate. I had a friend whose apartment got searched because the police had the wrong address. They broke two pieces of her deceased mother's china. She came unglued on them and waylaid one of the cops with a lamp."

"I like your friend," Emmaline said. "But I suppose she got arrested for the lamp stunt."

"Yeah, but the department had been running into some bad publicity at the time so they dropped the charges and wrote her a big check for the damage to keep it out of the newspapers. She's still mad, though, and that was a good ten years ago."

Emmaline put her hands on her hips and shook her head. "Well, I just think it's a shame that we pay our taxes and follow the rules and this is how we're treated. You can bet that someone at the ATF will be hearing from me."

I grinned. I'd pay to hear that conversation.

Chapter Eleven

With Emmaline back on guard at the hospital, I wasn't needed any longer. I could tell Carter wanted me to stay but wouldn't ask. I hesitated for a bit, wanting to stay a little longer myself, but I needed to check in with Ida Belle about our plans for tonight. She'd said she'd handle it, but walking into things blind with Ida Belle and Gertie was never a good idea.

Besides, my stomach had a reason to protest and my leg and shoulder muscles could do with another round of ointment. If I planned on going through with the storage facility break-in, I needed to be in the best shape possible. Sore muscles reacted slower. The more I could loosen them before tonight, the better my reflexes would be.

Downtown was still a mess, filled with voters and random fighting. I saw Deputy Breaux trying to break up a fight between two women with strollers. He looked as if he was ready to resign right there on the spot. I couldn't imagine how aggravating his job was right now. If I were there, I'd turn the fire department hose on the entire street, which was probably why it was a good thing that I didn't work with the general public.

I made a left turn and skirted downtown to get to my street. At least my house was far enough from the fray that it hadn't spilled over here. I pulled into the garage and headed inside, mentally running through the options in my refrigerator. There was leftover meatloaf and at least one piece of apple pie. I could do a lot worse than a meatloaf sandwich.

As soon as I opened the garage door and entered the house, the smell of barbeque wafted over me and I felt my knees buckle. I hurried into the kitchen and saw Ally opening up a huge tray of barbeque brisket.

"Emmaline told me you were at the hospital when she stopped by the diner," Ally said. "I figured you probably skipped lunch and would be starving."

"Ally?" I'd officially made up my mind.

"Yeah?"

"Will you marry me?"

She smiled. "How sad is it that you're the first person to ever ask?"

"Very, very sad. Because that means that all men are morons."

"You're great for a girl's ego. Sit down before you pass out. You're practically salivating."

She didn't have to ask me twice. I dropped into a chair like a death row prisoner presented with my last meal. Ally placed two plates on the table and another container that proved to be mashed potatoes. One last tray held garlic bread, and she topped the entire thing off with a jug of sweet tea.

Ally had barely slid into her seat before I'd heaped a pile of brisket on my plate and reached for the potatoes. "I owe you forever," I said. "I have no idea how I'll pay you back, but I'll figure out something."

"You're letting me live in your house. That's payment enough."

I shrugged. "It's not like it's my real house. Heck, I'm not even paying the bills. The estate is."

"The estate that you inherited," Ally pointed out. "You're still paying the bills, just not directly."

"I guess you're right." At least, she would be right if I were the real Sandy-Sue Morrow. "But still. It's hardly an inconvenience. In fact, my quality of life has increased quite a bit since you moved in, at least where food is concerned."

I stabbed a hunk of the brisket with my fork and practically inhaled it. An explosion of sweet and tangy with a touch of heat tantalized my taste buds. I didn't dare open my mouth to comment, but the brisket was too good to go without compliment, so I pointed to my lips and nodded.

Ally laughed. "Francine's secret BBQ sauce is almost as big a mystery as her banana pudding recipe. She's actually had people break into the café at night trying to find her recipe book."

I shook my head. Francine wasn't foolish enough to write her recipes down. I'd bet anything they were all stored safely in her head, and when she died, they would go with her.

"How's Carter doing?" Ally asked.

I swallowed the brisket and chugged down some sweet tea. "Better physically, but his memory is still blank from Saturday night on, except for a couple of minutes."

Ally's eyes widened. "He forgot your date?"

"No. He remembers all that and going home, showering, and turning on the television, but after that, it's all gone until he woke up in the hospital."

"That sucks."

"In a million different ways," I agreed and scooped up a helping of mashed potatoes.

"Walter told me he had to let the ATF in to search Carter's house. He was mad enough to spit when he came into the café. Said they made a right mess of Carter's place and talked to him like he was an idiot."

"That sounds about right. He should have let Tiny loose on them."

"He was tempted, but he was afraid the cowards would shoot the dog."

"Also sounds about right. Did he figure out how Tiny got out?"

"Yeah, there's a section of the fence that's broken. Best he could figure, Tiny was trying to get at something behind the fence line and broke it out." She frowned.

"What's wrong?"

"It's probably nothing, but I wondered if maybe it was some*one* Tiny was trying to get at."

"Could be, but don't people walk along the bayou all the time?"

"Yeah, you're right. It was probably an extra smelly rabbit or something equally as enticing to a big dumb dog. He told me about the burro incident. I haven't laughed that hard in years."

"It was a thing of beauty."

"It's a shame they aren't still trapped in the car. Anyway, Walter took Tiny to his house until Carter can get the fence fixed. The last thing he needs is Tiny running around Sinful, terrifying the residents. Aunt Celia would have more ammo for her 'fire the entire sheriff's department' campaign."

"You heard about that?"

"Hard to miss when she was carrying on with a microphone and speaker right down from the café. And residents kept coming in and talking about it."

"What are they saying?"

"Most people think she's being foolish. Unless there's widespread corruption, you don't just clean out experienced law enforcement."

"And the people who don't think she's being foolish?"

Ally sighed. "They're worried about everything that's been happening in Sinful, and frustrated at what they perceive as inefficiency on the part of the sheriff's department. But even then, they're not suggesting everyone be replaced. I think most would be happy if Sheriff Lee would retire and let Carter step in, then replace Carter with another young man, maybe one more capable than Deputy Breaux."

"I can't really say that I blame them, but if they want a younger crew protecting the town, then why do they keep reelecting Sheriff Lee?"

"No one runs against him. Carter has already said he won't run until Sheriff Lee retires. He'd see running against him as disrespectful, even though that's exactly what needs to happen."

"Maybe some of you could talk to Sheriff Lee about retiring. Make an argument that he's paid his dues and deserves a break."

"Ida Belle and Gertie have been trying for years, but Sheriff Lee is from the old school where real men dropped dead while working. He's not about to have it any other way."

"How old is he, anyway?"

"Heck if I know. I can remember Old Lady Crandal, who lived next door to me, calling him an old codger before she passed. I was only five years old then, and Old Lady Crandal seemed ancient. I guess that makes Sheriff Lee walking dust."

I laughed.

"I do know that his wife was the one exception in membership the Sinful Ladies Society ever made."

"Really?"

Ally nodded. "Gertie said that Sheriff Lee was so stubborn he would outlive Milly just to ensure she didn't get to be a member. So Ida Belle decided that Sheriff Lee hadn't influenced Milly since transistor radios were the rage and let her join. She passed away several years back."

My cell phone beeped and I pulled it out of my pocket and

checked the display. "Speak of the devil." It was a text from Ida Belle.

Get downtown. We have a situation.

I jumped up from my chair, grabbing a piece of French bread on my way.

"What's wrong?" Ally asked.

"Something's going on downtown."

Ally jumped up and grabbed her purse. "I'm going with you."

I gave her a nod and hurried out to my Jeep. It was easier to let her tag along than argue; besides, it was still broad daylight. It was probably more of Celia's election nonsense. At least, I hoped it was that simple.

The scene downtown was both confusing and somewhat frightening. A huge cluster of people gathered at the end of Main Street, surrounding the area where Celia had been speaking earlier. Parking was nonexistent so I just stopped in the middle of the road as close as I could get to the fray, and Ally and I jumped out and hurried toward the mob.

I caught sight of Ida Belle waving at us from about five feet up the town flagpole. She shinnied down as we approached. "What the heck is going on?" I asked.

"Those idiots with the ATF decided Deputy Breaux couldn't control the town and called in the state police. They've been arresting people left and right and shoving them on a bus for transport to New Orleans."

"I bet Celia's loving this mess," I said.

"Not at the moment," Ida Belle said. "I tried to stop her but Gertie came down here full of piss and vinegar and ready to take Celia down a peg or two."

Ally's hand flew over her mouth. "Oh no!"

"Oh yeah," Ida Belle said. "They're just yelling right now,

146

but if we don't break this up fast, they'll both be on that bus with the rest of Sinful's miscreants."

Ida Belle shot me a hard look. I knew exactly what she was trying to convey. Gertie could prove to be a liability at times, but for what we had planned tonight, we needed a lookout. The risk of breaking into that storage facility with just Ida Belle and me was too high. We needed Gertie. She was the eyes in the backs of our heads.

I pushed through the crowd toward the park bench Celia had been standing on earlier, Ida Belle and Ally close on my heels. As I drew closer, I could make out Celia's voice and then Gertie's, and it sounded as though things were escalating. The first slap echoed through the crowd like a gunshot and I shoved the last of the crowd out of the way and burst into the tiny open area surrounding the two fighting women.

I had wondered at first who threw the first punch, but the red mark on Gertie's cheek and Celia's open hand, reared back for a second blow, was a dead giveaway.

"You think that hurt, you old hag?" Gertie yelled. "I've been hit by mosquitoes that hurt worse."

"I could do it again," Celia yelled back.

"You could try. But I'm warning you, I'm a lot harder to hit when my back's not turned."

"Ladies," I yelled, waving my hands at both of them. "This is not the avenue you want to take."

"Who the hell are you calling a lady?" Celia asked. "Because I only see one standing here."

"I'm glad you recognize," Gertie said. "That's probably the only honest thing you've said all day today."

Celia's face turned a shade of red that I didn't think was even possible. I could practically see the steam coming off her head.

She pointed her finger at Gertie. "You are a disgrace to the women in this town. It's bad enough that you show your butt with your shenanigans, but today, you're quite literally showing it to the entire town."

"You think this is showing my butt?" Gertie shot back. "Heck, I'm barely giving you a peek, but I can fix that." She spun around and leaned over, flipping what remained of her tattered skirt up over her hips, giving Celia a clear view of the camo underwear.

"That does it," Celia shouted. She rushed over and grabbed Gertie's skirt with both hands and gave it a hard tug, apparently attempting to cover Gertie's butt.

Unfortunately, no one accounted for the fact that the dress was older than the planet and probably dry-rotted. I heard the fabric rip and cringed, praying that it was just a hem that pulled loose.

No such luck.

The entire dress split right down the middle. A stunned Celia backed up, jaw dropped and clutching one piece of the dress in each hand.

Gertie popped up and swung around. "You ruined my homecoming dress!" She reached into her purse and I said a silent prayer that she wouldn't start slinging those Chinese stars. I felt only a speck of relief when I saw her clutching a white tube, mistakenly thinking it was breath spray. Then that second of incorrect identification passed and I realized Gertie was about to blast Celia with Mace.

No way that could end well.

I jumped toward Gertie, attempting to grab the Mace from her hand, but as I leaped, she moved forward and my aim was off. Instead of grabbing her hand, I got the handle of her purse. Already off-balance, I lurched forward, pulling the handle with me and spinning Gertie around. She cried out and involuntarily clenched the Mace, sending a shot of it directly in my face.

I released the purse, flinging my hands over my eyes, but it was too late. The burning mist coated one of my pupils and I fell to the ground, yelling for water. With my good eye, I saw Gertie spin around as I released the purse strap, still depressing the canister.

Directly in the face of a state policeman.

The policeman screamed—a less than manly response—and grabbed Gertie by the arm. Another cop, this one much younger, came running up to see what was wrong and slid to a stop, clearly confused by what he saw.

"Sir?" the younger cop asked. "What happened?"

"She sprayed me with Mace. Arrest her and the other one in the pink suit."

"Wait!" Ida Belle shouted at the young cop as he handcuffed Gertie and motioned for another officer to do the same with Celia. "It was an accident."

"They can work that out with the judge down in New Orleans," the young cop said. "My orders are clear."

He tugged on Gertie's arm and she shot us a wide-eyed stare before stumbling through the crowd toward a school bus where the state police were apparently loading up offenders for transport to New Orleans. Celia wailed as the other officer cuffed her, and part of the crowd cheered. A couple of people booed.

Ally stared in dismay. "I'll go find Deputy Breaux," she said and dashed off into the crowd.

Ida Belle crouched down beside me and dumped a bottle of water in my eye. I sputtered and jumped up from the ground, flinging water as I went. "You could have warned me before you did that."

She grabbed my arm and tugged me toward the bus. "No time. If they put Gertie on that bus, we got bigger problems than we can fix."

I stumbled along behind her, my blurry eye making hurrying a bit of a challenge. When we arrived at the bus, the younger officer who had Gertie in custody was arguing with the older one she'd sprayed with Mace.

"The bus is full, sir," the young officer said. "I can't, in good conscience, force two old ladies to stand all the way to New Orleans in the middle of a bunch of redneck men. Especially when this one doesn't have on clothes. Our legal department would have my badge."

"Then get them over to the sheriff's department," the Maced officer yelled, "but do not release them. If you do, *I'll* have your badge."

Ida Belle and I followed behind as the policemen escorted Gertie and Celia into the sheriff's department. "At least they're not on the bus to New Orleans," Ida Belle said. "Maybe we can get them to release Gertie."

Myrtle was still at the front desk and looked as if she would drop from exhaustion at any minute. Her mascara trailed down her face, adding to the dark spots under her eyes. Her silver hair was mashed completely against her scalp in some places and standing straight on end in others. "I tried to stop them," she said, "but they weren't having any of it."

"Where did they take Gertie?" Ida Belle asked.

"To the drunk tank. With only two cells back there, we run out of space quick. The state police brought in the bus and started loading everyone up to carry to New Orleans. I've never seen such a mess in all my years living here, and I don't know how much more of it I can take."

Ida Belle gave her a sympathetic look. "You're overwrought

and overtired. I'm going to call for some help." She pulled out her phone and called Marie. "I need you to come help Myrtle down at the sheriff's department."

A couple seconds later, Ida Belle slipped her phone back into her purse. "Marie will be here in five minutes."

I took a moment to marvel over Ida Belle's command over her minions. Talk about respect and trust. No one except Gertie ever questioned her. The SLS women just jumped into action, automatically assuming that whatever Ida Belle asked for was necessary.

"Thank you," Myrtle said. "I don't know how much more of this I can take. I can't even keep up with the paperwork, and New Orleans will be expecting a list of those arrested and what they're being charged with."

She lifted a stack of assorted paper clumped on her desktop. "This is what I have to go on. Some of the arrest information is literally written on bubble gum wrappers."

"Don't worry about all that," Ida Belle said. "Marie is in her element with paperwork."

"That's true," Myrtle agreed, looking a tiny bit hopeful.

"Can we head back to the drunk tank?" Ida Belle asked. "We need to see about springing Gertie."

"Fine with me," Myrtle said. "Hell, tell them I sent you. Bunch of commies, rolling in here and taking over like it's a police state."

I grinned as we headed back to the drunk tank. The two cops who had hauled Gertie and Celia in passed us in the hallway without even giving us a second glance. They looked as exasperated as we did.

Another state policeman, this one tall and with gray hair, stood in front of the two cells. Gertie occupied one and Celia the other. It was a good thing both cells were empty. Separated by bars was probably best for everyone concerned. The state policeman glanced at Gertie and cringed, his expression a mixture of horror and "why me?"

We stepped up behind him and Ida Belle started to speak, but then the arguing started.

"I can't believe you're just sitting there like that," Celia said.

"You mean on my butt?" Gertie asked. "That's pretty much the accepted method of sitting for those of us that don't have a stick up it."

"I mean without clothes."

"You're the one who ripped off my dress, so what you see is what you get."

Celia's face turned red and she swung around to face the state policeman. "I'm not sitting in here with her half naked," Celia yelled.

"What the hell are you bitching about?" Gertie asked. "I'm the one with a chill."

"At least throw a blanket over her," Celia said.

"I'm not letting some prison blanket touch my bare skin. No telling which Sinful drunk sweated on it last."

"If I have to stay in here one more minute, I'm filing sexual harassment charges against the city."

"If you're elected mayor, that means you'll be suing yourself."

The policeman narrowed his gaze on Celia. "You're running for mayor?"

"Yes. I've been trying to tell you people that ever since you hauled me in here. This woman attacked me while I was giving a campaign speech. I'm the victim here."

Gertie snorted. "You've got to be kidding me. The only victims in this equation are everyone who's spent more than a minute in your presence."

The policeman, whose badge read Officer Crawford, opened the door and motioned for Celia to step out. She shot a smug look at Gertie, then walked past Ida Belle and me, not even bothering to hold in her grin as she exited the cellblock.

"Where is she going?" Ida Belle asked.

"I'm releasing her on her own recognizance," Crawford said.

"Just like that?" I asked.

He sighed. "Look. I'm retiring in two weeks and she's a mayoral candidate. I don't need the kind of grief keeping her locked up would bring. And she looked like a hell of a lot of grief."

Ida Belle and I glanced at each other and I shrugged. We couldn't really argue.

"What about Gertie? Aren't you going to release her, too?" Ida Belle asked.

"No can do. She assaulted a state policeman. I have to wait and see if he wants to press charges."

"And where is he?" I asked.

"Escorting the other detainees on the bus to New Orleans. It will take hours to book them all, so I don't anticipate he'll return until tomorrow."

My heart dropped. "You're keeping her in here all night?" Without Gertie, there was no storage facility visit.

"I don't have any other choice," he said.

"Can we at least bring her some clothes?" Ida Belle asked.

"I would appreciate it if you did. Bring her a toothbrush and dinner if you'd like." He glanced over at Gertie and winced. "Look, it's not like I want to keep her here, but the officer she Maced is a real hard-ass. If I turn her loose, he'll make trouble for me. It's just the way he is."

"We understand," Ida Belle said.

I looked over at her. "We do?" Gertie and I spoke at the same time.

"Sure. We can't fault the man for doing his job," Ida Belle said, her voice much nicer than normal.

Which meant Ida Belle had a plan.

"If you say so," I said and looked over at Gertie. "Don't worry. We'll get you some clothes, bathroom stuff, and something to eat and be back in a jiffy. Is there anything in particular you'd like?"

"Is it okay to have my knitting basket? I'm trying to finish a baby blanket for a shower this weekend."

Crawford nodded. "Sure, why not."

I held in a smile. He had mistaken Gertie for a woolly-headed old woman who baked cookies and knitted and got into fights with other old women. He didn't see her as a threat. Boy, was he wrong on that count. I'd put Gertie and her knitting needles up against al-Qaeda any day.

"I'll be back," I said in my best Arnold voice.

Gertie grinned. "Excellent choice."

Chapter Twelve

Ida Belle and I hurried up the sidewalk to the sheriff's department, her clutching two tote bags and me a pillow and blanket. Between the state police presence and the closing of the polls at the end of the day, the residents had seen no further reason to stand around in the heat and humidity and had made their way to their homes. The street was littered with paper plates, streamers, election flyers, and soda cans, sprinkled with the occasional illegal beer can.

"Who has to clean up this mess?" I asked.

"The town will hire people to do it. You ask me, they ought to get that lot in New Orleans released and make them do it."

"Do you think Gertie can work her magic with the knitting needles?"

"Oh, she'll have no problem opening the cell. We just have to hope these brownies send that policeman guarding her to the can long enough for her to escape."

"You put enough ex-lax in them to keep an elephant in the bathroom all night."

"Yeah, but it's safer than drugging him to sleep. They might test for that. An upset stomach after gorging on brownies is something he isn't even likely to admit to."

"True."

"Did you have any trouble giving Ally the slip?" Ida Belle asked.

"Tons of trouble. She's what's referred to as a Stage Five Clinger according to some man on television. Anyway, I finally convinced her to go see Carter in my place. I told her it would make him feel better if I sent her to personally explain that I was tied up trying to get Gertie out of jail."

"And she bought that?"

"I don't think she thinks it will make a whit of difference to Carter whether I sent her or gave him a call, but she wants to do me a favor so badly that she didn't question my silly idea."

"Whatever works. I talked to Emmaline earlier. She said Carter has been hell on wheels ever since Dr. Stewart said he had to stay another night."

"I know. When I talked to him, I could practically feel steam coming out of the phone."

"If the swelling hasn't come down enough, the hospital is the best place for him."

"We all know that. Even Carter does, although he's not about to admit it."

"He's a man, after all," Ida Belle said.

I nodded and we hurried into the sheriff's department. Marie greeted us from the front desk. "Where's Myrtle?" Ida Belle asked.

Marie pointed behind the desk and we leaned over to see a prone Myrtle softly snoring. "Since I'm not an official employee," Marie said, "they wouldn't let Myrtle leave, but I got tired of her leaning on me, so I made her lie down behind the desk. That way no one knows she's there unless she gets to snoring loud again."

"We brought Gertie some clothes and dinner," Ida Belle said. "Is it all right to take it back?"

"Please do. That Officer Crawford is fit to be tied over Gertie's lack of clothing. So far, she's refused a blanket, my sweater, and a tarp. Crawford even got desperate and offered her his shirt. He kept asking what was taking you so long."

"I had to bake some brownies," Ida Belle said, then leaned across the desk and whispered, "Do not eat the brownies."

Marie stared for a moment, then her eyes widened. "Oh. Right."

"And order the nice policeman a sandwich," Ida Belle suggested. "I'm thinking chicken salad."

Ida Belle gave her a wink and we headed back to the drunk tank. I gave her a high five as we walked down the hallway. The woman had serious moments of brilliance. If Crawford ate chicken salad and the brownies, he'd have no way of pinning down which one made him sick.

Gertie was stretched out across the bench, in all her glorious half nudity and snoring like a freight train. Crawford sat in a chair turned at an angle where he could clearly see the door but only see Gertie if he turned his head a little to the right. He wore an aggrieved expression that I recognized oh so well. I'd worn it many times when I was dealing with Gertie. He rose from his chair as we approached.

Ida Belle held up two tote bags. "We come bearing clothes, food, and knitting supplies."

Crawford looked relieved. "I'm happiest about the clothes."

Ida Belle laughed and pulled a Tupperware container out of one of the totes before setting them next to the cell. I banged on the bars to awaken Gertie, who popped up off the bench, flailing around like a half-naked chicken caught in a tornado. It took her a couple of seconds to wind down and focus.

"Oh, it's you," Gertie said. "What the hell took you so long? There's a draft in here that blows straight down the back of that bench. If you sit for too long, your butt crack freezes. Had to lie down and save myself."

Crawford blanched and shifted his gaze to the floor. Ida Belle shoved the Tupperware container at him. "I made these for you. I figured you could use a little reward for drawing this detail."

Crawford pulled back the edge of the lid and smiled. "Brownies. My favorite."

"Everyone's favorite," I said and shoved blanket, pillow, and tote bags through the bars to Gertie, praying that Crawford didn't ask to look through them.

"I really appreciate the pick-me-up," Crawford said, happily distracted with his container of dessert. "This detail is far from my usual beat."

"What's your usual perp?" I asked.

"Murderers. I'm a homicide detective, but I pissed off my captain and he sent me down here to this mess. I'll be glad to get back to murderers. They're more predictable."

I nodded. "Marie is ordering you a sandwich from the café. It should be here soon."

For a moment, I thought he was going to burst into tears. "That's great. You know, this is one strange place but some of you are really nice. No one would have ever thought to bring me food back in New Orleans."

"You got too many Yankees moving into the city," Ida Belle said. "Some of us haven't forgotten our proper Southern upbringing."

Gertie pulled on a pair of yoga pants and a T-shirt, then stuck her entire head in the tote. "Hey, how come I didn't get any brownies?"

Ida Belle put her hands on her hips. "Because all this stress has probably got your blood sugar through the roof. I brought you a peanut butter sandwich, soup, and an apple. That's sweet enough."

"Whatever," Gertie said and pulled the sandwich out of the tote along with her knitting needles and a roll of baby-blue yarn.

"Well," Ida Belle said, "I guess we'll get out of your way and let you get back to work."

Crawford lifted the Tupperware container. "Thanks again for the brownies…and for bringing her clothes."

"You're welcome," Ida Belle said. "Hopefully you'll be on your way back to murder and mayhem tomorrow."

"Your lips to my captain's ears."

We headed out of the drunk tank and back up front. Marie glanced down at the still-snoring Myrtle, then leaned across the desk. "Is there anything I need to do?" she whispered.

"Nope," Ida Belle said. "The less you know, the better. Just deliver the sandwich to Crawford and pretend you don't see or hear anything unless someone makes direct contact."

Marie nodded. "I can do that."

"What now?" I asked after we exited the sheriff's department.

Ida Belle pointed to Francine's. "We have dinner and we wait. You put my cell phone in the pillowcase, right?"

I nodded. The police had confiscated Gertie's purse with her cell phone in it. "She'll be able to call as soon as she gets out. Assuming she manages to get out at all."

"She'll get out," Ida Belle said.

"What happens when Crawford notices she's gone? He won't be in the can all night."

"I put a blow-up doll and gray wig in one of the totes," Ida Belle said. "Gertie will stuff it under the blanket so Crawford will think she's sleeping."

"Do I even want to know why you have a blow-up doll lying around?"

"Not me. My next-door neighbor found it in her teenage

son's closet. She was ranting to me about youth and perversion last week."

"You stole it from your neighbor?"

"Of course not. I asked her to borrow it so that Gertie and I could use it as a portable mannequin for clothes alterations. The solid ones take up a lot of space and aren't so easy to move around."

The mental picture of a blow-up doll wearing one of Gertie's flowery dresses popped into my mind and I cringed. "Good God."

Ida Belle grinned at my discomfort. "I threw in a spare pair of the camo undies so that she can leave part of the butt peeking out. Crawford won't come near that cot."

It was an unsettling mental picture, but then unsettling is exactly what might keep Crawford at bay long enough to pull this off. I opened the door to the café and we took a table next to the front window where we had a clear view of the sheriff's department.

"Can Gertie blow up the doll without passing out?" I asked.

"It comes with one of those battery-operated air compressors. It's small but the doll's not that big."

Between the blow-up dolls that came complete with their own air compressors and the thought of Gertie dressing one in camo underwear, I was starting to lose my appetite.

Francine strolled over with her pad, her big blond hair drooping a bit. "Ladies," she said. "How's Gertie holding up in Shawshank?"

"She's fine," Ida Belle said. "You know Gertie. She fares as well in a tank of sharks as she does in church on Sunday."

Francine nodded. "Those state police are holding her just for spite. A judge is going to take one look at her and tell the cop to grow a pair. Assault, my fanny."

"My guess is it won't even get that far," Ida Belle said. "If that cop presses charges, he'll catch hell forever for accusing a granny of assaulting him."

I heard a wail across the room and looked over to see Laurel lifting her crying baby from his high chair. An older woman sitting next to her pulled out a bottle and passed it to Laurel. Francine glanced at them and frowned. "Poor kid. He's usually one of those happy babies that never cries. I guess he's picking up on his mom's stress."

"You heard about the boat?" Ida Belle asked.

"It's pretty much made it around town. I mean, we all knew that boat was sitting on bottom somewhere, but it feels different when you got proof. One of the shrimpers that brought up the sheriff department's boat was in earlier. He said that roughneck who dives has offered to go back down and look for the...you know."

We nodded.

"It's nice of him to offer," I said. "It might make things easier if they could have a real service...I mean, complete."

"I agree," Francine said.

"Who's the woman with her?" I asked.

"Hank's mother," Francine said. "She's sorta a wreck. I can't imagine, losing your child... Anyway, you two didn't come in here to get depressed, so what's it going to be? Chicken-fried steak?"

It was so tempting to blurt out a "yes" to my favorite of Francine's dinners, but with a busy and physical night ahead of us, fried food probably wasn't the best option. "I better keep it light tonight. I'll have the grilled chicken with rice."

"Make that two," Ida Belle said.

Francine raised her eyebrows. "All sorts of odd things going on in Sinful today." She shoved her pad into her apron and headed for the kitchen.

The bells above the door jangled and the guy I saw with the fish on Saturday walked inside and up to the counter. What was his name?

"Lucas?" Hank's mother called across the restaurant.

Lucas. That was it.

He turned around and gave them a wave before heading over to their table. "Mrs. Eaton, Laurel," he said, shoving his hands in his jeans pocket. "I, uh, heard about the boat. I'm really sorry." He looked at the floor the entire time and shuffled his feet as he spoke, clearly uncomfortable.

"Thank you," Hank's mother said. "I haven't seen you in a long time. I hope you're doing well."

"Yes, ma'am. Shrimping is good, and I caught a mess of speckled trout last weekend."

"That's good to hear," Hank's mother said. "You drop by sometime when you get a chance."

"I will," he said. "Y'all have a good night." He gave them a nod before heading back to the counter to pay for a to-go order. He collected the bag and left the café.

Ida Belle leaned over toward me. "Lucas was best friends with Hank since the crib. He was supposed to go out with Hank shrimping that day, but broke his hand the day before. He was never the friendliest sort, but he withdrew completely after Hank disappeared. I think he feels responsible."

I watched out the window as Lucas climbed into a beat-up pickup truck and backed up. That surly look I'd always seen him wearing made more sense now. "That's rough."

Francine appeared with our dinner and we dug in right away, since we had no idea how soon Gertie would make a break for it. When we finished, we asked for coffee, paid our tab, and sat lost in our own thoughts, waiting for something to happen. It was probably the most silence I'd experienced since I'd arrived in Sinful.

When my phone beeped, I practically jumped.

Pick me up at the split oak tree.

"We're up," I said and tossed some tip money on the table. Ida Belle grabbed her purse and we headed out to my Jeep, which we'd deemed a better option for our nightly excursion than Gertie's ancient Cadillac. Not to mention my night and day vision was considerably better.

Gertie ran out from behind the oak tree before I even pulled to a stop and crawled into the back. "That hog Crawford downed the sandwich and half those brownies in twenty minutes. Didn't even offer me a single one. Serves him right to sit on the throne all night."

"So I guess the brownies kicked in?" I asked.

"Oh yeah," Gertie said. "I think they kicked a hole in his stomach. He was sitting in that chair, half asleep, then all of a sudden, he shot up like he'd been electrocuted. His face turned pale and he ran out of the room like people were shooting at him. I aired up the mannequin first, figuring I could hide it under the cot if Crawford finished up too soon. The way he ran out, there was bound to be a round two."

"And a three and four," I said.

"Maybe so," Gertie said, "but he was still out on one when I let myself out of the cell. I went out the back door and Marie locked up behind me."

"Good Lord!" I said. "I hope you didn't kill him, Ida Belle."

Ida Belle shot me a worried look. "Give me my phone," she said to Gertie.

Gertie handed her the phone and Ida Belle sent a text. Several seconds later, a reply came in.

"Marie says he's alive and sitting on a chair outside the

men's room," Ida Belle said. "He hasn't even been back to the cell to check on you."

"That doesn't surprise me," I said. "He thinks he's stuck in redneck Mayberry watching Grandmother Time. His guard is down."

Ida Belle nodded. "Let's hope it stays down until Gertie can sneak back in."

"Marie wouldn't give me my purse," Gertie said. "She let me have my cell phone but said Crawford might ask to see my bag and if it wasn't there, Myrtle would get in trouble."

"And she's right," Ida Belle said.

I held in a grin. If Ida Belle hadn't called Marie with specific instructions regarding Gertie's illegal weapon collection handbag, she probably would have handed the entire thing over when Gertie asked. But Ida Belle figured Gertie had already caused enough problems with her bag of tricks and wasn't about to risk her blinding either one of us, or worse. I was pretty sure I'd seen a Taser in there.

"What's the skinny on the storage facility?" I asked.

"I sent one of the Sinful Ladies over there this afternoon," Ida Belle said. "Under the guise of needing to rent a unit for her elderly aunt who was moving in with her. It's five rows of buildings, all one-story, but only one has units large enough to house a boat. She asked about car storage and found out only two of the big units are currently occupied."

"Great. So we only have two units to check. What about security?"

"There is a security system, but we figured as much. All she could tell me about it was that there was a panel on the office door with a blinking light."

"Probably a perimeter alarm."

"Does that mean we can't go over the fence?" Ida Belle

asked.

"Yeah, but they probably didn't wire the top of the office building. We can get in over the roof."

"Good thinking."

"How are we getting on top of the building?" Gertie asked.

"We aren't," I said. "You are going to keep watch and be ready to start the Jeep and haul ass out of there if things go south."

"How come you guys get to have all the fun?" Gertie groused.

"Because when we let you do things your way," I said, "you fall out of trees and get thrown in the drunk tank."

She sat up in between the front seats and glared at me. "I didn't realize you were so particular about how I carried out our criminal activity."

"Enough complaining," Ida Belle said. "This is about Carter, remember?"

Gertie slumped back in her seat.

"Here's our turnoff," Ida Belle said. "The storage facility is about a mile down. The road ends at the facility, and all of the side roads are dead ends as well, so this is the only way out."

"Got it," I said. It wasn't the kind of situation I liked. I preferred to have at least one alternate escape path, even if it was a difficult one. But I could work with this. I didn't have a choice.

"There's a side road up here on the left," Ida Belle said. "It's the last turnoff before the facility…about fifty yards away. I figure we should stash the Jeep there."

I located the road and pulled in, then swung the Jeep back around and eased it as far over as I could without running into the ditch that framed both sides of the road. A huge cypress tree with hanging moss completely cut off the little bit of moonlight available and blocked it from the view of traffic on the main road.

I cut the engine and handed Gertie the keys. "Unless someone turns down this road, they shouldn't be able to see you."

"How's your signal?" Gertie asked, checking her cell phone.

"One bar," I said.

"Me too," Gertie said.

"Me three," Ida Belle said.

"Crap." I shook my head. "When this is over, we have got to buy some good radios."

"That's a great idea," Gertie said. "I wish you would have come up with it sooner."

"I did," I said, "but I kept thinking all this cloak-and-dagger stuff was over. Now I'm resigned to the reality that I'm a criminal activity magnet."

Ida Belle pulled out gloves and beanie caps and I twisted my ponytail into a knot and shoved it under the hot wool. "We need to get some beanies made out of cotton. With all the heat and humidity here, this wool makes my scalp itch."

"I'll make some," Gertie said. "We can all have signature colors."

"Yeah, black," I said. "You know, the color you use when you don't want people to see you?"

I hopped out and hefted my backpack and a loop of rope from the back of the Jeep. Ida Belle grabbed a flashlight and a crowbar. Gertie moved from the backseat to the driver's seat and stuck the key in the ignition.

"We'll try the phones if we have to make a run for it," I told Gertie, "but we may not get a connection. I need you to be on alert. If someone is after us, we may have to break for it in the woods, so we could be approaching the Jeep from any direction. Watch all of them."

Gertie nodded. "Don't worry. I got this."

Ida Belle and I set off down the shoulder of the main road toward the storage facility. "Does it worry you," I asked, "that we just left the one of us with the worst vision to be lookout?"

"Oh, it worries me, but not as much as it would if she were skating over that roof. You need the better set of eyes watching your back once you're in that unit. Besides, Gertie isn't breaking any laws sitting in a parked car."

"Except for the fact that she's supposed to be in jail?"

"Well, there's that."

The security lights on the front of the storage facility shone brightly across the parking lot in front of the office building. I paused behind a hedge on the side of the road and studied it for a moment. "Lots of light."

"Too much light," Ida Belle said.

"But no car. No security guard?"

"The manager said they have roaming security that checks several properties during the night."

"Maybe we'll luck out and be done before he makes it back around here." I reached into my backpack and pulled out a BB pistol, took aim at the floodlight on the left side of the building, and squeezed the trigger. The light exploded and that side of the building went dark.

"Nice shot," Ida Belle said.

I grabbed the backpack and we hustled over to the office building. I pulled on the drainpipe and was happy to find it solid. "This hurricane construction comes in handy," I said as I shinnied up the pipe and onto the roof. "You want the rope?"

"No," Ida Belle said. "I got this."

She tossed me the flashlight and crowbar and grabbed hold of the pipe. Her ascent wasn't as quick as mine, nor as stylish, but I was still impressed. "Not bad," I said as I helped her over the roofline.

"Since you arrived, I've upped my workout," Ida Belle said, looking pleased with herself. "I tied a rope in my oak tree last week and have been climbing it at night when no one can see. Looks like it came in handy."

"What if one of your neighbors sees you?"

"One of them already did. I told them I was hunting squirrels for a stew."

I shook my head as we started across the roof to the back of the building. Only in Sinful would that explanation fly.

At the back of the building, I squatted down and checked the ground about fifteen feet below. A porch light next to the back door provided enough light to see the entire back of the building, but the area was completely free of hurricane-ready drainpipes or any other object large enough to use for a downward traverse. I could drop-and-roll it, but I wasn't sure asking Ida Belle to do the same was a good idea.

I lifted the rope from my shoulders and handed one end to Ida Belle. "Tie this off on that vent."

I tied a few knots in the other end of the rope and when Ida Belle gave me the thumbs-up, flipped it over the side of the building. I hoisted the backpack over my shoulder, lay flat on the roof, and swung my body around until my legs dangled over. Clutching the rope, I started down and hopped off a couple feet from the pavement. As soon as my feet hit the ground, Ida Belle dropped the crowbar and flashlight to me and started down the rope.

A couple seconds later, she dropped next to me and pointed to a row of tall metal buildings across the back of the lot. We grabbed our gear and hurried down a row of buildings for the back. "It's a good thing they don't have a guard dog," I said.

"Rumor has it that Big and Little are afraid of dogs."

"I guess they don't need them as long as that bodyguard's around. If he was fighting a grizzly bear, my money wouldn't be on the bear."

"Mine either."

We got to the end of the row and I scanned the taller units in both directions. "Which way?"

"From what she could make out on the computer screen, it looked like the units were on the end on the right."

"Okay. Check for locks as we go. If there's nothing inside, it shouldn't be locked."

We slipped around the corner and hurried down the row of units, scanning for locks as we passed. So far, the information appeared to be correct. None of the units we'd passed so far had a lock. Until we got to the end. The last two units had padlocks on the doors.

"It would be easier to back a boat into the end one," Ida Belle said.

"Yep." I pulled a set of small tools out of my backpack and went to work on the padlock. It took me a couple of minutes, but finally, I heard a faint *click*. I pulled down on the padlock and it slid open. "Bingo."

I grabbed the door and lifted it up high enough to crouch under. "Head to the front of the row and keep watch in case the guard makes his round."

Ida Belle gave me a nod and headed off down a row toward the office building. I dropped to the ground and rolled underneath the door. I supposed pushing it up farther and walking in would have been easier, but old habits died hard. I jumped up and clicked on my flashlight, shining it at the center of the unit. The mangled boat rested on a trailer. It was still dripping through cracks in the side, and pools of water formed below the battered structure. The stench of Louisiana mud and salt water filled the enclosed space.

I stepped closer to the boat, shining my light across the hull. Halfway down the front, I found the first bullet hole. I put my face up close to the hull, inspecting the size of the hole and the way the metal bent as the bullet entered and exited. Then I hurried to the other side of the boat and located the matching exit hole.

I stepped back from the boat. I knew what had made that hole. I'd seen it too many times before. An AK-47. Not exactly the kind of weapon that Walter could order for you down at the general store.

I blew out a breath. At least I knew why the ATF was here. If someone was running AK-47s through Sinful it could only be one small piece of a much larger puzzle. They'd probably had different areas down the coastline under surveillance for a while, trying to connect all the dots. It was no wonder they came running when they heard someone had opened fire on a deputy. They were afraid what Carter had done jeopardized who knew how many months or even years of planning.

My phone vibrated and I pulled it out and checked the display.

ATF on grounds. Hide!

Chapter Thirteen

Hide? A second later, I heard a car engine. I sprang for the door and shoved it down just as headlights swept across it. Where the hell was I supposed to hide when I was locked inside with the very thing they were coming to see? I scanned the unit with my flashlight, trying to locate anything to hide behind, but the only thing in there was the boat. Desperate for an out, I pointed my flashlight to the ceiling and saw big steel rafters.

It wasn't optimal, but it was all I had. I threw on my backpack and jumped onto the trailer, crawling up to the top of the spotlight frame on top of the boat. Carefully, I put my feet underneath me and reached for the rafters above. My shoulders and biceps strained with the effort, but I managed to pull myself onto the rafter just as the door to the unit flew up.

"You were supposed to lock it," Riker complained.

I pulled my legs straight and lay flat along the length of the rafter, praying that they didn't shine a light up. The rafter was wide enough for me to easily balance on top of it, but not wide enough to totally hide my body.

"I did lock it," Mitchell said.

"Then why wasn't it locked? Jesus, why don't you just park it at the curb and put a sign on it so the smugglers can pick it up?"

"You act like this is relevant. Who else is going to shoot a military rifle at a local cop but our guys?"

"Maybe I think it's a stupid thing to do," Riker said, "calling attention to yourself that way."

"If the cop saw something important, then taking him out wouldn't be stupid on their part at all."

"Maybe not, but a lot of good it does us if he can't remember what he saw."

"Can't remember, or won't tell us," Mitchell said.

"I don't know. Temporary amnesia is common enough with a concussion, but I find this one to be very inconvenient. Even if Mr. LeBlanc's memory returns, I seriously doubt he'll rush to inform us of it. He's a cop and someone tried to kill him. He's got more than one reason to want to nail the shooter himself."

"I guess. What are we doing here, anyway?"

"I wanted to check that ice chest that we confiscated at the last exchange."

Riker headed to the back of the unit. I leaned as far over as I could to try to see what he was doing, wishing that I was lying in the other direction. I saw the white top of an ice chest flip open, but I couldn't twist my head far enough back to see what was in it.

"See," Riker said. "This is what I'm talking about."

"What? Looks like the same weapons we confiscated last time."

"Not even close. The others came from Russian distributors. These are from the Middle East."

My chest tightened so hard that it almost squeezed the breath out of me. Could Ahmad be moving guns through Sinful? Was that even in the realm of possibility?

"So what?" Mitchell asked. "You think they're changing suppliers?"

"Maybe. Something happened to cause this slipup. New supplier, new personnel…something."

"Well, if you got what you came for, can we get out of here? I'm starving."

"Yeah, let me grab one of these to take back to headquarters."

Riker bent over and rose back up with one of the weapons, and the two of them headed out of the unit. They made it halfway before the whole shebang went to hell in a handbasket. Riker had left their car—a newly issued, non-burro-damaged one—still running and parked directly in front of the unit, the fog lights on. The yellow lights that had reached almost all the way to the back of the unit started to retract.

"Someone's stealing our car!" Mitchell yelled.

Riker set off at a dead run but on his second step, hit a puddle of slimy water dripping from the boat. His right foot shot out from under him and he flung his arms up, trying to maintain his balance. At the same time, he pulled the trigger on the AK-47 and bullets flew past the right side of my head.

Involuntarily, I lurched to the left to avoid the spray and dropped straight off the rafter and onto Riker and Mitchell, sending them sprawling onto the floor. I leaped up from the ground, grabbing the AK-47 from Riker's hand as I went, and gave him a good kick on the back of the head while striking Mitchell with the butt of the gun. It wasn't hard enough to seriously injure either of them, but it was a good enough blow to make their vision blur.

I sprinted out of the unit, as Ida Belle jumped out of Riker's car. I slammed the door shut behind me, clicking the padlock into place. "The gate!" Ida Belle yelled and pointed. "I jammed it when they came in. We can squeeze through."

In the dim light, it looked closed to me, but I rushed to it anyway. When I was about ten feet away, I saw the crowbar stuck in between the gate frame and the post. It was vibrating as the gate tried repeatedly to close. "Hurry," I said. "I don't think it's going to hold much longer."

Ida Belle ran up and sidled through the gap. I tossed my backpack through, then slid through the opening. A second after I made it through, the crowbar popped off and clanged onto the pavement. Gunshots rang out and I heard bullets hitting metal. I reached back between the wrought iron spikes and grabbed the crowbar.

"They're shooting their way out," I said. "Haul ass!"

We sprinted across the parking lot and into the woods, taking the direct route to the Jeep. I took a half second to mentally praise myself for choosing long sleeves before pulling out my cell phone and pressing speed dial for Gertie. Ida Belle ran ahead of me with the flashlight, trying to pick a path through the dense foliage. I stayed on her tail, trying to run and clutch the phone to my head at the same time, which is much harder than it sounds when giant branches are slapping you in the face every few seconds.

The phone went to voice mail and I cursed.

"Emergency evacuation!" I yelled before disconnecting, then prayed the message would go through.

We burst through the brush and tumbled into the ditch, both of us rolling into the muddy water at the bottom before springing up the other side. We popped out of the ditch right next to the Jeep and Gertie screamed.

"Jesus Christ!" she yelled. "You scared the crap out of me. And where the heck did you get the assault rifle?"

Ida Belle ran for the passenger's side door and I dived over the side of the Jeep and into the backseat. "Go! Go! Go!" I shouted.

Gertie started the Jeep and floored it, the back tires spinning on the gravel road as she shot out onto the main road.

"I called and texted when that car went by. Sent at least three to both you and Ida Belle, but I never heard a thing. I thought maybe there was another turnoff we didn't know about and it was just a resident, and then you two materialize next to the Jeep like ghosts."

"That car belonged to Riker and Mitchell."

"Crap!" Gertie stomped harder on the accelerator.

"I called but the phone went to voice mail."

"Did Riker and Mitchell see you?" Gertie asked.

"You could say that," I said. "Just get us back to Sinful and I'll tell you all about it."

She spun the wheel to the right and rounded a corner, then slammed on the brakes. "That might not be as easy as it sounds."

I leaned forward to peer out the windshield and saw Big and Little's Hulk of a bodyguard, Mannie, standing in the middle of the road with a shotgun pointed right at us.

He shifted the shotgun to one hand and held up a spotlight with the other. "I'm going to have to ask you to come with me," he said.

"What about my car?" Gertie asked.

He motioned his head to the side and a man jumped out of the black sedan behind him. "Your vehicle will be taken care of. If you'll come this way." He motioned to me. "And honey, you're going to want to put that baby down really slow-like."

I held my empty hand up and slowly lowered the AK-47 onto the seat. We all climbed out of the Jeep and made our way over to the Cadillac, where Mannie took our weapons and ordered us into the backseat.

"This is it," Gertie whispered as we climbed in. "They're going to kill us all and a blow-up doll is wearing my best underwear."

Mannie climbed into the driver's seat and locked the doors.

He looked back at us. "Just in case any of you get the idea that I can't drive and shoot you at the same time, I'm going to go ahead and assure you that I can. They don't call me backhanded Mannie for nothing."

He turned the car around and shot off down the road. I glanced back and saw the Jeep pull in behind us. "Where are you taking us?" I asked. If they were going to kill us, I saw no reason to sit silently awaiting my fate.

"To see the bosses."

Even though I knew the answer before he said it, my pulse spiked. We would have been safer with Riker and Mitchell than Big and Little Hebert. I frowned. Or maybe not. Riker would have cuffed us and sent us straight to New Orleans where the ATF would have done a serious background check on all three of us. I wasn't sure how well my cover would stand up to a federal search, especially from the ATF, since I'd worked with them in the past.

Gertie, who was sitting in the middle, sighed. "If I'm not back in jail by morning, Myrtle is going to be in trouble."

Ida Belle and I exchanged glances. Apparently, Gertie thought we were on our way to tea and crumpets. "All Myrtle has to do is lie," Ida Belle said, "and she's a pro at it. She didn't see or hear anything. It's not the dispatcher's job to keep up with prisoners. That Officer Crawford is going to catch it for this one."

"Excuse me," Mannie said, "am I understanding you correctly—that you broke out of jail?"

"Not all of us," Ida Belle said and pointed to Gertie. "Just her."

"She's a wily one," I said.

Mannie stared at us in the rearview mirror, his expression a mixture of disbelief and confusion. "I'll just let Big and Little sort this out."

"I wish someone would," I said, feeling slightly better about things now that I'd thought them through. Big and Little were businessmen with a vested interest in staying out of prison and keeping business up and running. So we'd trespassed on their property and taken a peek at an ATF asset. Killing us would be the most foolish solution to a problem that wasn't really affecting them, outside of the loss of a floodlight.

Mannie took a right turn onto a narrow road, and I recognized it as the road to the warehouse where we'd spoken with Big and Little before. A garage door lifted as we entered the parking lot and he pulled into the building, then directed us upstairs to Big's office.

Big was sitting on his heavy-duty park bench behind his enormous desk. Little jumped off his stool as we entered the room and shook his head. "Ladies. We'd hoped to see you again, but under different circumstances. Please take a seat." He gave Mannie a nod and the giant left the room, his relief apparent.

My head started to itch under his scrutiny and I realized I was still wearing the beanie hat. I pulled it off and sighed as cool air hit my scalp. Big looked at me and smiled.

"Much cooler, no?" he asked. "I always hate wearing a hat, but a man of a certain caliber is expected to for some events. You all look a little tired. Would you like some refreshments?"

Ida Belle and I shook our heads. Gertie perked up. "Heck yeah! What do you have?"

Big waved a hand at Little, who opened what looked to be a storage cabinet but turned out to be a minibar. "What's your pleasure?" he asked.

"Bourbon and Coke," Gertie said.

Ida Belle sighed and looked up at the ceiling. I knew she was praying but had no idea exactly what she expected God to do about this situation. He'd had darn near a century to work on Gertie and he'd only made it this far.

Big nodded his approval. "A woman with good Southern sensibilities and tastes. Are you sure I can't offer the two of you something?"

"What the hell," I said, "pass me a bottled water." It wasn't as if being parched was going to make this go any easier or quicker.

"Fine," Ida Belle said. "I'll have a bourbon and Coke, too."

I looked over at Ida Belle and raised my eyebrows.

"What?" she asked. "You're the designated driver."

Little passed me the water and served the rest of them bourbon. I took a sip of my water, casting a wistful glance at Gertie's drink. It was really good quality bourbon. I bet it was going down like honey.

Little took his seat and looked at Big, who finished a big drink of bourbon, then cleared his throat. "You ladies have caused a bit of excitement at our storage facility. I assume you were responsible for dispatching one of my floodlights, and those ATF agents managed to shoot up a perfectly good door trying to get out of the container you locked them in."

I opened my mouth to protest and Big raised his hand. "Don't even bother trying to deny it. You see, the perimeter alarm on the fence is a deterrent, not the ultimate in protection." He reached for a remote on his desk and pressed a button. A television lowered from the ceiling to the right of us. A second later, video of Ida Belle and me scaling the office building flashed onto the screen. Big hit Forward and the next shot showed Ida Belle moving the car and me slamming the unit door closed and locking it before running off.

"Quick thinking," Big said and gave Ida Belle an appreciative look. "If you were thirty years younger, me and you would be talking about a position on my security team."

"Oh," Ida Belle said, looking a little pleased with the compliment. "Thanks."

Big leaned forward and studied us for a moment. "So the big question is what do the three of you find so interesting about a sunken boat that you're willing to risk arrest by the ATF or trouble with me in order to get a peek at it?"

"The deputy that went down in that boat almost drowned," I said. "He's our friend."

Little narrowed his eyes at me. "I heard about that. You're the one who saved him, aren't you? Ain't too many great-looking broads around Sinful, especially with those kinds of skills. You got a diver's body."

Big jabbed him with his elbow. "Manners. Even though she broke into our storage facility, she's still a lady."

"I'm not offended," I said, "and you're right. I'm the one who got him out of the boat."

Big inclined his head and stared at me for a moment. "That must have been a risky move. So maybe more than just friends?"

I felt a blush creep up my neck. "We had a date. It's not a thing. Yet. Or maybe never. But I care about him enough to take the risk, if that's what you're asking."

Big nodded. "I like a woman who's willing to take action. I believe we either walk through life or walk in it. If you have people you're willing to put yourself on the line for, then you're walking *in* life. More heartache, but much more satisfaction."

I blinked. Big Hebert, mobster extraordinaire and philosopher?

The worst part was that what he said made absolute sense, and perfectly summed up feelings I'd been grappling with since my arrival in Sinful. The irony being that my walk through life was completely centered on being a woman of action. Just not a woman with a personal stake. "I agree with you," I said.

Big gave me a satisfied smile. "So, you broke in to take a look at the boat—why?"

At this point, I saw no point in being dishonest, at least not about our reason for the break-in. "We wanted to see if any of the rounds fired at our friend hit the boat."

"For what purpose?"

"To identify the weapon used. We figured if the ATF was involved it was going to be something illegal, possibly military. Our friend has a concussion and amnesia, but he wants to know what happened to him. As you can imagine, the ATF is being less than forthcoming with that information."

"They're rude and lack class," Little said.

Big frowned. "And what do you three broads know about military weapons?"

I glanced over at Ida Belle, hoping she'd catch on and take the lead on the weapons part. My cover as a librarian didn't exactly qualify me for identifying bullet holes.

"Gertie and I served in Vietnam," Ida Belle said. "And I like to keep up with things."

Big's eyes widened. "Please accept my thanks for your service. Men and women like you are the reason my son and I can have the life we do today."

I was fairly sure the Vietnam agenda didn't include defending the freedom of the Mafia, but I could tell that Big was sincere with his thanks.

"Are you going to turn us over to the ATF agents?" I asked.

"Good Lord, no!" Big said.

Little nodded. "Serves those two goons right, coming in here flashing their badges and talking to us like we're peons. Knowing they were bested by three women has made my week. I won't be able to look at them without smiling."

"The state police?" I asked.

Big shook his head. "I'm not a fan of the state police either."

"What about the security tapes?" I asked. "The ATF agents will get a warrant if you don't hand them over."

"Ah." Big smiled. "See, the thing about our security system is it's been on the blink. We just recently installed it and haven't gotten all the bugs out. It doesn't record half the time."

"Like tonight," Little said. "Tonight would be one of those half times it didn't record."

"Then you're going to let us go?" I asked. It seemed entirely too easy.

"Yes," Big said, "but with a warning. Your activities tonight only disrupted ATF business and didn't expose you to any of Little's and my endeavors. If things had gone differently...say if you'd entered the wrong unit...the outcome would have been different."

My gut clenched and I said a silent prayer that we'd gone straight to the right unit. Big's insinuation wasn't lost on me. If we'd discovered any of his illegal activities, then he would have made a completely different decision than he was now. "We understand," I said.

"Good," Big said. "Then you can collect your car keys from Mannie and you're free to go. Your weapons are in your vehicles. Just don't forget our conversation."

We all rose and after thanking him for his hospitality, filed toward the door.

"And ladies," Big said.

We stopped and turned to look at him.

"In the future, if your business is in direct opposition with law enforcement, and there is a way I can be of assistance, I suggest you simply ask for my help. My answer may surprise you...or not." He grinned and winked.

I smiled and we hurried out of the office and back downstairs, where the dour Mannie handed over my Jeep keys. We hauled it out front to where the Jeep was parked and jumped inside. "Let's get the hell out of here," I said as I took off out of the parking lot.

"So what happened inside the unit?" Ida Belle asked. "It sounded like a small war going on in there."

I explained about my compromised rafter hiding place and my impromptu drop onto Riker and Mitchell.

"Holy crap!" Gertie said. "Do you think Riker made you?"

"I doubt it," I said. "There was a lot of confusion and not a lot of light. Besides, Riker won't leap to us as potential suspects. He's going to think whoever fired on the boat is the culprit."

Ida Belle nodded. "Sounds right. So was all this a waste or were you able to find anything out?"

"I found a bullet hole. It went through one side of the boat and out the other."

Gertie whistled. "Not your standard Sinful fare."

"No," I agree. "I knew it was an AK-47 even before Riker removed one from the ice chest. Damn it! Mannie must have confiscated the rifle I grabbed from Riker. I just realized it wasn't here with our other weapons."

"What's wrong?" Ida Belle asked.

I told them about Riker and Mitchell's conversation about suppliers and the mention of the Middle East. "I grabbed the gun on the way out because I wanted to see if I could figure out the supplier."

Ida Belle glanced back at Gertie then back at me. "Do you think it could be the guy who's after you?"

"I don't know. It seems impossible, but I suppose nothing really is."

"All the more reason for us to be more careful," Ida Belle said, "especially you, Fortune. If anyone working for the man hunting you is in Sinful, they will know about the price on your head."

"But surely," Gertie said, "they won't recognize her. She looks completely different."

Ida Belle nodded. "They won't recognize her as long as she's acting like a regular resident, but if they catch her in action and involved in illegal arms transactions, they're going to take a closer look. Extensions, makeup, and clothes make a huge difference, but her bone structure is still the same."

"Ida Belle's right," I said. "I need to be more careful about detection. The way I was dressed tonight, with my hair up under the beanie, gave me more risk of discovery than walking around all girlie."

"Probably true," Ida Belle agreed.

"It's all a moot point now," I said, frustration taking over. "We don't have another lead. We're officially at a dead end."

"Unless Carter remembers," Gertie said.

"*Until* Carter remembers," I corrected and turned off the highway toward Main Street.

Ida Belle's cell phone went off and she frowned at the display. "It's Emmaline." She answered the phone. "What's wrong... Good Lord, is he hurt? We're on our way!"

I clutched the steering wheel. "What happened?"

Ida Belle looked over at me, her eyes wide. "Someone attacked Carter."

"In the hospital?" Gertie asked. "That's crazy."

"Let Gertie out at the tree," Ida Belle said. "We have to get to the hospital."

"No!" Gertie protested. "I'm going with you."

"You can't," Ida Belle said. "We've drawn enough attention

to ourselves already. Come tomorrow morning, I'm sure they'll turn you loose just to avoid the headache of doing more. But you have to get back in there before Crawford figures out you're gone."

Gertie was clearly unhappy when she got out of the Jeep, but she couldn't argue with logic. Ida Belle glanced back as I pulled away.

"Maybe next time," Ida Belle said, "she'll think twice before pulling a fool stunt like that."

"You mean like the stunt we pulled breaking into Big and Little's storage facility?"

"That's different," Ida Belle said. "Our stunt had a good reason behind it. Gertie was showing her weakness in going after Celia. The woman's not worth getting into trouble over. Carter is."

I couldn't argue with that. I pressed the accelerator down to the floor and the Jeep lurched forward. A million thoughts raced through my mind, none of them making sense. How did someone get to Carter in the hospital? The critical care unit was secure entry only. Why risk exposure by attacking him there?

Which brought me right back around to, what the hell had Carter seen?

Chapter Fourteen

Carter's room was packed with people when we arrived, all of them talking at once. Dr. Stewart was there along with a nurse, trying to check out Carter, but Carter was busy waving his arms at the state police and trying to dish out orders. Emmaline stood to the side of the fray, her hands clenched together in front of her mouth, her face pale.

I hurried over to her, and she grabbed my hand and squeezed it. Her hand was shaking.

Ida Belle and I huddled close to her. "What happened?" I asked.

"Carter was sleeping," Emmaline said, "so I went to the lobby to get some coffee. I stopped to chat with Lisa, the young lady at the nurse's station. She just moved here from Idaho and was asking about the food...and that doesn't matter."

"Take your time," Ida Belle said.

"I was giving her a recipe for gumbo and we heard something crash down the hall. My first thought was that Carter had tried to get out of bed and fallen, so I took off down the hall. I was halfway there when someone ran out of Carter's room. He shoved me out of the way and ran for the exit. Poor Lisa tried to stop him but he pushed her so hard she flipped over the desk and knocked herself out."

"Jesus," I said. "Are you all right?"

Emmaline nodded. "I'll probably have a bruise or two

tomorrow, but I didn't get the worst of it."

"Did you get a good look at him?"

"No. He was wearing a ski mask."

"Height?" I asked. "Build?"

"He was taller than me by several inches," Emmaline said. "Over six feet. And he was solid."

"Clothes?"

"Jeans and a black T-shirt. And gloves. He was wearing black gloves."

I ran one hand over my head. Basically, any man in Sinful who was in good shape. "What did Carter see?"

"He said noise in the room woke him up and he saw a shadowy figure standing next to his bed. I figure he turned the light off in the room before he entered. At first, Carter thought it was the nurse, but when he spoke, he didn't get an answer. So he reached for his cell phone to turn on that flashlight app thingy and the intruder knocked it out of his hand. Carter grabbed him and they struggled and knocked over the table, which is what Lisa and I heard."

I glanced at Ida Belle and could tell that Emmaline's story had her as scared as it did me. "Does Carter have any idea what he was trying to do?"

"Carter didn't, but the nurse found a syringe that got dropped and kicked under the bed. It had something called pan…pancro…"

"Pancuronium?" I asked.

"Yes, that's it. You've heard of it?"

I nodded.

"Dr. Stewart said it would have killed him," Emmaline said, her voice cracking. "What is going on? Why does someone want to kill my son? He doesn't remember anything."

"I think someone wants to keep it that way," I said.

"What are we going to do?" Emmaline asked. "Dr. Stewart won't let Carter leave. The attack has put his blood pressure up so high he refuses to release him, and Carter's insisting he's not safe here and neither am I."

"Give me a minute," I said and inched over to the bed where Carter, Dr. Stewart, and the state policeman were all engaged in a testosterone fest.

"Quiet!" I yelled.

They all stopped talking and turned to stare at me. "No one gets his man card revoked for not getting his way. Carter, you're not going anywhere until Dr. Stewart says you're healthy enough to. I'm sure you don't want to add any more stress to what your mother is already suffering."

Carter, who'd been staring at me as if I'd lost my mind, looked slightly guilty at my last statement. His jaw clenched but he didn't even try to argue.

"Dr. Stewart," I continued. "I don't care what the hospital's rules are about the number of people allowed in critical care or the visitation hours. As many people as we'd like are going to stay here in this room, and if anyone wants to, climb right in bed with him—armed."

"Wait a minute," the state policeman started.

"Sssshhhhh!" I waved my hand at him. "Your only responsibility here is to figure out how the intruder got into a locked-down unit of the hospital and to post a guard in the hall. Unless you want the death of a law enforcement officer on your jacket?" I stared at him.

"No ma'am," the officer said. "I'll call for backup and a forensics team."

"Great," I said, "then it's all settled. Now, everyone get to their jobs." they all stared at me and I clapped my hands. "Come on now, hurry."

The state policeman left the room, clutching his cell phone. Dr. Stewart checked Carter's vitals and his injuries and told the nurse to get him some medicine to take his blood pressure down. He gave me a wink before heading out of the room with the nurse.

Emmaline looked at me and smiled. "You're good."

I waved a hand in dismissal. "I just don't like wasting time. And it's late. If I wanted to listen to that drama half the night, I'd be at a sporting event, or hanging out with Celia Arceneaux."

"Damn straight," Ida Belle said. "So how do you want to play this?"

"Hey," Carter said, "I'm the cop here."

"Not tonight," I said. "Tonight you're the patient. Emmaline will stay here in the room. Ida Belle can take the lobby."

"What about you?" Ida Belle asked.

"I want to do some looking around. The intruder got in somehow. If Lisa says no one came through the front door, then he got in some other way, and I'd like to know how. The state police will put a guard outside the door, but I think one of us should walk the hallway. Ida Belle and I can trade off so each of us gets a rest."

Ida Belle nodded and pulled her Glock out of her purse to check the magazine.

"You locked and loaded?" she asked.

I nodded.

Carter groaned. "I don't need to hear any of this. Am I supposed to feel safer knowing you two are roaming the hospital with guns? That's the way most of my nightmares start."

I looked over at him. "I suppose you could arrest us…"

"Jesus." He flopped back on his bed. "For the love of God, just remember there's oxygen tanks in here. One misfire and you could send the whole place up in flames."

"Then our problems will be over, right?" I said and smiled.

He stared at me for a couple seconds, and finally the smile broke through. "You're impossible."

"That's what they tell me," I said.

"So what happened with Gertie?" he asked.

"She's still in lockup," Ida Belle said. "I figure they'll let her loose tomorrow morning, but that Officer Crawford wasn't sticking his neck out to let it happen tonight."

Carter frowned. "I thought she got into a fight with Celia? Why did they cut Celia loose and not Gertie?"

"There was this small incident with Mace and a state policeman," I said.

Carter stared. "You're kidding...no, never mind."

The nurse came back into the room and handed Carter some pills and a glass of water. Ida Belle and I took the opportunity to head out into the hallway.

"What do you think?" Ida Belle said.

"Stupid. Risky. If someone stronger and faster than Emmaline or Lisa had been here, he wouldn't have gotten away."

"Or someone armed, like most people around here are."

I nodded. "He wasn't counting on Carter waking up."

"Thank God he did!"

"Yeah." My chest clenched and I felt a spike of anger and fear rush through me. It had been a close call. Way too close.

"What was in the syringe?" Ida Belle asked. "That thing you knew?"

"It's an extremely powerful muscle relaxer. It can be used as a paralytic, but at even higher concentrations..."

Ida Belle blew out a breath. "So not something sitting around the average guy's medicine cabinet."

"Not even. It's one of the components used for lethal

injection. You can't pick up a bottle at Walgreens."

"This isn't some amateur criminal who panicked that we're dealing with. To even know about that drug and get access…that's someone walking the dark side."

"Yeah," I agreed. "I'm going to take a look around, check out the windows in all the rooms on this hallway. If Lisa is still at the front desk, talk to her and see if you can get anything else out of her."

"You got it. And Fortune?"

"Yeah?"

"Be careful."

I nodded and set off down the hall in the opposite direction from the lobby. The likelihood of the intruder's still being in the hospital was slim, but it was still a possibility. He was brazen enough to attempt to kill a man in a critical care unit. A deputy. And his method was advanced. Not just anyone would use something like pancuronium to dispatch their target.

I checked the rooms one by one, making sure the windows hadn't been breached. Carter was the only patient in the critical care wing at the moment, which made the search a bit easier. No other patients to bother with my inspection. I quickly determined that the patient rooms didn't contain windows. There was a small window near the ceiling of the janitor's closet, but it was too narrow for a man the size Emmaline had described to fit through.

The windows in the break room were normal-sized and could have easily allowed a large man passage, but I could see no sign of tampering with the locking mechanism on any of them. I supposed it was possible that someone gained entry during the day and left the window unlatched, but if the intruder had entered this way, I would have expected him to leave the window open for quick escape once he'd administered the drug. He could hardly stroll out through the lobby without Lisa seeing him.

I walked back into the hallway and saw the state policeman sitting in a chair outside Carter's room. He'd probably been assigned to guard shift until someone could replace him. I checked on Ida Belle, who had taken a seat in a corner of the lobby where she had a clear view of the front door, the hallway, and the front desk. Lisa had been relieved by a night nurse from another unit and sent home, so she hadn't been able to talk to her. I doubted Lisa would have been able to tell us any more than we already knew, so it was no big deal.

I headed back down the hallway and stepped into Carter's room. The cop narrowed his eyes at me as I passed, probably putting the blame for this less-than-stellar assignment squarely on my shoulders. He'd get over it. Or not. It didn't matter to me either way.

Emmaline sat next to the bed, her hands clenched in her lap. I was surprised to see Carter's eyes closed. "Is he all right?" I asked, worried that things were worse than Dr. Stewart had originally thought.

"He's fine," Emmaline said. "The nurse gave him something to sleep along with the med for his blood pressure." She looked a bit guilty. "We didn't tell Carter about that part."

"You're a good mother, and a smart woman."

She gave me a weak smile. "Some days I don't feel like either. I know it's foolish for me to think I can protect him forever. I couldn't protect him when he was overseas and I can't protect him from his job now."

"I get the desire," I said. "At least, I think I do. I don't have children, so I can't say for sure."

Emmaline nodded. "A mother's desire to keep her child safe is an overwhelming one that never goes away, even when they're adults. But I see your desire to protect him. It's because you care. You, Ida Belle, and Gertie. You're all doing everything you can to make sense of this impossible situation. You're a good friend, Fortune, and an intelligent one."

I felt a blush start on my neck and before it traveled onto my face, I smiled and backed out of the room. As I walked down the hall, I thought about Emmaline's words. It was true that I cared about Carter, despite all the risks. My halfhearted attempts to keep my feelings at bay were more revealing to me than the fact that I found myself attracted to Carter in the first place. In so many ways, he was the perfect fit for me. He was strong and capable and didn't take a moment of my crap. I understood completely why I wanted him. What I didn't quite get was why I allowed myself to let my guard down in the first place.

Was I not as happy with my old life as I'd thought? Had I made attachments in Sinful as some form of passive-aggressive rebellion against the only life I'd ever wanted or known?

You're a good friend, Fortune...

But was I really? Almost everything Carter thought he knew about me was a lie. If you kept these sort of monumental secrets from someone, were you really their friend? Or were you just taking advantage of what they were offering you based on false assumptions?

I lifted a chair from the break room and stuck it against the wall at the end of the hall. It was a good vantage point. I could see anyone coming through the secure access from the hospital wing or anyone entering the unit through the break room. I checked my pistol at my back waistband and slid down onto the cold, hard metal chair. It was going to be a long night with nothing to do but mull over my own thoughts. Maybe before morning, I'd have a moment of clarity and all of this would make sense.

I sighed. More likely, Gertie would admit she needed new

glasses before that happened.

It was a long and uneventful night at the hospital. When the full staff started arriving at six, Ida Belle and I let Emmaline know we were taking off. Carter was still sleeping and everyone agreed he should remain that way as long as possible. The swelling on his brain needed rest to diminish. As much as it pained him, Carter had to stay put and relax in order to get what he wanted, which was out of the hospital.

The drive back to Sinful was a somber one. Neither Ida Belle nor I had experienced a burst of clarity, illuminating the answers we so desperately wanted. Things seemed to be advancing around us but we were stuck in place, grasping at straws.

"What now?" I asked.

Ida Belle shook her head. "Shower, food, sleep. Spring Gertie later on this morning, assuming they release her. Beyond that, I don't know. I hate to admit it, but maybe this one is beyond us. Gertie and I are good at ferreting out things happening in our town because we know these people and their history, and what we don't know, we can find someone who does. But this is a federal crime…"

"Which means it might not involve people from Sinful but only Sinful as a drop point."

"Exactly. And even if we could find it, I don't know what locating the drop point would do for us."

"Likely nothing but make us a target if the smugglers saw us. So I guess we hope that Carter wakes up with his memory intact."

"That seems to be the only viable option remaining."

I pulled into Ida Belle's driveway and let her out. She gave me a halfhearted wave as she walked up the sidewalk and let herself inside. I backed out and drove home, feeling more defeated than I ever had before.

Ally was at the café, and I was grateful that she wasn't off work today. I didn't feel like trying to address questions I didn't have answers for, and the more I dwelled on them, the more confused I became. As much as I hated to admit it, I needed rest just as Carter did. My mind wasn't functioning at full capacity. It needed a break to refresh and get centered again.

Being the typical caretaker, Ally had left me a plate of pigs in a blanket and a tray of blueberry muffins. At least I knew that no matter what happened, I wouldn't starve while dealing with it. I considered a shower, but decided on breakfast first. If I got upstairs under hot water, I didn't think I'd manage walking by my bed without climbing in. Then I'd awaken starving and with a headache. Best to top off the stomach, then get some z's.

I popped two of the sausage rolls and a blueberry muffin into the microwave, hauled out the butter, and poured myself a huge glass of chocolate milk. I must have been starving because I barely took time to appreciate how good everything tasted before washing it down with the milk and heading upstairs.

I could have wept for joy when the hot water hit my aching back. That metal chair from the break room could have doubled as a torture device. The cushioned one in the lobby hadn't been much better, although I think at that point it was less about the furniture and more about my aching body. After thirty minutes of standing in steam, I donned a T-shirt and underwear and poured myself into bed, not even pausing to close my blinds. At this point, a spotlight directly on my face wouldn't keep me from sleeping.

I am pretty sure I was out before my head ever hit the pillow.

Chapter Fifteen

I had no idea how long I'd been asleep when I awakened. It felt like only minutes before, but my alert mind and stiff body told me I'd been there much longer. I glanced at the clock and was surprised to find five hours had passed and it was past lunchtime. I reached for my cell phone on the nightstand and felt a wave of relief pass over me when I saw no messages or texts waiting for me. No drama while I was out. Thank God.

Ida Belle must have been as exhausted as I was, but I figured I'd hear from her as soon as she was up. I swung my legs over the side of the bed and stretched, thinking about our fiasco at the storage facility the night before. Now that I'd had a break from the event and could process it more clearly, my respect for Ida Belle shot up about ten notches. She was in seriously good shape for her age. I hoped I was that lucky.

My doorbell rang and I peered outside and saw Gertie's ancient Cadillac in my driveway. I grinned and pulled on a pair of shorts before heading downstairs. The ole girl must be out of Shawshank.

I let Ida Belle and Gertie in the house and they trailed off to the kitchen. Ida Belle clutched a big paper bag and from the smell wafting out of it, I assumed she'd made a stop by Francine's before heading my way.

"Burgers and fries," Ida Belle said and put the bag on the

kitchen table. "I figure we'd all be starving and no one would feel like cooking."

"I don't even feel like making a sandwich," I said, "but the sleep was stellar."

Ida Belle nodded. "I got in a good four hours. Older bladders don't allow for much more without interruption. It's just as well. Gertie called right after I woke up."

I looked over at Gertie, who was unpacking the food and sliding it across the table. "I guess that cop decided not to press charges?"

Gertie nodded. "Myrtle told him he'd have to come back here to file the report. I guess he wasn't interested in a return trip."

"Or admitting on paper that an old woman got the best of him," Ida Belle said.

I handed out canned colas and took a seat. "I guess you managed to get back inside without Crawford noticing?"

Gertie shook her head. "Poor Crawford. He shouldn't have been such a glutton with those brownies. He spent the entire night groaning and running for the bathroom. I finally shoved yarn in my ears so I could get some rest."

"But he's all right?" I asked.

"Oh, yeah. He was pale and a little shaky this morning, but the worst is over. In a day or so, he'll be back to normal."

"Good," I said. "I felt a little guilty over that one. Crawford didn't seem like a bad guy."

"Collateral damage," Gertie said. "It happens, and there's a lot worse things than spending a night on the throne. Ida Belle filled me in on what happened at the hospital."

"Lots of drama and very little information," I said and took a bite out of my burger.

Ida Belle nodded. "Now that you've had time to sleep on it,

have you come up with anything?"

I shook my head. "I had these wild dreams all night...like there was something right there on the edge and I couldn't quite grasp it."

"Something your subconscious is wrestling with that your conscious hasn't put together," Ida Belle said. "Isn't that what you said about Carter?"

"Yeah, I guess I did. But aside from that, I know I've forgotten something but for the life of me, I can't remember what."

"You should try deep hypnosis regression," Gertie said, "like they did on that *X-Files* episode."

"That's it!" I jumped up from the table and grabbed my laptop. "The television. Remember, we wanted to know what Carter was watching Saturday night. Emmaline said the television was on the History channel, but with everything else that was going on, I completely forgot to check and see what was on."

I accessed the website for the History channel and looked at its schedule. "Monday, Sunday, Saturday." I scanned through the day and into late night. Then I sat back in my chair and frowned. "They were doing a twenty-four-hour marathon. Missing persons files."

"Missing persons?" Gertie said. "I don't see—"

And then it hit me. I sprang up out of my chair again. "I'm an idiot!"

Ida Belle looked up at me. "I'm going to hold off on agreeing with that statement until after I hear what you have to say."

I sat back down. "I read Carter's note as 'He shouldn't have been there' but it wasn't 'he' it was 'HE'—the first two letters were capitalized. I thought it was lazy typing."

"What do you think it is now?" Ida Belle asked.

"Initials. HE—Hank Eaton."

Ida Belle's eyes widened and Gertie sucked in a breath.

"But Hank's been missing for over a year," Gertie said.

"Maybe he wasn't missing," I said. "Maybe that's just what he wanted everyone to think."

Ida Belle's lips set in a hard line. "Then that would make Hank the smuggler."

I nodded. "And the man who tried to kill Carter."

"Poor Laurel," Gertie said. "First her husband disappears and she's left with all those bills and now this. What in the world is she going to do when she finds out he didn't die at all but ran off to be a criminal?"

"Even worse," Ida Belle said, "what's she going to do when the insurance company tells her she has to pay back those life insurance proceeds?"

"How could he do that to her?" Gertie asked, clearly dismayed. "What is wrong with men?"

"Plenty," Ida Belle said. "Which is why we don't have any."

"He's not doing it without help," Gertie said. "I mean, Hank has the knowledge to move the product in from the Gulf without raising suspicion, but no way could he have gone unseen all this time if he was doing more than that. He may have been dropping the guns here, but someone else was picking them up and carrying them out."

The ice chest of AK-47s from the storage unit flashed through my mind, followed by the memory of an ice chest of fish. "Lucas Riley?" I suggested, and told them about seeing him Saturday evening with the ice chest of fish.

Ida Belle blew out a breath. "Whew. You could be onto something."

"You said they go way back, right?" I asked.

"Yep," Ida Belle said. "Best friends from the crib."

"Did Hank hang around anyone else?" I asked.

"Not that I can recall," Gertie said. "It was always just those two. They never got on much with the other students."

"So the only person in Sinful that Hank would trust is Lucas."

"And vice versa," Ida Belle said. "I don't think Lucas ever trusted anyone but Hank."

Gertie shook her head. "It just doesn't seem like Hank. He was such a nice boy. I can certainly believe it about that Lucas, who was always trouble. I never understood why Hank and Lucas were friends. They didn't seem to have anything in common."

"That's what people always say," Ida Belle said. "They want to blame one person for being the bad influence that turned the other person into something they're not. I don't agree. I'm going to stick with the old saying that water seeks its own level. Something was just as broken in Hank, or he would never have taken up with Lucas."

Gertie sighed. "I suppose you're right, but I still can't believe he left Laurel and the baby like that."

"You said his son was sick, right?" I asked Ida Belle. "Maybe he figured it was the perfect solution. Laurel would collect the insurance and use it for the baby and he'd become the master criminal he always wanted to be without the domestic responsibilities that had become more than he bargained for."

"Looks like the time stamp on the perfect solution just ran out," Ida Belle said.

"Yeah, and I have no idea what to do now," I said. "Even if we tell Carter, we still don't know if he'll remember, at least not until the swelling goes away."

"True," Ida Belle said, "and if he does remember, then it will make him more anxious to get out of the hospital and track him down, which is the last thing he needs to be doing."

"What about Riker?" Gertie asked. "Where do you think he stands on this?"

"Riker is sure Carter saw the smuggler, but I don't think he has any idea who the smuggler is. That's why he's so hell-bent on digging out Carter's memory."

"If we told Riker who it was," Gertie said, "he wouldn't listen."

"True," Ida Belle said, "and even if he did listen, he wouldn't know where to start looking."

"So what the hell do we do?" Gertie asked. "We can't just sit around and wait for Hank to make another attempt on Carter, and until Hank is dead or behind bars, Carter is going to remain his biggest threat."

"What about Lucas?" Gertie asked.

"What about him?" Ida Belle asked. "His involvement is only speculation on our part. Granted, I think we're right because it's the only thing that fits, but Riker isn't going to take our word for it. If he goes in half-assed, it will tip Lucas off."

"And then they'd both disappear," Gertie said.

"Probably," I said, "but maybe not in the way that you think."

"What do you mean?" Ida Belle asked.

"If Hank and Lucas are smuggling guns from the Middle East, they're dealing with people who do not leave loose ends—loose ends being the kind that talk. If their supplier gets even a hint of an idea that either of them has been made, they'll clean house. Hank, Lucas, Carter, Riker, Mitchell, maybe even Emmaline, Dr. Stewart, and us…basically anyone who might know anything at all about the product."

The blood washed out of Gertie's face. "You're talking about a bloodbath."

I nodded. "Arms dealers are the most ruthless form of sociopath I've ever seen. They make serial killers look pleasant."

"What can we do?" Ida Belle asked. "It sounds hopeless."

"Maybe not," I said. "What we need is to break the chain."

"What do you mean?" Ida Belle said.

"If Riker arrested Hank, then Carter would no longer be a target because Hank's identity would be known."

"Or if Riker killed him," Gertie said. "I'm okay with that if Hank's the one who tried to kill Carter."

I nodded. "Either would take the heat off Carter and anyone else in Sinful. If Hank rolls on Lucas, Riker will arrest him. If he takes too long, the supplier will eliminate the threat, but with Hank exposed, the supplier won't have any reason to kill Carter."

"Because the only thing Carter will have on him is that he's supposed to be a dead man," Ida Belle said. "Brilliant."

"Yeah," I said, "except for the part where we need Riker to arrest Hank."

"And Riker doesn't even know he's looking for Hank," Gertie said, "much less where to look."

"And we're right back around to how to get Riker to find Hank without alerting Lucas that he's onto them," Ida Belle said. "Even if we could convince Riker that Hank was their man, he's not equipped to locate someone in these bayous."

"You think Hank is hiding somewhere nearby?" I asked.

"Not permanently," Ida Belle said. "It's too risky given that everyone in Sinful knows him, but I bet he has a sort of safe house to use if things get hairy. A problem could be as simple as a storm blowing in that prevents him from heading back out right after a drop."

"Or as serious as a deputy seeing a dead man," I said.

Ida Belle nodded. "You said yourself that the supplier

would clean up this mess, so I figure Hank won't leave until he thinks he's no longer in danger of being fired, so to speak, by the supplier."

"This whole thing is making my head hurt," Gertie said.

"Then let me sum it up for you," Ida Belle said. "We need to find Hank's hideout and get that idiot Riker over there to arrest him before the supplier gets word of the problems here and comes to clean house."

"My head hurts worse now," Gertie said.

"Mine too," I agreed.

"But at least we have a plan," Ida Belle said. "Sort of."

"A sort of plan is what we live for," Gertie said.

"Does anyone have a sort of boat?" I asked. "Because the last time I checked, none of us had wings."

"We could borrow Walter's," Gertie said.

Ida Belle shook her head. "Not this time. Hank knows Walter's boat."

At first, I didn't get her comment but suddenly, it made sense. "And Walter is Carter's uncle. If Hank saw the boat, he'd automatically assume Walter was looking for him. So what now? Ally has a boat, but it's a small one and wouldn't provide much protection."

"No, we need something larger and with a cabin," Ida Belle said. "Fortune can stay out of sight, but use a scope to search the banks. You and I will don stupid floppy hats decorated with lures and blend with the other fishermen."

"That sounds great," I said, "but unless cabin cruisers are sitting around for rent, I don't see how that helps us."

"I might know where one is just sitting around," Ida Belle said.

By the glint in her eyes, I knew I wasn't going to like the answer to the next question, even before I asked it. "And where might this boat be sitting around?"

"The dock behind the butcher shop."

"You want to steal the butcher's boat?" I asked. I'd been in the butcher shop. The knives in that place were scary, and the butcher wasn't any better.

"It's not his boat," Ida Belle said. "He's leasing it from the owner until he can put together the money to buy it."

I frowned. So far, it didn't sound so bad. "Can he lend us the boat if he's only leasing it?"

"Of course not," Ida Belle said. "And the owner would never lend it to us. We'll have to steal it."

Okay. It was getting worse.

"Who's the owner?" I asked.

"Celia."

I blinked. "Celia Arceneaux? Your sworn enemy?"

Ida Belle grinned.

"Surely there's another boat with a cabin in Sinful," I said.

"Only shrimp boats," Ida Belle said. "Celia's departed husband owned the only cabin cruiser used for fishing in Sinful. Everyone else uses a regular bass boat."

Gertie chuckled. "I still remember the day he drove into town towing that boat. Celia had forbidden him to purchase it, but then his uncle died and left him some money. He went straight from the estate attorney's office to the boat shop. Celia stopped him in the middle of Main Street and yelled at him for twenty minutes before Sheriff Lee managed to drag her out of the road."

Ida Belle laughed. "Ally said Celia made him sleep in the boat for a month."

"Probably the best month of his life since marrying Celia," Gertie said.

"So let me get this straight," I said. "All we need to do is load up on weapons, binoculars, scopes, and fishing gear, then head downtown and in broad daylight, steal a boat from a dock just a couple of buildings down from the sheriff's department."

"It's not like Deputy Breaux can chase us," Gertie said. "The sheriff department's boat is in Big and Little's storage facility."

"And we can put all the weapons and gear in your backyard and pick it up on our way out," Ida Belle said.

If it had been about anyone but Carter, I would have said no, a million times no. But it *was* Carter, and it was life or death. And beyond that was my own vested interest. The last thing I needed was a Middle Eastern arms supplier sending cleaners to Sinful. One chance crossing of paths and I would be dead before I could even request extraction.

"Fine. Great," I said. "We'll steal a boat."

After all, it had been at least twelve hours since I'd broken the law.

Chapter Sixteen

"Hurry up." Ida Belle looked back at a lagging Gertie. "We're burning daylight."

Since we were going to take the stolen boat to pick up our equipment, we'd decided to leave the cars at home and walk to the dock. That way, one of our vehicles wouldn't be parked on Main Street all day, potentially causing questions. Gertie had fallen behind a half block into the walk and Ida Belle had been razzing her for it ever since.

"I'm tired," Gertie said. "It's been a long week."

"It's only Tuesday," Ida Belle said.

"All the more reason to be complaining about being tired, then," Gertie said. "Imagine how I'll feel if I make it until Friday."

"What are you bitching about? Tired? At least you got to sleep all night," Ida Belle said.

"With a blow-up doll on a prison cot. Hardly the Ritz."

I grinned. "Wonder how many angry wives have heard that one before?"

When we got to downtown, we skirted the side of the flower shop and headed behind the row of shops that ran along the bayou. Toward the end of the row was the butcher shop dock, complete with Celia's cabin cruiser. "Nice," I said as I took in the good-sized vessel.

"I heard it even has a toilet," Gertie said.

"You should use it," I said. "Just to spite Celia."

Gertie pulled a roll of toilet paper out of her purse. "Ahead of you on that one."

"Crap," Ida Belle said and pulled up short.

"I don't have to yet," Gertie said.

"What's wrong?" I followed her gaze down the bayou to the activity at the back of the butcher's shop. "He's cooking?"

"Hogs," Ida Belle said. "Not everyone has a spit big enough for a whole one, so they pay him to cook it for them. It's a long, boring job, so he usually waits until he has two or three on order then does them all the same day."

"So you're saying he's going to be out back, twenty yards from the boat we need to steal, all day long."

"He will unless we figure out a way to get rid of him."

"I have an idea," Gertie said.

Ida Belle and I both gave her a skeptical look.

"No, seriously," she said. "Remember those dogs that ran over me and Celia on Sunday? They belong to the guy renting the old Cooper place."

"That place right past Main Street that looks like half of it is caved in?" I asked.

"That's the place. If those dogs were to get loose, with all those smelly hogs cooking..."

"Sounds like a plan," I said. "Since I'm the quickest, I'll let the dogs out. Can you hot-wire the boat?"

Ida Belle nodded. "Gertie and I will head down the bank toward the dock. As soon as the dogs cause a commotion, we'll board the boat and get it running."

"If you find an opening to get the boat away from the dock without the butcher noticing, don't wait for me," I said. "Take it. I can sprint back to my house and you can pick me up there."

I took off down the bayou, doing my daily jogger imitation,

and gave the butcher a wave as I passed. He was struggling to lift an enormous side of meat wrapped in plastic wrap onto a folding table and barely noticed me. All the better.

The old Cooper place was about fifty yards from the butcher shop, set back into the swamp a good twenty yards in. The swamp allowed good coverage for my approach, and I was happy to see that the carport was empty. Hopefully, that meant the renter was away. As I approached the backyard, the dogs hurried to the back fence, barking their greeting.

"Hey, fellows," I said, looking over the fence.

The two hounds looked up at me and wagged their tails. At least they weren't scary, like Tiny. These two were younger versions of Bones, the ancient hound I'd inherited and who had unearthed the bone of a murder victim before I'd even had a chance to unpack. Bones was living out the rest of his sleeping days with Marie, who'd loved him since he was a puppy.

"You guys want some excellent dinner?" I asked. "I know a great place...more meat than you can eat."

They both barked and wagged harder. I took that to mean they were up for the challenge. "Okay. Let's go." I opened the gate and took off running back through the swamp toward the butcher shop. I stopped at the edge of the swamp, but the hounds didn't even notice. They'd already locked onto the smell of the cooking pig and leaped out of the tree line in a dead run at a glorious dinner.

The butcher looked up from the spit when he heard the dogs barking and his eyes widened when he saw them bearing down on him at full speed. He stepped in front of the spit, waving his arms to stop them from attacking his cooking pig. While his back was turned, Ida Belle and Gertie ran down the dock for the boat.

And one of them made it.

Ida Belle sprinted to the end of the dock and leaped into the boat as though she'd been running hurdles for a living. Gertie sprinted, sort of, almost all the way down the dock before her giant purse gained too much momentum and swung up, smacking her directly in the face. She pitched forward and her purse flew off her arm and right into the back of Ida Belle's head. The weight of the purse sent Ida Belle sprawling to the bottom of the boat deck as Gertie lost her footing and tipped off into the bayou.

I heard the giant splash all the way over where I was hiding and swung my head back toward the fray at the butcher shop to see if he had seen the dock drama. Fortunately, the dogs had his complete attention. The smart hounds had given up on the spit and went for the side of hog on the folding table. One of them was on each side of the table, clenching a wad of the Saran wrap in their jaws and pulling it like they were engaged in an Olympic-sized tug-of-war contest.

The butcher alternated yelling and spraying the dogs with the water hose, but they weren't even remotely fazed. I heard the boat fire up and looked over to see a dripping wet Gertie drop over the side and crash onto the bottom of the boat. Then the butcher let up a huge yell and I turned back to see the hounds pull the pig completely off the table and race off down the back of the shops, each of them clutching the pig in its mouth. All the racket had Walter hurrying out the back of the general store, some patrons close on his heels.

The last one out the door was Celia Arceneaux.

She was also the only one who lacked the good sense to stay close to the building and out of the way. Holy crap! It was like watching a train wreck. She pushed past Walter and the other patrons, and I could see her mouth wide open, yelling as usual. I couldn't make out what she was saying, but it didn't matter. With

Celia it was always the same sort of thing.

Her second step out from the pack landed her smack in between the running dogs. And they weren't the least bit interested in stopping. The side of pig hit her at full speed, flipping her legs completely out from under her. Her pink skirt flew up to her waist and she crashed down onto the ground, her giant white underwear shining like a full moon over the bayou.

As the patrons rushed to help Celia up, Ida Belle took off in the boat, ducking low behind the driver's column and speeding past the fray. Walter watched the boat as it passed and shook his head. I figured I had been standing there long enough and set off for the front of the building and sprinted down Main Street for my house. I could hear Celia's wailing and ranting two blocks away.

I made the run in five minutes flat. Gertie was tossing the last of the fishing equipment into the boat when I ran into my backyard and leaped inside. "Get down," Ida Belle said.

I ducked through the cabin door and sat on the floor just inside. Gertie climbed back into the boat and Ida Belle set off at a good pace down the bayou toward the lake, which is where we agreed was the best place to start our search. My cell phone beeped and I pulled it out, then noticed Ida Belle and Gertie were both doing the same. It was a message from Walter to all three of us.

You just stole your new mayor's boat.

Crap.

We all started talking at once.

"Oh my God!" I said.

"My worst nightmare," Ida Belle said.

"It's the rise of the Antichrist," Gertie said.

"Well, the Antichrist just mooned all the customers in Walter's store." I told them about the dogs hitting Celia with the side of hog, and Gertie laughed so hard she literally sat down and rolled onto her side, heaving with laughter.

"Serves her right," Gertie said when she came up for air. "It was all her fault half of Sinful saw me in my skivvies. If they'd all seen her giant white underwear before the election, they might not have voted for her."

"Call Marie," Ida Belle said. "I haven't heard from her, and that makes me think something is up."

Gertie dialed Marie, who must have started talking the instant she answered the phone because all Gertie managed was nodding and the occasional "uh-huh." But I could tell by her expression that whatever Marie was saying wasn't good. Finally Gertie disconnected the call and looked up at Ida Belle.

"We got trouble," Gertie said. "Marie's pissed."

I stared. "What does that look like exactly?" I'd seen Marie scared, anxious, worried, and upset, but I had no idea what outright pissed entailed.

"It's not pretty," Ida Belle said. "What's up?"

"Sarah Gunderson said Wilma Tillery voted for Celia."

Ida Belle's eyes widened and she made a hissing sound.

"What did I miss?" I asked.

"Sarah Gunderson is a Sinful Lady," Gertie said. "Also one of the vote counters. There are representatives from each side— to keep things on the up-and-up. Wilma Tillery died six years ago, so Sinful has its own election episode of *The Walking Dead* going on. It looks like someone stuffed the ballots."

"What can you do about it?" I asked.

"Marie is already filing a motion for an audit," Gertie said.

"But until then," Ida Belle said, "we're screwed."

"What do you mean?" I asked.

Gertie shot me a worried look. "I mean that this was an emergency election, so until that vote is recounted, Celia is mayor of Sinful. Which means Carter's job is on the line."

"One situation at a time," Ida Belle said. "Let's make sure no one is going to try to kill Carter again and then we'll worry about his continued employment. Fortune, we're almost to the mouth of the lake. Head to the front of the boat and use the binoculars to scan the bank. The cabins near the bank aren't our mark. They're too visible. If he's got a hiding place, it's going to be back some from the bank and hidden in an area with thick foliage and trees."

"So I'm looking for a point of egress," I said, "not the structure itself."

"Exactly, and it's not going to be easy to spot. Hank will cover his tracks."

Ida Belle pulled the boat over as close to the bank as she could and cut the engine speed to a bare minimum. She motioned for Gertie to hand her a fishing pole and cast the line in the water off the back of the boat. Gertie pulled a mangled straw hat out of her purse and plopped it on her head. Between the awful hat and her wet clothes hanging on her, she looked like a pitiful scarecrow.

I pulled the binoculars and a scope out of the duffel bag and opened a porthole on the front of the boat. It was easy to discard most of the bank as it consisted of mostly tall reeds, and there's no way a boat could have docked there without leaving a trail. I scanned ahead and saw a long stretch of reeds ahead of us that slowly turned to muddy bank after about fifty yards. I was about to lower the binoculars until we reached the mud when I caught a glint of light about two hundred yards away.

I lifted the scope and zeroed in on the object creating the glare. It was a shrimp boat.

Lucas Riley's shrimp boat.

"Ida Belle," I called.

She ducked her head in and I motioned for her to come over. "About two hundred yards ahead and to the left. That's Lucas Riley's shrimp boat."

Ida Belle peered through the scope. "He's coming straight at us." She hurried out of the cabin, pulled on a ball cap and cut the engine to the boat. "Get ready," she told Gertie as she picked up her fishing pole. "Lucas Riley is going to pass us in about thirty seconds."

I closed the porthole and ducked down below the line of circular windows. Someone peering out of a porthole might look a little odd. It was best that Lucas only register two old ladies fishing. I heard the engine approaching and was happy that he seemed to be moving fairly fast. He probably wouldn't give our boat a second glance. I watched out the cabin door as he approached and saw Ida Belle and Gertie lift a hand in the air as he passed about twenty yards away from us. I saw his arm go up in the air, but he didn't even bother to turn his head.

Ida Belle watched until he rounded the bend, then dropped her pole and jumped over to the steering column to start the boat. "Let's see if we can figure out where he came from," she said.

As she took off across the lake, I popped the hatch on the top of the cabin and poked my head up with the scope. I scanned the surface of the lake, looking for the ripples left from the wake from Lucas's boat. As we neared an inlet, the ripples dissipated. I hurried to the back of the boat and pointed out the channel to Ida Belle.

"I think he came out there," I said.

Ida Belle cut the engine speed and directed the boat into the smaller channel.

"Do you know where this goes?"

Ida Belle shook her head. "There's hundreds, maybe

thousands, of channels like these off the lake. They sometimes shift with time."

I watched as the channel grew narrower, until it was probably only forty feet across. Trees started to sprout up along the bank, replacing the tall reeds and marsh grass. In some places, cypress roots created banks, pushing the land above the channel by a couple of feet. I climbed onto the seat across from Ida Belle and lifted the binoculars, alternating my scan of both sides of the bank.

"Wait!" I said and jumped off the seat to grab Ida Belle's arm. "I think I saw something."

Ida Belle cut the boat engine off and I grabbed the cypress roots to stop our progress. "Look there," I said and pointed to a section of roots about ten feet behind us. "There's a piece of rope tied to that big root on top."

Ida Belle leaned over the back of the boat and looked where I was pointing. "Looks like someone tied off there and the rope broke."

"The break's recent," I said. "The ends of the rope haven't frayed enough for it to have been that way long."

"Then what are we waiting for?" Gertie asked. "Let's check it out."

I looked at Ida Belle. "What do you think? Is this the hiding place or the drop-off location?"

Ida Belle studied the area and frowned. "I'm more inclined to say hiding place. This channel is shallow. When the tide goes out, a larger boat wouldn't be able to travel down this without hitting bottom. I don't think they'd choose a drop location that was cut off every time the tide went out."

I pulled my Glock out of my waistband and checked the magazine. "I think we should assume that if Hank is hiding here, he's well armed."

"We're not going to walk up and sell him Girl Scout Cookies," Ida Belle said. "We just need to get close enough to verify he's there and then we get the hell out of here and call Riker. This is no time for any of us to play the hero. Our necks are already stuck out enough."

I nodded, relieved that Ida Belle and I were in agreement on how this should play out. We could not afford a showdown in the middle of the swamp, especially one that was smack-dab in the middle of ATF business. Besides which, we were neither qualified nor sufficiently equipped to come up against an arms dealer's security unit. If the supplier had gotten wind of problems and dispatched more personnel to Sinful, they would be as skilled as me and there would be more of them.

"What if Lucas comes back?" Gertie asked.

"Already thought about that," I said. "As soon as Ida Belle and I take off, I want you to move the boat down the channel around that bend. Take point on the bank behind the foliage and watch for anyone approaching. Make sure the boat is far enough around the bend that it can't be seen from this channel, and turn it around so you're ready to haul butt this direction to pick us up."

"We've got no cell service out here," Gertie said. "How do I signal you?"

"Worse case, if Lucas returns, wait until he enters the swamp and shoot a flare. We'll keep a watch for one. Same thing on our end. If we need a quick evacuation, we'll fire a flare and you get to this bank as fast as possible."

"Got it," Gertie said.

I jumped out of the boat and onto the bank, Ida Belle close behind. As we stepped onto a path in the swamp, Ida Belle turned around and looked at Gertie. "Now might be a good time to start praying Lucas doesn't return."

Gertie nodded and started the boat. Ida Belle and I slipped into the swamp, and the boat disappeared from our sight. The path was narrow and rarely traveled. In fact, only someone adept at tracking would have noticed it at all.

"Someone's been down this recently," Ida Belle said.

"You've got good eyes."

"I've done my share of hunting…here and in Vietnam. You think they have any kind of security out here?"

"Unless they're running a generator, they wouldn't have the power for cameras. Sound from a generator would carry for miles out here, and I haven't heard anything."

"What about trip wires…you know, military sort of stuff."

"It's certainly possible, and for the drop site, I'd say more likely, but if this is only a hideout, then I don't know that much security is necessary. You'd only have one person out there and the hideout was probably constructed with a view from every side. With good visibility of anyone approaching and a store of weapons that will cut a human in half, they probably don't need anything else."

Ida Belle nodded. "I guess with all the storms and flooding, they'd be running a risk of coming up against their own security if they set up anything like that out here."

"The risk definitely increases in hostile weather environments." I pointed to a branch in the path. "The right side was traveled more recently," I said as I veered off in that direction.

"He's trying not to leave a trail, but he's not that good at it."

"Not when he's up against professionals." I stopped short and put my finger up to my lips, then pointed to our left.

Ida Belle nodded and followed me as I crept into the brush and followed the noise. It hadn't been much—a scratching sound like two pieces of wood rubbing together—but in the stillness of the swamp, it stood out. I eased between the cypress trees, pushing aside the hanging moss and dense weeds, then drew up short.

About ten feet away, the trees thinned out. Behind them I could see the edges of a square structure. I pointed and pulled out my scope. Ida Belle nodded and did the same. I locked in on the structure immediately. It was a small building—maybe ten feet square—constructed of plywood and tin, with long narrow windows on the two walls I could see. I had no doubt the other two walls contained the same windows, giving someone the ability to check the entire perimeter.

I lined my scope up with the window I had the best view into and scanned slowly across the opening, looking for movement. When I reached as far right as I could go, I saw a shadow move along the back wall.

"Someone's in there," I whispered, "but I can't see clearly from this angle. Move right."

Ida Belle nodded and I eased over, choosing every step for maximum silence, until I had the right angle to see the other side of the structure. I lifted my scope and scanned right.

And then I stopped cold.

Chapter Seventeen

I lowered the scope and motioned to Ida Belle to look for herself. She lifted her scope and scanned to the point I indicated, then dropped her scope and stared at me.

"What the hell?" she whispered.

I shook my head, at a total loss.

The man inside was Hank Eaton. I recognized him from a picture Gertie had shown me. But he was bound and gagged.

"Do you think the supplier did that?" Ida Belle asked.

"Maybe...I don't know. If it was the supplier then how does Lucas fit in? His presence here can't be a coincidence."

"Maybe Lucas has orders from the supplier?"

"It doesn't work like that. Delivery boys and cleaners are two different jobs and two different types of people. Something is so very wrong with all of this. What are we missing?"

"I don't know, but we can't leave him there like that. By the time we send Riker here, Lucas could have returned, killed him, and tossed the body in the swamp. Everything we say will sound like the rantings of crazy people."

"So what? We stroll in there and free the man who tried to kill Carter?"

"We take him prisoner."

"What?" It was all I could do not to yell. "You want to kidnap a gun-smuggling murderer? And do what, take him to Francine's for dinner?"

"Turn him in to Riker."

A felt a rise of panic. "I can't hand someone over to the ATF. They'd unravel my cover until I was standing naked on Main Street."

"You're right. Okay, then we get him back to town and Gertie and I will turn him over."

I shook my head. "He'll tell the ATF I was involved."

Ida Belle bit her lower lip. "I'll blindfold him and we'll tell Gertie not to talk. That way he hears two voices, and that's it. By the time this goes to trial, he won't know the difference between you and Gertie on the stand, and even if he makes claims, who's going to believe him?"

I took in a huge breath and slowly blew it out. It was a big risk with too many things that could go wrong, but what was the alternative? Leaving him here for the supplier to do a kill-and-dump? Then Carter was unprotected and all of this was for nothing.

"Okay. I'll get closer and make sure the structure is clear. You enter and blindfold Hank, then I'll come in. Try to do all the talking. If I have to, I'll whisper and attempt a Southern accent. That will make it harder for him to match later on."

Ida Belle nodded. I lifted my Glock and crept up to the edge of the structure, from the far left side. I eased down and slid over until I could peer directly into the narrow window.

Hank sat in a chair to the right of my position and facing a door on the wall just around the corner from me. His hands and feet were bound with handcuffs and duct-taped to a metal chair that was chained to the floor. A bandanna was stuffed in his mouth with duct tape wrapped around his head. From everything I could see, he presented no risk to anyone entering the structure.

I motioned to Ida Belle, who crept out of the swamp and to

the front door. Hank froze, his eyes wide, when he heard Ida Belle outside. I could see beads of sweat rolling down his head and neck. Then Ida Belle swung the door open and stepped inside, and his expression went from stark fear to ultimate confusion.

"I'm going to remove this from your mouth," Ida Belle said, "but if you yell, I will shoot you. Do you understand?"

His expression said that he didn't understand in the least, but he nodded. Ida Belle cut the duct tape and pulled the bandanna from his mouth. He sucked in a huge gulp of air, then coughed violently, shaking the chair.

"Ida Belle?" he asked, his voice raspy. "I don't understand."

"Yeah, well, neither do I," Ida Belle said, "and things are only going to get more confusing from here on out. I'm going to blindfold you."

"No!"

"You don't have a choice. You're less of a threat to me if you can't see to maneuver. So it's the blindfold or I turn around and leave you here just like I found you."

"Fine. The blindfold is fine."

I could hear the desperation in his voice. He had no idea why Ida Belle was there, but I don't think he cared. His only thought was probably whether or not she could get him out of there alive.

Ida Belle took the bandanna that had been stuffed in his mouth and unrolled it, then tied it around his eyes. She checked it for stability, then motioned for me to come in.

"My partner is here with me," Ida Belle said, "and we need some answers. First, did you fake your death so that you could smuggle guns through the Gulf and into Sinful?"

"Yes, but—"

"Just yes or no for now," Ida Belle interrupted.

I bent down and went to work on the cuffs and duct tape around Hank's legs.

"Were you in this with Lucas Riley," Ida Belle asked, "and is he the one who tied you up?"

"Yes and yes."

"Do you know when he's coming back?"

"No. He said he had to get the boss, and then they'd take care of me."

I looked at Ida Belle and shrugged.

"Who's the boss?" Ida Belle asked.

"I don't know what he's talking about," Hank said. "My boss isn't here. He's never been here that I'm aware of."

"I assume you're referring to the man representing the supplier. Would Lucas have a way to contact this man?"

"Not that I know of. Lucas was the pickup man. That's it. I deliver. He picks up. No one knows more than one contact forward and back along the chain. That's how it's done."

Ida Belle looked over at me and I nodded. His description was typical. It was always in a criminal organization's best interest if its supply lines knew as little as possible of and about one another. That way if under duress, an employee could only provide information about two other employees, no more.

I finished with Hank's legs and moved to his arms, removing the duct tape but leaving the handcuffs in place.

"Why did you do it, Hank?" Ida Belle asked.

His expression turned sad. "It was stupid. I know. But the baby was sick and without health insurance, we couldn't get the treatments he needed. I was shrimping one night a couple miles off the coast and a man approached me with an offer."

"To smuggle guns."

Hank nodded. "I should have said no, but it's like he knew exactly what to say. He told me that if I disappeared and my boat sank, Laurel could collect the life insurance money and get my son the treatment he needed."

"But you'd never be able to return to Sinful," Ida Belle said.

"The amount of money he offered me was stupid. I thought if I could stockpile enough of it, then I could take Laurel and the baby and disappear. You know, like those shows you see on TV—new town, new identity, everything. The money would buy us the credentials we'd need and time to start over somewhere else."

"Away from everything and everyone you ever knew. Just like that?"

"Laurel doesn't have any family left to speak of, and my family already thinks I'm dead, so it wouldn't have changed anything for them."

"Except their grandson disappearing."

"Yeah, look, I know it sounds bad, but at the time, it seemed like the only way I could keep my baby from dying."

"So Laurel knew you were doing this?"

"No! I couldn't put her at risk. Better she think I'm dead than something go wrong and the people I work for come after her. It was only supposed to be for a year. That was my plan."

"But Lucas knew."

"Yeah. My boss needed someone in Sinful to pick up the weapons. I suggested Lucas. That way, I could have him look out for Laurel, feed her money along as she needed it."

"How did he do that without telling her where it came from?"

"He told her it was charity—anonymous donations and stuff."

I tapped Ida Belle and motioned to the door. I wanted answers as much as she did, but I was more concerned about Lucas's return with the boss.

"Okay," Ida Belle said, "this is what's going to happen. We're going to take you into Sinful and turn you over to the ATF, who are here looking for you. I know that wasn't your plan, but I figure they're a better option than the boss."

"The ATF is in Sinful?" he asked.

"Yeah."

His shoulders slumped with relief. "I didn't think they'd believe me."

Ida Belle stared. "Wait. You brought the ATF to Sinful? What about your escape plan?"

He shook his head. "It wasn't going to happen the way I'd thought. These men I'm dealing with…the deeper in I got, the more I realized I didn't have the knowledge or the connections to get off their radar."

"You were going to turn state's evidence in exchange for immunity and a new identity."

Hank nodded.

"One last thing," Ida Belle said. "Did you shoot Carter LeBlanc?"

"What? No! I swear."

His surprise was genuine. I looked over at Ida Belle and shook my head. He wasn't lying. I mouthed "Lucas" and Ida Belle nodded.

"Let's get you out of here," Ida Belle said.

We each grabbed an arm and helped him up from the chair. His legs were weak from being bound so long, but with one of us on each side, we were able to get him out of the cabin and into the swamp. The farther we walked, the more his mobility returned until he was able to walk without losing his balance, albeit much slower than I would have liked.

We were about twenty yards from the bank when I saw the flare. I pointed up and pulled Hank off the path and into the brush, yanking Ida Belle along with him.

"What the hell—" Hank started.

"Someone's coming," Ida Belle whispered. "Get down and stay quiet."

Hank clamped his mouth shut and dropped into a squat. Ida Belle and I sank down behind him and listened as footsteps approached. A couple seconds later, Lucas passed by us at a fast clip. I held up a finger to Ida Belle and waited another five seconds before hauling Hank up and hurrying down the path to the bank. About ten feet from the edge of the bank, while we were still hidden by the swamp, I pulled out my flare gun and waited.

Five seconds. Ten seconds. Fifteen seconds.

Two minutes is what I figured it would take Lucas to reach the cabin. I wanted him as far away as possible before we made a break for it, but I knew as soon as he saw that Hank was missing, he'd come running. When I hit one minute fifty seconds, I lifted my flare gun and fired. A second later, I heard the boat roar to a start and race down the bayou. I waited until Gertie had almost reached us, then burst out of the swamp and tossed Hank into the bottom of the boat.

He hit the bottom with a thud and didn't move, but a couple of bruises or a bump on the head were the least of his worries. I bailed into the boat to the left of him, and Ida Belle jumped off to the right. Our feet barely touched down before Gertie took off. I half shoved, half dragged the unconscious Hank into a corner between the passenger seat and the cabin wall while Ida Belle took over as boat captain. I took a step down into the cabin where only my head was visible above the back of the boat, and reached for my binoculars. As long as Lucas thought only Gertie and Ida Belle were on the boat, I was still at an advantage.

I trained my binoculars down the channel, praying that Lucas had boat trouble or fell and broke his leg. Something. When we reached the intersection of the channel and the lake, I saw Lucas burst out of the swamp and jump into his shrimp boat. A second later it shot away from the bank.

"He's coming," I said.

Ida Belle swung the boat around into the corner into the lake, sending Gertie sprawling onto the bottom. She flopped around and managed to get upright about the time Ida Belle got the vessel straightened out. Ida Belle pressed the accelerator down and the boat leaped forward and rushed across the smooth top of the lake. Gertie flipped over backward and crashed into the back of the boat.

"I'll just stay here," she said.

I lifted my binoculars and kept watching behind and saw Lucas's boat swing around the corner far sooner than I'd hoped.

"He's gaining on us," I said. "Can't you go any faster?"

"It's already floored," Ida Belle said. "It's a cabin cruiser. It wasn't made for speed."

I hurried to the front window of the cabin and peered outside. My hands clenched the trim around the window and I realized I was pushing it, as if to try to make the boat go faster. "The radio!" I dashed back and pointed at the CB under the dash. "Call for help."

Ida Belle changed the channel on the radio and brought the mouthpiece up. "Mayday! This is Ida Belle and Gertie. We're headed southwest on Lake Pete and are being pursued by gun smugglers. They are shooting at us. Send help. Repeat, this is Ida Belle and Gertie and we are being pursued by the man who shot Deputy LeBlanc. Send help now!"

"You think someone will hear it?" I asked.

"That's the sheriff's department's channel. There's a CB at

dispatch."

A couple seconds later, Myrtle's voice came over the radio. "The ATF was here when your transmission came through. They're en route now. Can you give me your position?"

Ida Belle glanced around and shouted off some landmarks to Myrtle.

"I'm calling for more backup," Myrtle said. "Keep your head down and the boat floored."

I looked at the radio and shook my head. The woman was fainting in the hospital two days before and now she was barking orders like Dirty Harry. I glanced back and saw that Lucas had closed the gap by half. Unless I did something, by the time backup got here, it would all be over.

I grabbed the binoculars and tossed them to Gertie. "Sight for me."

She rose to a kneeling position at the back of the boat and put the binoculars up to her face. I pulled out my pistol and steadied myself as best I could and took aim at Lucas. I squeezed the trigger, then lowered my pistol and looked at Gertie. She turned around and shook her head.

"I think it went left."

I steadied myself and took aim again, squeezing off another two rounds.

Gertie turned around and shook her head.

Damn it. With a rifle, I would have had a much better chance, but a pistol combined with the distance and the movement of not one but two boats made the shot next to impossible. Because we'd only planned on surveillance, we'd only brought the light stuff—handguns, scopes, binoculars, and the fishing equipment. Did I wait for Lucas to get closer, increasing my chances at a good shot?

A second later, I had my answer.

"He's pulling out an AK-47," Gertie said.

A second later, a spray of bullets showered the boat, splintering wood and piercing holes through the safety glass windows. Gertie and Ida Belle hit the deck and I ducked lower in the cabin, throwing my arms over my head as the shower of plastic and wood came down over me. Ida Belle reached up with one hand to hold the steering wheel straight, leaving the accelerator on full throttle. She grabbed the radio.

"This is Ida Belle. We are being fired upon. I repeat, we are being fired upon with an AK-47."

"Holy shit!" Myrtle's voice came over the radio several seconds later. "I've yelled at the ATF to go faster and I'm trying to scramble a helicopter from one of the local oil rigs. Hang in there!"

I lifted my pistol and took aim, squeezing off another three rounds. I didn't have to ask if I'd hit. A second wave of bullet spray from the AK-47 was my answer.

"We're taking on water," Ida Belle said and pointed to the water seeping through the bottom and sides of the boat. "I don't know how much farther we can make it."

I ran to the front of the cabin and checked our position again. The island where Carter and I had our romantic dinner was just to the left about a hundred yards away. I rushed back to Ida Belle. "Head for the island. We can split up on land."

Ida Belle glanced over at Hank, who was bobbing around loose on the bottom of the boat. "What about him?"

"If that's what Lucas wants," I said, "he can have him. I'm not risking the three of us for a gunrunner."

Ida Belle gave me a grim nod. She didn't like it any more than I did, but what choice did we have? Our deaths wouldn't solve anything, but if Lucas got access to Hank, he may be smart enough to take him out, then bail before the cavalry arrived. He would expect us to call for help, which meant his time was limited and he knew it. I hoped if we scattered on the island, he'd choose to flee rather than pursue.

Another spray of bullets hit the boat and I cringed as the water poured in through the floor twice as fast as before. "We're not going to make it," Ida Belle said.

Hank started to stir and sat up. "What happened?"

"Your buddy is trying to kill us," I said. "This boat is about to sink. Get ready to swim for your life."

I ripped his blindfold off; no reason left to conceal my identity from him. He stared up at me, his dark brown eyes full of fear and regret. Too little, too late.

"We're done," Ida Belle said as the front of the boat crashed down on top of the water, bringing the entire craft to an abrupt stop.

Chapter Eighteen

I yanked Hank up from the bottom of the boat and shoved him overboard. His hands were still cuffed, but his legs were free. Ida Belle and Gertie both bailed over the side. I took one glance back and estimated Lucas at a hundred yards away.

He still hasn't seen you.

The cabin was already a quarter full of water and sinking fast. I waded through to the front and popped the hatch on top. I pulled myself up through the hatch onto my belly, making sure I kept my body below the cabin where Lucas couldn't see me. I checked the bank for an entry point and saw a reef of marsh grass about thirty yards to my right. I secured my pistol in my waistband and rolled off the front of the boat and into the water.

As soon as I dropped below the surface, I set out for the grouping of marsh grass I'd identified. Visibility was low, the sunlight making only the very top of the lake clear enough to see, but it was enough to gauge my depth. Direction was entirely up to me. I kicked with all my might, shoving my arms back with every ounce of strength that I had.

In the distance, I could hear the buzz of a boat motor and knew Lucas was getting close. I kicked again, feeling my lungs tighten from the exertion and the lack of air.

You're not at a hundred percent.

I tried to push the thought aside, but I knew it was true. My dive for Carter had strained my lungs and I wasn't back to full capacity. If I didn't make that grass soon, I'd have to come up for air. And it would all be over. I closed my eyes and gave one final kick and my hands sank into a slimy grass. I grabbed hold of the sharp blades and pulled my entire body into the clump before poking my head up to draw in a breath.

The air hurt as it hit my lungs and my hands stung from lacerations from the marsh grass. I blinked a couple of times to clear the water from my eyes and looked down the bank.

My heart sank.

I saw Hank, Gertie, and Ida Belle climbing up the bank just down from the spot where Carter had taken me. Directly behind them, standing on the bow of his boat, was Lucas, and he had the AK-47 trained right on them.

Lucas looked down at them and shook his head. "What the hell were you two old bats thinking? You must have lost your minds."

"Leave them out of it," Hank said. "This is between you and me."

"No can do, bro," Lucas said. "The boss doesn't like loose ends. You'll be coming with me, but the trail ends here for all nosy old women."

I pulled my Glock from my waistband and gently shook it. Chances were good it would fire. The question was whether or not it would fire correctly. I had one shot at Lucas, and it had to be perfect. Otherwise, he'd simply sling that AK in my direction and cut me and the marsh grass in two.

I leveled my gun at Lucas's head, zeroing in for the shot, when he jumped off the bow of his boat and onto the bank. "On your knees," he said to Gertie and Ida Belle.

They dropped down onto the muddy bank and I could see the stark fear on their faces. It was the end of the line. Lucas walked over in front of Hank and smiled as he glanced down at the handcuffs. I cursed silently, wishing I'd had time to remove them before we bailed. At least Hank would have been able to try a sucker punch. Something, anything, to change the balance.

I looked down my sight, but Hank was blocking me from a clean shot at Lucas. All that was visible was one arm and leg. I cursed again and lowered my gun, silently willing Hank to move over to the side.

"You can stop pretending to be the big man," Hank said. "You don't know the boss. You're not important enough."

Lucas smiled. "That's where you're wrong. I've known the boss for a long time. So have you." He waved his arm at his shrimp boat and I saw a shadow move in the cabin.

Then Laurel Eaton stepped out.

I'm not certain who was more surprised, but I would have put my money on Hank. He turned to look at his wife, his eyes wide, jaw dropped.

"Laurel?" Hank said. "I don't understand. What are you doing here?"

"Cleaning up your mess," she said. "Did you really think you could turn yourself in to the ATF and just walk away?"

"No. I came back for you…for our son. They promised us a new life. I have all the money I made smuggling. I was coming back for you. That was always the plan."

"That was always your plan," Laurel said. "I hadn't planned on a happy reunion."

"I don't understand. What are you doing here? How do you know about any of this? Did Lucas tell you?"

Lucas laughed. "He still doesn't get it, baby."

I felt a chill run through my body as it all fell into place. Lucas wasn't the delivery boy. Laurel was. All those trips to New Orleans, under the guise of care for her sick baby, were drop-offs. Laurel, who worked at the hospital, had access to the locked-down wing. Laurel, who had brown eyes like her husband Hank, but had a baby with blue eyes.

Like Lucas.

Hank's expression shifted from confused to shocked to sad. "You set me up?"

Laurel nodded. "I met the supplier's representative one night at the Swamp Bar. I was depressed about the medical costs and we got to talking. When he found out about the insurance policy, I knew he'd hit on a way for me to get the cash I needed right then and get rid of you in the process, so he found you the next night and pitched you the job. Deliverymen don't usually have a good life expectancy, but you proved to be more resourceful than most, much to my dismay."

Hank shook his head, completely defeated. "Why did you marry me?"

"Because you were steady. I needed a house and someone to take care of me and my son. Lucas has his good traits, but domestication isn't one of them."

"Got that right, baby," Lucas said and grinned.

"Anyway," Laurel said. "This has become a circus and I never liked the circus. Load up Hank, pop the two old biddies and let's get the hell out of this town once and for all."

I'd scanned Laurel up and down as she stood on the bow of the boat. I hadn't seen any indication that she was packing, but I had no doubt more weapons were stored on the boat. If I got my shot off on Lucas, I had to hope Hank retrieved the AK before Laurel came out with something equally deadly.

I leveled my gun at Lucas and waited as he motioned Hank toward the boat. Just another two inches and I'd have the perfect shot. I sighted in Lucas's head and my mind and body shifted into the zone. When the shot came, I flinched.

Mainly because I hadn't fired it.

Chapter Nineteen

I twisted my head to look behind me, where the shot had originated, and saw Riker standing on the bow of a ski boat that was easing around the corner of the island, his gun leveled at Lucas. Unfortunately, his shot had only nicked Lucas and had given him time to wrap his arm around Hank's neck, the AK shoved against Hank's temple.

The rest of us were frozen in place—Ida Belle and Gertie still kneeling on the muddy bank, Laurel standing stock-still on the bow of Lucas's boat, and me in my patch of marsh grass, as yet, still unknown.

"Throw your weapon in the lake," Lucas said. "Or I'll blow his head off. And you, driver, get up on the bow. Slowly and hands in the air."

Mitchell lifted his hands and inched forward to stand next to Riker.

"The weapon, Agent!" Lucas shouted. "Do you think I'm playing?"

I have no idea what Riker thought, but I was certain Lucas wasn't playing. If Riker didn't disarm, I had no doubt Lucas would shoot Hank and then swing that AK down and level the rest of us. Unfortunately, if Riker tossed his weapon, I expected the same outcome. Our only hope was if Hank could get control of the weapon, but he wasn't in a position to make a move. The slightest flinch and Lucas would pull that trigger.

I could see the indecision on Riker's face. He knew the score, but he didn't want to be the one responsible for the bloodbath.

"I just want this man," Lucas said, "and to leave. Once he's secured on board, I'll sink your boat and you'll never see me again."

I frowned. Yeah, it sounded good, and I'm sure that's exactly what Lucas wanted Riker to think, but I didn't believe for a moment that he'd leave anyone alive to pursue him. Lucas was going to create a path of bodies wide enough to get him out of Louisiana and probably somewhere with no extradition laws.

Riker moved his finger off the trigger. Damn it, he was going to take the bait. I had about one second to make a decision and execute it. With Hank in the way, I didn't have a clear line of sight to Lucas, so a kill shot wasn't an option. And given my submerged weapon and reliance on Hank to instantly react, I gave the only other option about a 1 percent success rate.

As Riker tossed his gun into the lake, I took aim and fired, hitting Hank right in the middle of the thigh. Bull's-eye!

Hank's legs involuntarily buckled, causing Lucas to lose his grip on Hank's neck. It was all I could do not to cheer when he grabbed the AK-47 on his way down. He'd done exactly what I hoped, but the battle was far from over. Lucas still had a good grip on the weapon and as Hank yanked on it, Lucas pulled the trigger, sending a spray of bullets over the lake. I ducked as low as possible in the weeds and saw Ida Belle and Gertie fall face-first onto the bank.

Riker and Mitchell dived off the sides of their boat as the bullets tore across the hull. Laurel crouched down on the bow of the boat, covering her head with her arms, like that was any defense against the wrath of the AK. I lifted my pistol to aim again but Hank and Lucas were struggling too close to each other for me to risk the shot. If I hit Hank instead of Lucas, we were right back where we started and I was exposed.

I watched as they fought, praying that Hank would get the better of Lucas, but the longer the fight lasted, the more I could see Hank's energy starting to lag. Being bound up for so long had made him weak. He was no match for the stronger, meaner Lucas. Hank made one last attempt to tear the rifle from Lucas and caused Lucas to squeeze off another round. Hank lost his grip and fell onto the muddy bank. Lucas stumbled backward a step and I zeroed in on him and squeezed the trigger.

The gun jammed.

I tapped the bottom of the magazine and pulled the rack back to release the lodged bullet and load a new round. I took aim again just as Lucas leveled the rifle at Hank. My pulse beat like crazy in my throat as I squeezed the trigger again. Last chance.

It didn't fire.

All the blood rushed out of my face as I saw Lucas's finger move to the trigger. Ida Belle and Gertie looked up, the finality of the situation registered in their expressions.

When the first shot rang out, I closed my eyes and tried not to sob. A second followed.

Then there was only silence.

I opened my eyes and blinked, certain I'd died and was dreaming.

Lucas lay flat and unmoving on the bank. Hank slumped beside him. Ida Belle and Gertie uncovered their eyes and looked up.

At Carter's smoking gun.

My heart leaped in my throat at the sight of him. He was pale and his hand holding the pistol shook slightly. I'd never seen someone sexier in my life.

Move over, Daniel Craig. Carter LeBlanc is the real James Bond.

Gertie and Ida Belle jumped up as Carter and Deputy Breaux leaned over Lucas and Hank, checking for a pulse. They looked at each other and shook their heads.

"No!" Laurel began to wail and crumpled on the bow of the boat.

"She's the ringleader," Ida Belle said.

Carter and Deputy Breaux looked over at her, their surprise clear, but Deputy Breaux climbed on board and cuffed her. She didn't even bother to struggle. It was over. All her carefully laid plans had ended in death.

"Help!"

I heard Riker shout and looked to the side to see him swimming around the front of his sinking boat, clutching Mitchell under his arm. "He's been shot!"

Carter ran down the bank and helped Riker get the unconscious Mitchell out of the water. I blew out a breath. I'd been hiding in this clump of grass for too long. It was time to face the music. Even though I knew exposing myself to the ATF ultimately meant I'd have to leave Sinful.

I looked over at Ida Belle and Gertie and saw Ida Belle looking straight at me. I shouldn't have been surprised that she figured out where that first shot had come from. Ida Belle was one sharp cookie, and she knew her guns.

"Go," she mouthed. "Hurry."

I looked behind me and saw that the area of marsh grass I was hidden in stretched all the way to the corner of the island. She was right; I could wade through the grass and walk away from the entire thing.

And then what?

I had no way to get off the island. Boats were sorta at a premium at the moment. I couldn't walk back to Sinful, and although I knew Ida Belle would come back for me as soon as she could, both she and Gertie would be tied up forever trying to sort this mess out with the ATF. I'd be waiting for hours, and there was no way Carter would believe I wasn't involved. He'd send someone for me right away, and when I couldn't be located, the gig was up.

So what?

I smiled. Yeah, so what? So it was the longest shot in the world that I'd actually get back to Sinful and never land on the ATF radar. It wasn't any more unlikely than the shot I'd made earlier, and Carter riding in to the rescue when it looked like everything was going to end with lights out for all of us.

I gave Ida Belle a thumbs-up and turned around, easing myself through the marsh grass, keeping only my head above water. It took several minutes of slogging through the thick mud, especially since I had to keep the noise to a minimum, but eventually, I rounded the corner of the island and climbed up onto the bank. I didn't even glance back before disappearing into the swamp.

The smartest thing for me to do now was put some distance between myself and the fray. Backup would be on its way, and I didn't want to risk a random sighting by law enforcement. So I stayed inside the tree line but close enough to see the bank and skirted the side of the island. If I remembered correctly, it was only a mile or so long. The other side ought to be far enough away to escape detection. I would get there, then sit down, lean my exhausted body against a tree, and rest until the Swamp Team 3 cavalry arrived.

But when I reached the far side of the island, another option presented itself. I had no idea why Sheriff Lee was fishing just off the bank, but there he was, Methuselah wearing a fishing hat and packing up a rod.

"Sheriff Lee!" I shouted as he made his way back to the outboard motor of the bass boat. He didn't so much as flinch, so I ran down to the edge of the bank and yelled louder.

He turned around and looked at me, frowning, then squinting. "Is all that hollering necessary?" he asked.

"You didn't hear me the first time. Can you give me a ride back to town?"

"Where's your boat?"

"Sank."

He shook his head. "I ain't running no taxi service, but I suppose it wouldn't be right to leave you stranded. Get in."

I waded into the lake and climbed over the side of the boat. "Are you off today?" It seemed an odd time for any of the local law enforcement to have a day off.

"What the hell are you talking about? I'm off every day. Been retired for almost thirty years."

I blinked. It had finally happened. His mind had turned to dust. "You're the sheriff. At least you were yesterday."

He gave me a disgusted look. "I oughta make you get out of the boat, confusing me with that old coot. I am not my brother." He turned around and started the motor and took off down the channel.

I clenched the metal bench and stared. Brother? There were two of them? That was some seriously long-lasting DNA.

"Sorry," I yelled. "I didn't know the sheriff had a brother."

He waved a hand at me. "Women."

I laughed, and all the tension slipped away.

Life in Sinful was back to normal.

Chapter Twenty

It took hours and hours for Carter and Riker to sort everything out. While I was hiding in the marsh grass, Ally had called me a million times in a panic, certain that I'd been killed in the showdown. Fortunately, I had been smart enough to leave my cell phone at home, otherwise it would be swimming in Lake Pete. I returned her call and feigned having been asleep due to not feeling well, then rushed up to the sheriff's department, hugging Ida Belle and Gertie and surprising myself when I managed some real tears. For good measure, I threw in some butt-chewing about them taking off to look for Hank without me. They'd been shocked when I burst in, clearly expecting me to still be sitting on the island, but had covered it quickly.

Despite the best attempts by the paramedics, Agent Mitchell didn't make it. It was an unfortunate loss for the good guys, but quick-thinking Ida Belle used it to my advantage by claiming it was Mitchell who had fired the shot hitting Hank in the thigh. Mitchell had been packing a nine-millimeter that wasn't recovered after their dive in the water, so there was nothing to prove it didn't happen exactly that way.

With both Lucas and Hank dead, Laurel broke down and gave up everything to Riker—the drop-off, her original contact, and how she was paid. I hoped if they offered her some sort of new identity, she was smart enough to leave her baby in Sinful with his grandmother. She'd admitted that after the first surgery and treatments, his heart was stable. The rest of the doctor's visits had been cover for her weapons drops.

Carter had finally remembered seeing Hank on the lake and had thought he recognized him, but couldn't place his face. Probably because he was trying to place that face on a live body, and Hank wasn't supposed to be alive. When he'd seen the missing persons show on television, it clicked why he recognized Hank and why it had troubled him. Hank knew that Carter had seen him and told Lucas to be extra careful around the deputy. Lucas had taken it upon himself to eliminate the problem.

I worried at first that Sheriff Lee's brother would tell someone he'd given me a lift back to Sinful, so I'd had him drop me off at the beginning of the channel instead of my house, to help hide my identity. I'd stepped off the boat and when I turned to thank him, he stared up at me with a completely blank expression and asked who I was and what I wanted. With that bad a memory, it was a wonder he made it back home every day, but it came in handy for me.

Carter, who'd finally remembered everything and sneaked out of the hospital prior to saving our collective butts, showed signs of extreme exhaustion and everyone told him to go home. He was so tired he actually agreed without arguing. Ida Belle, Gertie, and I were close behind, all of us close to collapse but incredibly happy. It was all over. We were all alive. Carter was going to be fine.

Things in Sinful were going to return to normal. Again. Hopefully for longer this time.

At ten o'clock the next morning, I climbed into my hammock with a book, with every intention of staying there until I was starving or had to use the bathroom. It was already hot, but a breeze blew in off the bayou, making it tolerable. I'd already had an awesome breakfast of muffins and eggs and had filled my cooler with beer and hauled it outside with me.

I got about two pages into the book before I dozed off.

"When you didn't answer your phone, I figured I'd find you out here."

I opened one eye and saw Carter standing above me, smiling. "It was the best place I could think of to be."

"It's a damned good choice."

"You're not working today, are you? You should be resting."

"No, I'm not working, and don't start nagging. My mom's got that covered."

His cell phone rang and he pulled it out and frowned. "Deputy Breaux." He answered the call and I could hear Deputy Breaux's voice booming over the phone. He sounded panicked. Carter listened until there was a break in Deputy Breaux's rant then said, "I'm off today. Tell her it will have to wait until tomorrow."

He stuck the phone back in his pocket and stared down at me. "You wouldn't happen to know anything about Celia's boat being stolen, would you?"

"I didn't even know Celia had a boat. Doesn't seem like her, really. I suppose she's giving Deputy Breaux fits?"

"Yeah. I think there might be a lot of that coming now that she's mayor." He studied me for several seconds and I could tell he thought he should help Deputy Breaux. "To hell with it," he said finally. "I've never liked the woman."

He grabbed the side of the hammock and rolled over into it with me. I laughed as the hammock swung out, thinking that any minute, we'd flip over and both be eating grass. But the swinging finally stopped. Carter stuck his arm out and I rolled over to nestle into his shoulder. He kissed the top of my head and I relaxed against him.

And we drifted off. Together.

The End

About the Author

Jana DeLeon grew up among the bayous and gators of southwest Louisiana. She's never stumbled across a mystery like one of her heroines but is still hopeful. She lives in Dallas, Texas with a menagerie of animals and not a single ghost.

Visit Jana at:

Website: http://janadeleon.com
Facebook: http://www.facebook.com/JanaDeLeonAuthor/
Twitter: @JanaDeLeon

For new release notification, to participate in a monthly $100 egift card drawing, and more, sign up for Jana's newsletter. http://janadeleon.com/newsletter-sign-up/

CPSIA information can be obtained
at www.ICGtesting.com
Printed in the USA
LVHW020051091121
702796LV00013B/419

9 781940 270197